# Serious as a Heart Attack

(Second Edition)

By Jeffrey Hornbull

# Table of Contents

## Emergency

## Post-Op

## Homeward-Bound and Home-Bound

## Getting Better

## <u>Life Goes On</u>

# Dedication

*This book is dedicated to all of you who encouraged me over many years to take a crack at this writing thing, including but not limited to: My mother, my father, my aunt Fran, my wife Nichole, Tom and Jamie Newman, Evan Howell, Cathy Clark, Alicia and Jeff, Chris Condon, Julius Strauss, Jonathan Conway, that guy Darin from Beloit, Angie, and my mentor and editor Alana Reynolds.*

*And you. Yes you. You know who you are. It is dedicated to you too. You thought I forgot about you, didn't you? But I didn't.*

# This Page
# Unintentionally
# Left Blank

*God damn Microsoft formatting!*
*How do you get rid of this shit?*

## Forward

I am not Winston Churchill. Nobody cares, or should care, whether this book is an historically accurate portrayal of events and characters precisely as they actually unfolded. They did not shape history. I could still drop dead for all history cares. I simply tried to string together the events and observations that were kind of funny in a way that is kind of funny. The reader should not be overly concerned about historical accuracy. But considering the likelihood that everyone who reads this is likely to know me well and be familiar with the events as they transpired, I foresee some nitpickery (get used to it, this book contains a lot of made-up words) regarding the veracity of the details. So, in the interest of forthrightitude (told you so), let me fill you, the reader, in on the approach taken by me, the writer.

In the year or so that followed my surgery, I regularly posted the occasional humorous tidbit on Facebook to assure my family and friends that I was doing well and was in good spirits and good humor, literally. I began to think, and was often told, the whole affair could make for an entertaining memoir. I thought if I could just frame a story compelling enough to draw the reader from one funny bit to the next, the laughs would be enough to make it a worthwhile read. My starting point for writing this tale was to paste all the Facebook posts into a document and use it as an outline.

I set out with the intention of writing a memoir, a factual account of events, factual as I see them at least. But being a first-time writer, I had a tendency to digress down dead-end paths that became omissions and re-writes. In my struggle to draw the reader from one funny bit to the next, I concluded that *entertaining* was far more important than *accuracy*.

I discovered, as many writers do, that it is simply tiresome to introduce fifty characters just so they can each get their one good line in. So, many characters were consolidated into composite characters, and events were strung together in a way that made a logical sequence of events for the reader to follow rather than a more accurate unintelligible jumble – as real life tends to be.

My sage editor and mentor, Alana Reynolds, explained to me that this approach led the work out of the traditional realm of *memoir* and into a different genre that is referred to as *complete and utter bullshit*. And she makes a good point: if it is fiction, then why be constrained by real events at all? Why not write a purely fictional novel that has a narrative arc with characters on an emotional journey to arrive at some sort of existential point?

The answer is simple: I ain't that good a writer (as evidenced by my use of the words *ain't* and *forthrightitude*). I am a first-time writer trying to coax you the reader from one funny bit to the next in any way I can so that you actually make it through all the funny bits, and that's about all I got.

So, what is real and what is not? For those of you readers who don't know me personally (this is likely to be no one at all), allow me to tell you about myself: just about all events are true, they are simply told through fictional and composite characters and not necessarily in the right order or time frame. In a nutshell, the book takes you from one moment, when I entered the emergency room, and then in two directions in time: forward through recovery and backwards reflecting on my life and how I wound up there in the first place. The events surrounding my dropping dead of a heart attack are all true – except of course I didn't actually drop dead or I wouldn't be here to tell you about it, and I didn't technically have a heart attack either since there was no permanent scarring on the heart tissue. But other than that, I really did drop dead of a heart attack and really had immediate emergency open-heart surgery on June 21st, 2016. Shakey is not a fictitious or composite character, he was a dear friend who really did drop dead of a heart attack right there in that same emergency room a few months earlier. He always had to one-up me. And, yes Virginia, there really is a Hornbullonia. The events of my life are true. I grew up in Brooklyn. I lived in Hungary for a long time and ate like a Hungarian (Hungarians eat a traditional diet rich in cardio-crappy food), I smoked like a Hungarian (they smoke a lot of cardio-crappy cigarettes) and I really did quit smoking by being stranded alone in the Alaskan bush without any cigarettes and the details of that are all true. I worked for FEMA for over twenty years and had the occasional bout of job stress to put it mildly. And I really did engage in, and lose, a battle of wits with a poo-flinging monkey.

I have come to embrace my editor's classification of my work as falling into the *complete and utter bullshit* genre, much to her chagrin (she seems to think I didn't fully comprehend her guidance in this regard). But it suits my needs and meets my humble goals. I had three modest goals for writing this story:

- Enjoy the process. Exceeded expectations here to the point I am now almost entirely uninterested in how many people ever read it.

- Learn enough about the process to take a better crack at another book in the future. Exceeded expectations to the point that I am so excited about taking a running start at the next one I no longer care about this one or what anyone thinks of it.

- Somehow convince a few hundred people to read it, hopefully a few dozen will actually enjoy it, and a few will find some sort of cathartic solace as it relates to their own experiences and lives. This expectation is nullified by the fact that, as I stated in goals one and two, I no longer care who reads it or what they think. But if you get a few good laughs out of it, we will all have met our expectations. I've had my fun, now it's your turn to take it or leave it.

With that said, I do hope you take it, and I seriously do hope you enjoy it. Just don't take it too seriously. And with that introduction, ladies and gentlemen, I give you... Serious as a Heart Attack.

# Emergency

## 1. Super Model

The closest thing to being treated like a super model that an obese, fifty-year-old male will ever experience is to walk into an emergency room and say: "Hi, I'm an obese, 50-year-old male with chest pains and shortness of breath."

"Right this way, sir. Please, have a seat in this wheel chair, I'll escort you to your private exam room. You, on the crutches, out of the way, an obese fifty-year-old male with chest pains is coming through."

If there were velvet ropes, they would be lifted up. The service is swift and customer-focused, nothing but full attention lavished on the all-important, obese, 50-year-old male.

A security guard snatched the admitting paperwork out of my hands: "You don't need those insurance forms, sir. I am sorry anyone gave those to you. Someone will come by later and fill them out for you."

The security guard had overheard me describe my symptoms to the triage nurse, took it upon himself to overrule her direction, followed me into the waiting area and escorted me by the elbow into a wheel chair. I was wheeled immediately to a private exam room with an ER nurse waiting just for someone like me to arrive. She apparently just sits there all day in this room decked out with an EKG, blood pressure monitor, all manner of other gizmos and there is almost a chilled bottle of champagne on ice – there isn't one, of course, but there almost is.

A tall, stern and serious-looking doctor swooped in a minute later with her entourage of technicians and interns. I think there may have even been a few paparazzi in the back trying to get a shot of the world-renowned obese 50-year-old. They drew blood, took baby pictures of my heart with a sonogram, took x-rays with a portable x-ray machine that saves the all-important fifty-year-old male the trouble of going to the x-ray room and they almost placed a tiara on my head and handed me a bouquet of flowers – they didn't, of course, but they treated me so special it felt like they almost did.

I highly recommend this experience for any obese, 50-year-old male with self-esteem issues. Feeling unattractive? Unappreciated? Just waltz into the nearest emergency room, grab your chest, stagger into the nearest emergency room and put on your best Redd Foxx's Fred Sanford imitation: "This is the big one! I'm coming to join you Elizabeth!" They'll make you feel really special.

I'll have to find more ways to take advantage of this: crowded restaurants, the DMV, long lines at amusement parks, the airport, velvet rope lines – clutching my chest: "this is the big one, let me get a table by the window, please." This is going to be great. I love being an obese 50-year male with chest pains and shortness of breath.

**

"I was on my way to my primary care physician on 86th Street to get checked out for these chest pains and shortness of breath. You know, better safe than sorry. But as I was walking there, I live on 82$^{nd}$, I kept having to stop and catch my breath."

"You're from 82nd Street?" the doctor asked. She probably thought.

"I'm actually from Brooklyn originally. I know I look more like a lumberjack than a Brooklynite, all burly with a beard and all. But I'm from the other Brooklyn, 1970's Brooklyn. I'm from the Brooklyn where people thought I might be dangerous when I said I was from Brooklyn. Nowadays they think I might have a discerning taste in latte when I say I'm from Brooklyn. But I get it, there are more latte drinkers than lumberjacks in Brooklyn nowadays."

"Welcome to the twenty-first century, Mr. Hornbull, we have much to teach you here in the future," the doctor said, "What I need to know is did you walk here?

"I tried. But after a few blocks, I couldn't make it half a block without stopping for air," I continued. "And the chest pains were getting worse and worse."

"What kind of chest pains?" the doctor looked up from the chart.

"Like heart burn but up here," I said pointing to my sternum. "And radiating out though my arm bones like a dull ache and up my neck like my head was going to pop off."

"Has your primary care doctor treated or examined you for these symptoms before?"

"I've never been to that doctor. My old primary care doctor dropped my insurance plan. I didn't know where to go, so I looked up a new one this morning on the insurance company website. I don't know this doctor, but once the chest pains got that bad, I figured he was going to do one of two things: call an ambulance; or nothing at all. So, I figured I might as well just come over to the ER myself."

"Well you did the right thing coming in to get checked out," the doctor said matter-of-factly. "We are going to do a full range of tests and talk about what to do from there."

I had been scared, on that walk, not knowing if I could even get to the ER. Should I ask a stranger for help? On the streets of New York? I was getting some disconcerting looks of concern from strangers passing me by on the street, but God knows what sort of psychopathic dumb ass I might have entrusted with my life, or what kind of scene might have been created around me. It sounds silly, but I was worried it would be embarrassing to be at the center of a concerned crowd of on-looking oglers being loaded into an ambulance, especially if I looked like there is nothing wrong with me. What would they think?

But what if I couldn't make it to the ER by myself? New York City is famous throughout the world for stepping over dead people on the street for days before anyone thinks to wonder if maybe this is not a drug-addict con man luring passersby close enough to bait some do-gooder into a sham law suit.

I thought they were making too big a deal of it

all, I only came to get checked out. I assumed I would be out of there within a couple hours with a prescription and a referral to a cardiologist – or better yet, maybe they would just call me an out-of-shape fat slob in need of some Roll-Aids and send me on my way. I told my wife, Nichole, I had diverted to the emergency room on my way to the doctor but not to bother coming. Surely, I would be out of there within a few hours anyway. She swore she only wanted to keep me company and wouldn't be a worry wart. If she was willing to leave the Antique shop in the hands of her parents, clearly she was worried. But I figured the tedium of the emergency room wait would surely calm her nerves.

Nichole arrived in concerningly short order sans calmed nerves looking awfully hot and bothered. She burst through the door making a disheveled, panicked entrance worthy of Jackie Gleason, her arms throwing back the privacy curtain, her blouse untucked and her curly hair all unruly. "I'm calling your mother," she said as she burst into my exam room.

"Slow down, Sweetie. Look at you, your hair looks like your toe is plugged into an electrical socket.

Nichole fumbled through her purse, pulled out her cell phone and started pacing the few short steps of the exam room.

"No, don't do that Nichole, it'll only needlessly freak her out if you tell her I'm in the emergency room with chest pains. In two hours, I'll be home, I'll be fine, and we'll call her and tell her I'm home and I'm fine and then tell her what happened once I'm home and fine." I assured her. Nichole plopped onto the stool next to my exam table. "I know you told me you were going to the doctor, but when you told me you were in the emergency room it really freaked me out and I ran out of the shop and found a cab," Nichole started talking very fast as she does when she is nervous or upset.

"Wait a second, how fast did that taxi drive, anyway? You made it here in like fifteen minutes. Are you alright?"

"Am I alright? What is going on with you, Jeff? Are you alright? What have you found out?"

A nurse was strapping the Velcro around my bicep for the fourth time in the hour I had been there. "I'm about to find out how many times a human being can have his blood pressure taken in a single hour."

"So, what is your blood pressure?"

"I don't know, I have had a lot more tests than answers so far."

"What about your father?" Nichole asked. My father is a medical school professor and a logical persona to call in a medical emergency, but I didn't want to panic him either.

"No, I'll ask his opinion when we know what is going on. Right now, we don't need analysis, we need basic information for him to offer an opinion on."

"Nurse, what is Jeff's blood pressure?" Nichole asked.

"Are you aware your blood pressure is very

high?" said the nurse, removing the cuff.

"Yeah sure, it always runs high. Doctors have been bugging me about it for years, but I don't want to go on those drugs in my forties…"

The nurse's face looked grim, "Mr. Hornbull, your blood pressure is 230 over 190."

"230? 230 what?"

"Your blood pressure, Mr. Hornbull, is 230 over 190" the nurse repeated.

"How are you measuring that? What is that? Metric blood pressure?"

"I'm calling your mother," Nichole fumbled through her purse for her cell phone again.

"Nichole, put that cell phone away. 230 what? 230 blood pressure pesos? 230 isn't a blood pressure."

The nurse leaned in, looked me in the eye and annunciated: "That is the blood pressure of someone having a serious cardiac episode."

"I want to speak to the doctor?" Nichole said with a subtle crack in her voice holding back tears.

The doctor swept in with a clipboard full of test results. "Some good news, Mr. Hornbull. Your blood work shows you don't appear to be having a heart attack. But we do need to keep you for some more tests."

Good news of course but it also meant I lost my supermodel status and was expelled from my private exam room and cast down into the over-crowded bowels of the ER with all the common medical chattel. They removed me from my private exam room and downgraded me to a curtain cubicle, which I even had to share at times while I waited hours between tests. I even had to fill out all those dreaded forms finally. Very demeaning for a one-time celebrity obese fifty-year-old super model.

**

It was probably a good sign that they no longer considered me to be such a special case, but the sudden lack of special treatment made me feel uneasy and impatient with all the waiting. Nichole was nervously surveying our new environs, exploring outside the privacy curtain of my exam bay on the main ER floor. She looked out at the ward and exhaled deeply when she got her bearings and the memories came flooding back "You realize where we are don't you, Jeff?"

"Yes, I figured that out on the way in. It all happened in the exam area in the far corner."

Nichole peered again, "Oh my God, you're right."

We were in the same row in the same area of the ER where a few months earlier we watched in disbelief as doctors took turns performing CPR and administering electric defibrillating shocks on our close friend Shakey.

Three months earlier, at a Valentine's Day dance at his church, Shakey had collapsed and lost consciousness. A young man at the church called our regular bar to ask if anyone knew how to get hold of his family. I happened to answer the phone while the bartender was busy.

"What exactly is going on? What condition is he in? Are there EMTs there? No? You called the bar before you called an ambulance? Dude, call an ambulance, stay right there, I'll be right over."

Nichole and I took a cab the six blocks over to the church and arrived in time to meet the ambulance as they wheeled him out while they administered chest compressions and a breathing bag on him on the stretcher. We followed them to the emergency room and stood by, horrified while they performed CPR and administered defibrillating shocks for forty minutes. After the first twenty I looked at Nichole and rhetorically asked, crying: "Aren't they just going to call this already?"

They didn't 'call it'. They put him on life support and spent the next several days doing test after test on his body and brain to empirically prove there was nothing more to be done.

I resisted any temptation to travel down that particular path of Memory Lane or draw parallels to my current situation. I am conscious and breathing and my heart is still beating, I thought. And if things were to take a southerly turn, at least I would drop on the floor of the ER, not the dance floor at the church. Thankfully, there was plenty to distract me from the memories of that night. A steady stream of doctors, interns, nurses and you-name-its paraded through my cubicle making me repeat my medical history ad nauseum. My medical history consists of strep throat once in college and a sprained ankle, but they still want to hear "yes" or "no" to every question every time:

"History of heart disease? History of kidney disease? Cancer? Emphysema? Transplant recipient?" and on and on.

"No, no, no, no and for last time no to all of the above and all the below."

"Any of these symptoms in your family history? Have your parents or immediate family had heart disease"

"My eighty-year-old father still coaches rugby and my Canadian mother is my Mexican day-laborer at our place in the country, she digs ditches and hauls lumber better than I do."

The routine of questionnaires, poking, prodding and tests was growing tedious. Nichole and I whiled away the time in my ER curtain cube making passing diagnoses on my neighbors. "I'll bet the guy with the eye patch and the head bandage got his ass kicked by his wife," I ventured to guess.

"The crying teenage girl probably has the clap, don't you think?" Nichole pondered out loud as she perused her phone researching medical conditions for our surreptitious diagnoses of my curtain cubicle neighbors. "What's new on the outside world?" I asked.

"What's on Facebook?"

"Facebook says Joe and Ro are going to Bahama Mama tonight for Margarita Madness."

"Do you think the doctor will accept Margarita Madness as an excuse for early release?"

"Tom Newman posted pictures of him and his girls camping in the Adirondacks. It's Irish Brian's birthday. And oh look, the Emperor has commanded the Sun to set a little earlier each day."

I had declared myself Emperor of our plot of land in the Catskills, anointed myself Jeffonius Hornbullonius Maximus the First, ruler of Hornbullonia. Mostly, my empirical duties consisted of splitting wood, drinking beer around the campfire and generally living like a savage in the woods. But I had also assumed the responsibility of commanding the Sun Gods to obey the solstices via Facebook post. If you want to one day be emperor of more than a few acres in the Catskills, woo-ing and wow-ing all the Sun-worshiping pagans on Facebook seemed as good a place as any to start.

"Maybe if there is really something wrong with you, you can get a medical leave of absence and we can spend a chunk of time in Hornbullonia this summer," Nichole said.

"Well don't get your hopes up." I thought there must be something wrong with my work-life balance if my wife is yearning longingly for me to be an invalid to keep me home.

"I'm just saying maybe this is a sign you should quit your job and live a calmer life. We could get a dog and live in Hornbullonia."

"Let's hope that's a little premature. But, look, here comes a doggie to tide you over for now."

A happy smiling volunteer with a friendly tail-wagging volunteer dog in an official-looking service dog vest popped into the exam area from behind the curtain. The volunteer seemed peppy and enthusiastic enough, but the dog was the most decrepit looking animal I have ever seen in a hospital. He was a small, black, wiry little thing kind of like Toto if he were a crack-addict stray. He just seemed unsanitary and out of place in a hospital setting. If you stuck a broom stick up his butt, he'd look like a filthy mop. I would have expected a well-groomed shitzu with a hair bow or a peppy Jack Russell jumping and doing tricks. But this poor, mongrel didn't look like he was any happier to be there than I was. He would probably rather be taking a long hot flea bath at a doggy day spa, or maybe he'd happily settle for being rung out in a mop bucket.

The tall, swift no-nonsense ER doctor swept back in with her clipboard and more questions: "How long have you had these symptoms?"

"Well, over the past three weeks or so I have had a series of episodes like I had today: walking down the street and suddenly feeling like I was running a marathon through molasses. And I had a pain like heartburn in my chest. I don't how many Tums I consumed thinking it was heartburn, but the three or four inches that separated my stomach under my diaphragm and the sensation under my sternum was strangely alarming for such a subtle distance. At times the pain radiated down my arms in a throbbing ache and up into my jaw like it was going to build up pressure and pop my head off like a champagne cork."

"These are classic signs of an impending heart attack. Didn't you realize at this point this was a serious problem?" The doctor asked.

"I did at first but each time I sat down and caught my breath I felt fine, so I breathed a sigh of relief and thought 'ok, I guess it was nothing.'"

"No, that is a sign of an unstable angina, a much more serious symptom than a stable angina not caused by exertion. The fact that it was clearly caused by the exertion was a really bad sign that you should have gone to an ER immediately," the doctor explained.

So little did I know that on one occasion I tagged along with a work friend, Gus, who was walking the four miles from World Trade Center up to Penn Station. I felt I really needed to get more exercise. It seemed no matter how hard I tried I just couldn't get back into shape. I had been using the Citi Bike bike-sharing service to get to work but it became more and more strenuous until I just couldn't do it. I thought the walk would be a more manageable pace. I made it about two blocks before I felt like I was in some near-light-speed experiment where I was moving in a different time continuum than the rest of the world. I finally asked Gus to stop and he held me by the elbow and walked me toward a bench.

"You alright?" he asked.

"Yeah, just let me sit here on this bench for a minute, I'll be fine." I was panting, flushed and sweating.

"I hate to ask this, but should I call an ambulance?" Gus asked.

"No, calm down. This will go away in a minute. This has happened a couple times before, lately. It goes away."

"Is this what happened when you were with Nathan last week?" John asked.

"Yeah, and I sat for a few minutes and I was fine. And we got back on our merry way to Maxwell's and drank our faces off all night. No problem."

Sure enough, I was fine in a couple minutes and we set on our merry way, but only about halfway to Penn Station and drank our faces off at the Whitehorse Tavern where Dylan Thomas famously drank his face off until he dropped dead.

**

The ER doctor returned a while later with a pack of interns who had been taking turns repeatedly and redundantly taking my medical history. "This is the patient whose test results we have been reviewing. How are you feeling Mr. Hornbull?"

"I'm fine as long as I'm sitting still – I'd never know anything was wrong."

"We were just wondering how you got here." One of the interns asked..

"How I got here? Well, for the last few weeks I have experienced a series of episodes of heart-burn-like pain and shortness of breath..."

"No, I mean how did you get here today?"

"I was on my way to the doctor to get this checked out and..."

"I mean, did you come here by ambulance?"

"No, I took a cab."

"Oh my God, he was a walk-in!" and there was a collective gasp and whispers from the pack of interns and a steady grumbling as they shuffled back behind the doctor and slid away from the exam area.

"What was that about?" Nichole asked.

"We need to do one more test before I can say..." the doctor began.

"Fine, but what do all the tests we've done all day say so far?" I interrupted.

"Well, you're not having a heart attack and it doesn't look like any permanent damage has been incurred." The doctor continued.

"Look, Doctor, with all respect, I'm all for getting everything checked out, that's why I'm here. But, if there's any way to finish these tests at another time … it's getting late and if this is all going to end with a prescription and a referral to a cardiologist can we just skip ahead to that part so I can get home tonight in time to call my mother and tell her I'm home and I'm fine? I mean rather than wind up being admitted, can't I get out of here and come back tomorrow? If I'm not having a heart attack…?"

The doctor grew a little impatient with my pushiness: "I said you are not having a heart attack right now, this very instant.I didn't say you weren't going to fall flat on your face dead on the sidewalk if you try to walk out of here, which is exactly what I think will happen if you do."

I rolled my eyes, thinking the doctor was overdramatizing to make a point, or just to cut me off. Nichole took it differently. She bit her lip and looked at me: "Can I call your mother now?"

And I realized I was probably not going home that night.

**

I spent the better part of the next hour being passed back and forth in a CT scan tube. The chatty technician told me she was not supposed to diagnose or discuss results with patients but not to worry, she'd let me know if she could see that everything was fine. She fell very silent as the results came streaming across her monitor. She quietly dashed out of the room and returned with a couple other technicians, radiologists or whoever they were.  They mumbled to each other and pointed at the monitor but said nothing more to me until

I was wheeled back to my ER curtain cube.

The doctor returned to my ER bay and stood at the foot of my exam table, a group in white lab coats peered out from behind her.

"How did the CAT scan look, Doctor?"

"These folks are from the Radiology Department and had a few questions for you if you don't mind taking a minute."

"Not at all."

"Actually, we are the entire Radiology Department on duty. I assembled the group to review your imaging results," The apparent group leader clarified.

"Nice touch of customer service," I said with shifty-eyed suspicion, growing uncomfortable with the renewed attention on my case and the lack of information on the results. "What are the scans telling you?"

"We're going to do another CAT scan but this time with a dye injected directly into your heart from a catheter inserted into you groin. The same catheter can then insert a stent if the scan shows that to be the course of action."

The entourage left the exam area and left me frustrated with the job of trying to calm Nichole's nerves under the shadow of their ominous silence on the test results.

"I'm calling your mother!" Nichole said clutching her cell phone.

"No, sweetie, don't. Not now. That'll freak her out even worse. I'll still be home by the end of the night and I'll still be fine, and we'll call her and tell her I'm home, I'm fine, and maybe I got a stent, but I'm fine. Just another CAT scan."

"I don't know what they saw in the first CAT scan," Nichole continued, her voice cracking, "but I don't like the fact that the entire Radiology Department felt the need to get together to ogle at it and pay you a personal visit."

"It's just another test, sweetie; and maybe a stent, maybe."

## 2. The Ultimate Sacrifice

My entourage of doctors, interns and radiologist wheeled me on the gurney into the operating room. The room was tiled and sterile, the walls were lined with neatly organized surgical implements and electronics. A large display hung over the operating table where a team of doctors in surgical gowns and masks were waiting.

"I am Dr. Surya," said a tall doctor with an Indian English accent, politely revealing his face from under his mask to introduce himself.

"We are going to insert this catheter into your femoral artery in your groin," said Dr. Surya in the calm voice of a surgeon. "We will need to shave the area," he said with raised eyebrows. "Is that all right?"

"You mean? Shave the nether regions?" I asked with a wince. "Sure, I understand it's all hip and trendy to do that nowadays."

The electric razor gave an embarrassing tickle down there that I've never experienced in public before. The needle broke the skin and the doctor slid the catheter in what felt like 5000 yards into my crotch. The insertion came to a stop and the doctors all looked up at the large display screen above the table.

"You can watch on the screen if you like. We are viewing the imagery on the big screen behind you." I craned my neck upwards and around to get a view of the big screen with a projection of my undulating heart. It was an awe-inspiring image to literally look into my own heart, like taking flight for the first time. I marveled at the technological and biological mastery it took to produce this image and at the same time was comforted to see it was still beating, and comforted that if anything goes wrong now, I was in the right place in damn good hands.

"We're going to inject the dye now." Suddenly all the arteries of the heart appeared in sequence as the dye moved through the vessels feeding the heart. You didn't have to be a highly trained medical technician to see something was wrong. Even looking at it upside down over my head with an untrained eye I could tell the major artery I was looking at seemed to just stop and then start again an inch later. Once the doctor pointed out this was a blockage, I realized there was a thin channel the width of a human hair connecting the two bulging dead ends of the artery. The stent insertion might be a simple procedure, but to me it was clearly going to be a life-changing event. I wouldn't say my life flashed before my eyes, but my mind did a very quick and thorough introspection of what the hell I might have done to myself throughout my life to cause this to happen.

"This is a problem," said Dr. Surya.

"No shit Sherlock," said my brain onto itself as my mouth said: "Yes Doctor I see the problem. Is that where you will put in the stent?" "I'm afraid a stent is not really the best option in a case like this. This is a 98 percent blockage of a major coronary artery. You also have an 80 percent blockage of a second and a 60 percent blockage of a third. We could stent the other two, but stents could cause complications in years to come. If blockages continue to form the stents could complicate future attempts at angioplasty, stents or even by-pass surgery if there is already wire mesh in the arteries."

"You think I might need by-pass surgery in the future?"

"We have to recommend we perform by-pass surgery right away. The 98 percent blockage must be addressed immediately. We don't like to wait in cases like this, anything could happen while waiting for surgery. The longer we wait…"

"Whoa! By-pass surgery? Just to be clear, you are talking open-heart surgery?"

"Well, yes…"

"Crack-me-open-like-a-crab surgery?"

"That's putting it graphically, but…"

"Open chest? Like a human sacrifice?"

"It is an invasive procedure…"

"And in what time frame are you thinking we need to do this?"

"Immediately. The soonest we can get the surgical team together is tomorrow morning."

"Tomorrow morning?! Tomorrow? Tomorrow is June 21st."

"Yes." Dr. Surya looked a little puzzled as to what the relevancy of tomorrow's date might be.

"The summer solstice?" You want to cut my chest open and pull my heart out on the summer solstice? What are you? An Aztec priest in need of a human sacrifice?"

"I'm afraid this is a serious and dire matter." Dr. Surya explained. "Actually, we will not 'pull your heart out.' We are pioneering a new type of by-pass surgery here in which we do not use a heart-lung machine and stop the heart. We simply graft onto the beating heart. It is far less invasive, and you won't be under anesthesia for nearly as long."

"Well, I guess if you figure that it's not too invasive."

"We recommend triple by-pass surgery. You see, the trauma of by-pass surgery lies in the incisions, not in the arterial grafting. You have probably heard people talk about quadruple by-pass as if it is more traumatic or invasive than triple or single by-pass, but the truth is that it is the going in and out that is invasive, while in there we might as well graft all the arteries. By-pass is a much more robust and permanent solution. We could take care of the two lesser blockages with stents and medications, but the 98 percent blockage is the acute, immediate problem and if we are going in we might as well take care of all three blockages at once. You are young, strong and at relatively low risk for complications, so we recommend we take care of all three blockages at once.

"You have not suffered any scarring of the heart tissue as you would have in an actual heart attack. You should fully recover, stronger than before and if you take better care of yourself, it should never be a problem again."

"That makes sense, but… Oh my God."

"We need your understanding and concurrence to proceed. We need to begin assembling the surgical team immediately to be prepared for the morning."

"You make it sound like there is isn't any reasonable alternative.'

"I'm afraid that is the case."

"And the urgency of the situation doesn't seem to leave time for research and second opinions and bullshit like that."

Nods.

"Let's do it. Let's get it taken care of." It was a frightening leap, but I had to take it with faith in the doctors and confidence in my own decisiveness. So, I put my game face on and hid the fear, but it was there, threatening to drown out my thoughts and better judgement.

"Do you have any questions?"

"Yeah, will I become an immortal Aztec Sun God if I survive this?"

It was only when the doctors began leaving the

room, I realized there was something of an audience to this conversation. A few technicians, nurses and a more civilian-looking woman with a clipboard. The woman stopped the doctors and said: "I will need to talk to him now."

"I don't think that will be necessary. He understands the gravity of the situation and has made the right decision."

"But he has to come to acceptance…"

"Acceptance? I have never seen anyone come to understanding and acceptance quite that quickly He thinks he is a human sacrifice. I think he gets it." And they shooed her aside as they wheeled me out of the operating room. I suppose they were anxious that she might explain things to me in a way that would make me hem and haw my options or even change my mind.

"Would you like to talk to a spiritual advisor?" she asked as they wheeled my gurney past her. "Any particular denomination?"

"My parents raised me to be a godless New Yorker. Do you have one of those on hand I could speak to?"

It only struck me afterwards that she was asking if I wanted help coping with the fact that I might not survive all this. And I guess a godless New Yorker is probably not the spiritual advisor I would want by my side if things go horribly wrong. What would he do? Crack open a last beer for me, say "sucks to be you," curse out the doctor for botching the operation, maybe smack him around a little? Alright, I guess that is exactly who I want by my side in my final moments on the operating table. Beats some guy in a dress throwing holy water at me and mumbling in Latin. In fact, that is my spiritual commitment to myself: If I survive, and if there are no godless-New-Yorker spiritual advisors providing these atheistic lack-of-spiritual services, I will train to become the first. I'll dedicate my life to consoling the dying by cracking beers and cracking wise.

It struck me that my quick agreement to the most radically invasive of surgeries put a humbling amount of faith in the doctors and an equal amount of faith in my own ability to make such a consequential decision based on such scant information. No second opinions, no shopping around, no analysis – just faith.

I would not, however call this a leap of faith. A leap of faith is making a bold move with full faith it will end well. Sometimes, you take a leap with a pretty good idea that it may not end well. This requires balls, rather than faith and should hereto forth be recorded in the lexicon of the English language as: 'a leap of balls.' This could be part of my godless spiritual advisor schtick: "Put your balls in my hands, my son, and we will see this through together – or I'll kick your surgeon in his."

A leap of balls is necessary when the outcome is far from certain but decisive and immediate action is the better alternative than over-analyzing and delaying – no matter what action you decide. My father is the former coach of the US Rugby team, making him, as I often say, very famous among very few people. As he often says: "Sometimes you just have to make a decision, tuck your head down and keep running forward no matter what you're headed at: an opposing player, the opposing team, some idiot on your own team who got in the way, or head first into the goal post, whatever."

Dad's day job is medical school professor at Mt. Sinai. I immediately considered calling Dad the professor before making a decision, but I thought Dad the rugby coach would fully understand why I didn't call Dad the professor. The situation did not call for analysis, it called for immediate and decisive action. Sometimes any decision is better than no decision.

Dad the rugby coach really excelled at one thing medically-speaking: talking me into sucking it up rather than succumbing to any given trip to an emergency room or an inconvenient medical procedure. He has had more injuries than Evel Kneivel and has never been impressed by any of my injuries.

"A broken toe?" he once balked at me. "I toured Argentina with a broken toe."

"I toured South Africa after my back surgery, what bloody back pain are you complaining about?"

I once slipped on an icy dock in Hornbullonia and fell and banged my shin so badly I couldn't imagine any tibia ever breaking from anything if mine didn't break from that. I essentially took a flying leap in the air, bent my knee and landed squarely on my shin on the sharp corner edge of the dock. I crawled to a rake and used it as a crutch and hobbled hundreds of yards back to my car. I drove to the nearest cell signal, got hold of my dad and he said: "If you made it that far, it's not broken. It's probably got a contusion on the bone."

"I can feel a dent in my shin bone."

"That's the contusion, you crushed the bone. But if it's not broken, there's not much they can do. You can stay off it and keep it elevated and iced; or, you can go to the emergency room, get an X-ray of your bone contusion and they'll tell you to go home and stay off it, keep it elevated and iced. It's really just a matter of what a picture of your bone contusion is worth to you."

I honestly believe I could call him upside-down from a burning, flipped over car and he'd say: "I scored against New Zealand while upside-down in a burning, flipped-over car!"

It made me feel inadequate in a way, that I would never be able to impress my father with a bumbling accident. But this time it was serious. And it seemed obvious to me that he would not see the need to talk me out of this one. So, I consented and signed the admittance forms without consulting Dad. I didn't want to overanalyze, and I didn't want him to second guess, or talk me out of it. And I certainly didn't want to know how many points he scored against Zimbabwe with a spear in his chest, or against Fiji with his sternum ripped open and his guts hanging out or whatever shit he would come up with to one-up my story.

### 3. Tick-Tock-Tick-Tock-Tick...

They wheeled me out of the operating room on my gurney and into a room where I would spend the night awaiting the surgery. The route was circuitous, through several interconnected buildings and wings, multiple elevator rides. On the final elevator ride I realized where I was: "Oh, please don't get out on five" I thought. We did. "Oh, please don't turn right." We did. They were wheeling me right to the same corridor on the same ward I had spent an entire week by the bedside of my friend Shakey. He didn't have family on the east coast so I was tasked by chance and fate to take the role of medical proxy, liaison to his family and host to the endless stream of grieving visitors.

Shakey's room over that week was filled with a constant crowd of friends filling and spilling out into the corridor. They came from all walks of Shakey's life: church, work, theater, neighborhood bar, college friends. Some understood the gravity of the situation, some expected him to wake up any moment. I tried at first to explain the dire prognosis to people but was quickly schooled that people have to come to their own conclusion in their own time. One of his church friends burst out crying and yelling, accusing me of having no faith in the power of prayer. She was right, of course. God didn't make anyone more atheist than me. Having been raised a godless New Yorker, I hadn't been considerate of how others may need to come to acceptance and grieve on their own terms. I learned to convey information without trying to sway people over to my conclusions. And I came to understand why the doctors were going through such lengths to prove to the rest of us that everything that could be tried had been tried.

I felt guilty for being resigned to his doom and at the same time resentful that the medical practitioners were putting us all through this protracted end. But over a few days, watching the stream of loved ones pass through to say their good-byes, pray for his recovery or just hold his hand in hopes of comforting him, I grew quite touched that they took such extraordinary measures to comfort the rest of us and assure us that they had tried everything, even beyond any reasonable chance that he could possibly pull through. I realized they weren't doing any of this for Shakey's benefit, they were doing it for the rest of us. As far as I was concerned, Shakey had died on the dance floor that Valentine's Day night while doing what he loved best: shaking his funky thang on the dance floor to the delight of female dance partners and on-lookers.

His cardiac problems were different than my own. He did not have significant blockages in his coronary arteries, he had a high degree of deterioration of the heart muscle itself. This condition can be caused or exacerbated by heavy alcohol intake and anyone who knew or drank with Shakey might have logically made that association. People often assumed his nickname was a reference to his heavy, public and exuberant drinking habits, although it was actually derived from his passion in life: Shakespearean acting.

But he had a greater risk factor working against him: his father and older brother had both died of exactly the same thing at exactly the same age. As the doctors on this same cardiac ward explained test results and diagnoses to me one-by-one over those long days, I finally reached the inevitable and disturbing conclusion and asked the cardiologist in disbelief: "You mean he just went tick-tock, tick-tock, tick… and that was it?" And he just nodded with a grimace.

His mom had lost two husbands and two sons already. She was poised to lose a third and the fourth was unable to come to her side because he was undergoing cancer treatments.

His mom, 'the Mom' as she was known and addressed by Shakey's friends, flew in from New Mexico as soon as the prognosis had become clear. The Mom made the difficult decisions to remove life support and donate his organs. She was stoic. "He is too full of life to live like a vegetable," she said. They scheduled the procedure for the next day. We were each given a moment alone with him. I held his hand and promised to take care of the Mom and cried in a way I hadn't since I was a child.

The following morning, Shakey's mom, pastor, Nichole and I gathered by his bedside before they wheeled him out of the room – the same room they were wheeling me into. The Mom and his pastor went with him and the doctors and nurses to the operating room to remove the life support, wait and harvest his organs. After a week of corralling visitors, consulting doctors and difficult conversations with family and friends, Nichole and I were left alone, in silence, and in shock.

And when I arrived on the gurney Nichole was

waiting for me alone and in shock again in that very same room again.

"Did the doctors explain about the surgery tomorrow?" I asked.

"Can I call your god-damned mother yet?"

"I guess we better," I conceded.

We made the difficult calls to my parents and arranged for them to come over in the morning.

"Oh, thank goodness you got finally got it checked out," she gasped. "It sounds like you barely caught it in time. Should I come over now? Will someone be with you tonight? How is Nichole? Oh my goodness, Nichole."

"Don't come over tonight, Ma. I'm fine. Sure, you can talk to Nichole. I'd better call Dad."

I passed one phone over to Nichole and used the other to call my father wile the ladies commiserated on their own terms.

"By-pass surgery?" Dad exclaimed. "That's very serious business. Did the doctors explain to you what's involved in that?"

"Yeah, like Aztec human sacrifice surgery."

"The doctor called it human sacrifice surgery?"

"No, that was my way of telling them I understood how serious it is. And it's the solstice tomorrow, you know."

"Well I'm glad you're taking this seriously,"

Dad and I share a wry sense of humor and it helped break the tension. As an Englishman, he was always much more comfortable with sarcastic expressions of understatement than feelings. Nichole wrapped up the boo-hoo-fest with Mom and we all agreed to reconvene at the hospital in the morning.

"I'll go get you some food and come back and keep you company," Nichole offered.

"You'd better not, they told me not to eat. Besides, you should go home and get some sleep. Tomorrow is likely to be the long day, and there may be many more after that. Get some food, get some rest."

"What are you going to do here all by yourself?" she asked.

"I don't know. Run through the hospital corridors in my ass gown through the night like Roy Schreider in All That Jazz looking for Jessica Lange."

"Wasn't she the Angel of Death?"

## 4. The Next Thing to Go Wrong

The hospital fell very silent very quickly once Nichole left and the night nurses came on duty. I was left alone in my room and alone with my thoughts all night. The whole day had been a steady descent from bad to worse. Every step of the way, every test, every finding was another turn for the worse. It only really occurred to me then, alone in that dark room, that there weren't any more tests or procedures left after emergency open-heart surgery. The next thing to go wrong would be the last thing to go wrong for me.

Could this be it? An unceremonious end? Was fate trying to tell me I didn't do enough for Shakey by leaving me in his room on my last night alive, alone? What then? Just nothing? Not really. It occurred to me that even having been an atheist my whole life, I still had some sort of assumption that there is at least some sort of epiphany at the end: I would finally understand physics and the fate of the Universe if only for a split second, a glimpse of my life as a whole and a memory of every event in my life in one synchronous moment, or just have a moment of being at peace with myself without my life-long veil of self-doubt and worry. There is a certain amount of nervousness and self-consciousness that comes with being human – or at least it comes with being Jeffrey Hornbull – that I always imagined would lift like a veil before death in a moment of total conscious enlightenment like the kind promised by mystical spiritual hucksters everywhere.

I thought I would at least get a moment of silence from the panel of inner critics in my mind that perpetually debates what exactly it is that makes me such an asshole. But I guess I only get that when I rest in peace. I guess I don't get an everlasting moment of orgasmic intellectual stimulation and spiritual enlightenment. It all seemed so banal for a last day, if that is what things were coming to. But I guess my last moment really could be that plain since this really could have been my last moments for all I knew. Then nothing? No, it would not be the end of everything, and not the end of the things I cherish in life. All those things would go on. All my friends would live out their lives, history would unfold, and the Universe would meet whatever end it is destined for – just without me perceiving it. And I would get the gift of being able to ponder the end of history and the fate of the Universe in my final moments and indeed for my entire life. Not a bad deal, really. I have had a remarkable life. I could live with that – or peacefully die with that. I will not spend my final moments angrily renegotiating that deal.

**

Nichole returned the following morning with my parents in tow. On the outside they were nervous, on the inside they were surely terrified. My parents' presence was awkward. I felt guilty for not heeding every bit of my mother's lifetime of advice and counsel (nagging) about taking better care of myself. On the outside, she sat quietly composed like the polite Canadian that she is, but on the inside, she was wagging her inner index finger in admonishment and shouting: "Damn it Jeff, how many times did I tell you…" followed by every scolding she ever levied against me. Drinking, smoking, foul language and not putting my toys away all somehow contributed to the blockages in my coronary arteries.

Dad was uncharacteristically quiet as well. I was unsure if he felt snubbed that I didn't consult him before agreeing to the surgery or if he was simply content to distance himself from that responsibility. Either way, there was not really any other recourse to discuss.

Nichole was characteristically not quiet, trying to acquire as much information as she could from the doctors and nurses about every procedure and medication, taking notes and taking down names. As the morning went on, the stream of doctors, nurses and orderlies grew too steady to keep track of and before long, that became helpless as well and we all sat quietly and helplessly.

The awkward silence was broken when a disheveled looking doctor with unruly hair and an untucked shirt walked into the room and unloaded a loose arm-load of props at the foot of my bed. We were all unsure if he was going to put on a magic show or perform some sort of embarrassing medical procedure with the mysterious devices: breathing tubes, a breathalyzer-looking device with a ball in a tube and something that looked like a bong. "You will need to pay very close attention to what I have to say. Learning to control your breathing will be very important to your immediate post-operative recovery. When you first awake from surgery, you will have to show you can breathe on your own. Do as I do."

He slowly sucked in a breath like he was sucking on a straw. I imitated.

"No, wrong. Watch again. Now you try. No! Wrong!"

We repeated this drill until the breathing doctor put his hands on his forehead, walked a quick half-circle around the room, shook out his arms and took a deep relaxation breath.

"Ok, try this instead: PAH!" he said with an explosive, lip-flapping 'P' and his head tilted back.

"Ok, PAH!"

"NO! WRONG! This is very important, please try to do as I do: PAH!"

"PAaaah?" I repeated.

The breathing doctor threw his arms in the air and sighed. "I tried. Good luck."

With the breathing instructor out of the way I got back to breathing with an oxygen tube under my nose. I started feeling light headed and dizzy.

"That's the glycerin," my dad explained. "They feed you that through the oxygen tube to dilate your blood vessels and improve oxygen flow before the surgery."

"It's getting me really nauseous. I think I might throw up."

"That's good, they'll probably keep you on it until you do throw up." He fetched a waste-paper basket from the corner.

I was glad my dad was there to explain that, nobody else had. I was getting more nauseous than I've ever felt in my life. The room was spinning, and I was getting concerned I might lose consciousness. My dad held up the waste-paper basket as I threw up the few remaining contents of my stomach, having not eaten for almost twenty-four hours. Vomiting felt good, but I wished I had more to throw up. My mom fetched a nurse.

"Oh, you're supposed to use this, not the garbage can," the nurse held up a plastic tub.

How was I to know? Nobody told me about the glycerin, the nausea or the vomiting much less provided instruction on proper usage of the barfing tub.

"It's about time for you to be transported to the OR, the transport crew is here whenever you're ready."

I wiped my chin and nodded.

## 5. The Death-Penalty Gurney

Nichole, my mom and my dad walked along side my gurney all the way to the operating area. My dad, aside from being a professor at Mt Sinai, has had more surgeries than the Frankenstein monster. "Do you wake up refreshed like you had a good sleep, or groggy like you were drugged? Do you dream when you're under?"

"No, it's like no time passed at all."

The light banter was suiting Dad and I just fine but it wasn't working so well for Mom. It occurred to me my levity was backfiring. Maybe a recognition of the seriousness of the situation would have suited Mom better, but I didn't have it in me to confront the seriousness of the situation much less an even more distraught mother.

I raised a hand off the gurney to wave goodbye as they wheeled me past the sterile point of no return toward the waiting Dr. Surya and his cult of sun-worshippers, I mean surgical team. A realization washed over me as they fastened me to the gurney, arms outstretched on that crucifix gurney I have only ever associated with the death penalty, that I was literally putting my life in their hands. And I tried but could not imagine being a death row inmate in the same physical position, knowing that the doctors do not have your interest at heart in any way and in the full knowledge that you will submit to their mal-intent with or without your dignity. Those final moments must be more terrifying than death itself for those poor souls. Even the religious ones wouldn't believe in a positive outcome for their fate.

I eased my mind by switching my thoughts back to Aztec human sacrifices again. I have heard and prefer to believe the Aztec sacrifices were actually willing participants. At least they kept their dignity and trust intact, in fact their dignity and stature reached its pinnacle through the final act. Somehow, in relative terms, I found these to be soothing thoughts.

I was put under for the entire procedure of course, but I suspect as soon as I went under the ritual headdresses went on, the surgical gowns came off to reveal the ceremonial golden loin cloths and they held an obsidian hand axe up to the Gods. And I imagined I would reemerge a stronger more vivacious version of myself – Jeffreyetzl Hornbullatl, the immortal Aztec Sun God.

I don't really see how anyone can doubt this is what happened seeing as how there was nobody there to witness it. There was just me, who was unconscious and the suspected Aztec priests and priestesses, so there are no reliable witnesses or evidence to suggest otherwise, now is there? Were you there? I didn't think so. And if you were, I would place you among the suspected sacrificieers. Sacrificieers? I hope you didn't put that lexicon away.

The anesthesiologist finished up inserting needles into my arm. "We are ready to inject. Can you count backwards from one hundred?"

"Ninety-nine, Ninety-eight, Ninety-sev..." All went black as I watched the syringe plunger slowly, deliberately compress the drugs into my arm.

# Post-Op

## 6. Waking Up

I could hear a nurse saying: "Give me a breath, just one breath." My eyes remained closed, but I could feel a tube in my trachea completely blocking my throat. This sensation of a blocked wind pipe instilled a visceral sense of panic. And that topped by the very immediate sensation of my diaphragm not breathing, my chest not rising and falling. Was I dying on the operating table? Choking on this tube? I was in a state of absolute panic but had a complete lack of any ability to move or do anything about it.

"Breathe!" I commanded myself. "Pull that damn tube out of my throat! Can't these people see I am choking on this thing?"

I could hear Nichole. I could not understand her, but she sounded like she was crying. In my half-conscience state, I tried to convey that there was a tube blocking my throat as if it shouldn't have been perfectly obvious that the people in the room with their eyes open wouldn't have already known this. I tried to gesticulate writing, so I could tell them the tube was blocking my throat. Nichole got it and said: "He wants to write something!" I could feel someone give me a pen. I tried to write "I can't breathe" but wrote it in Hungarian in my delusional and panicked state. The nurse got the point.

I felt the nurse restrain my arms from grabbing at the tube. I heard her say: "we'll try this again in a couple hours" and I drifted back into unconsciousness. I never managed to open my eyes, and in that instant, I didn't know if I ever would.

Another timeless second, and presumably a couple hours, later, I heard the nurse again: "Just breathe! Just give me a breath. Just one breath"

I struggled to understand the nurse's instruction of "give me a breath!" Inhale? Exhale? Through my nose? My mouth? And how could I possibly do any of this with this damn tube clogging my throat. I tried to recall the instructions of the pre-op breathing doctor and thought maybe I guess I should have payed attention to the breathing lesson that quack doctor tried to give me. But what the hell was he talking about? How the hell was I supposed to say "PAH!" with a breathing tube in my mouth?

I couldn't shake the sensation of being choked by the damn tube and reached for it only to realize my arms had been restrained to the sides of the gurney since my last attempt to yank my life support out of my throat. The sense of panic eased as I realized the tube was pumping air into my lungs in a continuous stream. My chest did not need to rise and fall, I was getting air from the tube I thought was choking me. The panic eased, and I gave a more relaxed attempt to breath on my own.

It was a strong enough sign of free will that the nurse decided to go ahead and pull the breathing tube out. The only sensation more panic-inducing than having a breathing tube stuck in your throat is having one pulled out. It felt like a garden hose was coiled up in my lungs as it scraped its way out and was taking my trachea and lungs along with it. But my eyes finally opened, and I was finally awake.

I looked around the room for Nichole, but she wasn't there. I had no idea how much time had passed since my last awakening, I figured it must have been a long time if Nichole had left. The nurse untied my arm restraints. Should I look down and see the damage? It was a scary thought. I pulled at my gown and glimpsed down in fear and dread at my chest not quite knowing what I would see. The bandaging revealed how serious the incision was, but I was relieved I did not have to confront the actual cut or scar just yet. I surveyed the rest of my body and realized I had more wires, cables and tubes going in and out of me than the back of my TV.

"Holy shit, I look like RoboCop. What is all this stuff?"

The nurse explained There were three tubes in my abdomen to drain fluid from my chest cavity, an IV in my arm, air tubes leading to automated compression socks, oxygen tubes under my nose, an blood oxygen monitor on my finger, a catheter in my penis and even more intrusive than that: a thick wire in my neck that attached a defibrillator on one of the IV poles, into my carotid artery down to my heart where there was an electrode that would jolt my heart back into action if it suddenly stopped beating.

"You've heard of an EAD? External Automated Defibrillator? This is an Internal Automated Defibrillator," the nurse explained.

"I guess I'm kind of tied down for a while," I

figured I would be bed-ridden for days connected to all these gizmos.

"No, I need you to get out of bed right now, let me help you," she pulled my wires and tubes over to one side of the bed and held me by the elbow.

I had no idea they would expect me up and on my feet that day much less immediately upon awakening. I wasn't even sure I could sit up, in fact I couldn't. I realized that my chest muscles having been cut in two and my sternum sawed in half.

I had very little strength in my abdomen and quite a lot of learning to do as to how to use my remaining strength to do the simplest of things like sit up or roll over. Even breathing too deeply triggered a stark reminder of the state of my chest cavity. The nurse helped me sit up and gather my wires and tubes into more organized clumps and sat me on the edge of the bed. Once on my feet, things felt quite normal. I was able to waddle across the room to an armchair towing my IV poles and tubes and wires along with me.

They let me sit for a while and gave me some lemon Jello. I looked up to see Nichole standing in the doorway to my room. I don't where she had been, but she had clearly been in a dark place mentally. She looked tired, physically worn out and emotionally exhausted, her head slumped and her arms dangling.

"Want some Jello?" I offered.

She exhaled and deflated with relief to see me sitting up in the chair.

"I was so scared," she sounded mad at me for putting her through all this.

"Me too. But I'm fine. Already out of bed."

Then it was time to get up again and take a lap around the room. A couple times an hour they shuffled me around the room, eventually venturing into the hallway. By the end of the day Nichole helped me gather my wires, tubes and IV poles and carried them like a wedding train behind me as she walked me all the way down the corridor to my new room in the Cardiac ICU.

## 7. The Big One!

A slender young nurse with long hair and almond eyes helped me into bed, untangled my tubes and introduced herself. Her name was Elizabeth.

"Elizabeth? A Cardiac ICU nurse named Elizabeth? Really? You must get more than your share of Fred Sanford imitations around here," I asked.

"Who?"

"I guess you're too young for Redd Foxx?" She looked confused.

"I'm coming Elizabeth! This is the big one!" I shouted with hand clenched on chest.

"Oh that! People do say that all the time. What is that again?"

I explained to her the joys and nostalgia of Sanford and Son as she oriented me to my bed, station and various medical devices attached to my body. She gave me the dime tour of all the medications I would be on, half of which seemed to counter the side effects of the others. The technological and biochemical details were a bit over my head, so I focused on the Sanford and Son side of the conversation. Elizabeth was also, when not a nurse, a yoga instructor and proved very adept at explaining the relationship between open-heart surgery and breathing – far more adept than that quack who kept shouting "PAH!" at me in pre-op.

It is very difficult, tiresome and often painful to

breathe with a bifurcated sternum and severed chest muscles. Patients tend to breathe very shallow and as a result build up fluid in their lungs. The fluid can lead to further difficulty breathing and more fluid leading to pneumonia and lung infections. Thank goodness I had quit smoking ten years before, I couldn't imagine all the coughing while trying to regain lung capacity with a smoker's lungs.

Elizabeth showed me the ball-in-tube device and how to keep the ball suspended with a prolonged breath. "You need to do this every fifteen minutes, all day, every day to strengthen your breathing."

"You make it look so easy," I struggle to move the ball at all.

It seemed impossibly difficult and painful to exhale too deeply. But Elizabeth introduced me to my new best friend: a bright red, heart-shaped pillow. "Hold this against your chest and exhale deeply."

"The ball-in-tube and pillow are much further into my technological comfort zone than the blood-oxygen monitor and automated compression socks." I winced as I tried to exhale into the tube.

"Hold the pillow tight on your chest to force yourself to breath from your diaphragm, so you don't stretch your chest muscles."

"Oh, much better." I was pleased with myself for how quickly I was learning to breathe.

"Now to keep the fluid from building up, you're

going to have to give me a deep cough."

"Cough!?" I said in a panic. "I don't think I'm ready for the advanced placement level just yet. Can we work our way up to that tomorrow? That sounds really painful."

"You've got to start immediately, or fluid will build up in your lungs and it will just get harder."

I winced out a cough and fluid loosened setting off a chain of very shallow, very painful wheezing coughs.

"Keep the heart pillow tight on your chest and use your diaphragm, not your chest. You're going to have to master this before the time comes that you will inevitably have to sneeze."

"SNEEZE!!?!?? Are you crazy? I can't sneeze." I gasped for a breath. "An alien erupting from my chest would feel like a foot massage compared to a sneeze right now." I struggled to get the words out. "I think they did the surgery wrong, there is no way I can survive a sneeze!"

I tried to explain that I am known the world over for my spasmodic screaming sneezes by everyone who has ever had the displeasure of witnessing this spectacle. Sometimes, I expend so much energy into a sneeze I need a nap afterwards. When I sneeze from my hilltop campsite in Hornbullonia: "Waaaaah-chooooooo!" barking dogs echo back across the valley starting from our nearest neighbor a half-mile away: "Ow-ow-owooooo;" and rippling from farm dog to farm dog for miles and the coyotes echo from the mountains beyond: "Yip-yip-yeeeowee-yeep-yeep-yeeeeow." No one could possibly survive one of *my* sneezes following chest surgery.

What I would learn in time was that somehow the human body establishes some sort of unspoken truce among the nose, diaphragm, brain and heart to establish a biological moratorium on sneezing following open-heart surgery. It's like the various biological mechanisms involved in sneezing all look at each other and give that two-finger eye-to-eye gesture: 'Do we all understand each other here? This won't end well for any of us if it comes down to sneezing.' I felt the urge to sneeze periodically and grabbed for my heart pillow in horror and dread of the fateful sneeze that would surely turn me inside out. But it would just pass with a little shiver and a gently voiced exhalation – sort of like that little post-urination shiver after a really long leak. Oftentimes I would just walk around on the verge of sneezing for minutes on end, my mouth agape and tears streaming down my cheeks like someone was about to hand me a bouquet and crown me Miss America. It would be sixteen days until I actually sneezed and even that was more of a half-formed proto-sneeze – like my body was relearning how to sneeze without ripping my sternum back open. I guess Elizabeth omitted this just to put the fear of Sneezus into me so I'd follow through with my breathing exercises.

It is truly amazing how many violent and potentially painful spasmodic convulsive motions of the diaphragm we take for granted: coughing, sneezing, hiccupping, burping, gasping, yawning and vomiting

(God forbid) to name a few. These abdominal spasms are not my friends. Laughter is the only one that doesn't hurt – in fact it feels pretty good, the best medicine indeed.

## 8. Wally and the Beave

Nichole came into the room and slunk into the armchair by my bedside, visibly exhausted and emotionally drained. Not much energy to talk. "Your parents are coming up to see you if you are up for it."

"Sure, let's not keep them in any more suspense than we have to. Just help me up and into the chair."

I had been told to spend as much time upright as possible and to ask for help getting out of bed and into the armchair. It was a ritual that I would practice and perfect over time: Gathering all my tubes and wires into a bundle, rolling over on one side and getting my torso halfway up by twisting sideways and sliding my feet to the floor. I needed help from there to get into a sitting position, then I was fine. I just couldn't sit up in a sit-up motion with my sternum severed and my abdominal muscles punctured with tube holes.

My sense of decorum dictated maybe I should put on some underwear under my ass-gown for the occasion of my parents visit. Nichole fished a pair of boxers out of an overnight bag she had packed for me. I sat on the edge of the bed in a half-standing position, holding the underwear in front of, my arms out stretched, trying to lift one leg while balancing on the other while not bending any abdominal muscles.

"Christ, I feel like the Karate Kid perched on that old pier piling of his. How the hell am I supposed to do this?" I grumbled in frustration.

"Just let me help you." Nichole said snickering

at my expense.

"I hope that Karate Kid kept up those balance skills, he's going to need them to put on his underpants by the time he's fifty."

I stumbled into my underpants and Nichole fell away just in time for my ass-gown to lift up like a stage curtain just as my parents entered the room. They awkwardly excused themselves back into the hallway for a minute while I perfected the Karate Kid crane kick into my underpants.

"Nichole, we are going to have to exercise a strong degree of visitor control. I can't handle the Shakey shit-show of visitors parading through the room while I'm fumbling around in this ass gown."

"You're right, I get it. But everyone is going to want to come see you. And quite frankly, I could use the support. Can I at least call Wally in the morning?"

"Sure. Absolutely. But only Wally. One at a time."

Mom and Dad looked like they were going to collapse with relief that I was up and about and in good spirits.

"I've been reading up on Dr. Surya and his off-line surgery," Dad said. "He's really quite a pioneer in the field."

Dad continued on with graphic descriptions of open-heart surgery that did nothing to comfort my mother. She sat and stared at all my wires, tubes and bandages occasionally beginning to mouth a question but never getting it out before deciding she'd rather not know any more than that I was okay.

Mostly, we sat quietly until I fell asleep. When I awoke they were gone.

**

It was the first time I had been left alone by nurses, doctors and family to just rest and I had fallen into a deep sleep.

"Sweetie? Are you awake?" Nichole prodded me from the arm chair by my bedside. I had to take stock of where I was. I tried and failed to sit up to look around, constrained by my tubes and wires and incapacitated by my severed sternum and abdominal muscles.

"I don't know if you are ready, but I decided I really needed to call Wally and well, Wally rushed right over."

"Yeah, sure. Wally's here?"

My oldest, bestest drinking buddy Wally came peering around the edge of my privacy curtain.

"Nichole told me what happened, I can't believe this, look at you. I hope you don't mind I came right over but I couldn't let Nichole go through this alone either, you know?"

"Thank you, Wally. Thank you for coming and thinking of Nichole, of course it's fine."

Wally held out a wrapped present. "I thought I shouldn't show up empty handed. I thought I should bring something. I just grabbed it on the way over."

I unwrapped a copy of the book <u>The Subtle Art of Not Giving a Fuck</u>. "It seemed like it might have some important life lessons for someone with heart issues." Wally said with a chuckle, a choked throat and watery eyes.

"Oh my God, are you going to cry."

"Well, I'm really shocked and upset…" and the tears started flowing.

"Oh my God you are such a wimp."

"I'm not a wimp, I'm a girl!" She said with a mock punch.

That's right, Wally is a girl. I can't hide it or avoid using pronouns any longer, so I might as well admit it now, my best drinking buddy over the last twenty years is a chick – a hot chick, no less. She says if she were blonde she would be the spitting image of Brittany Spears. You might even think she was sexy if you didn't think of her as being more like a sister, or think of her as being like Brittany Spears.

When Wally and I met and we were both single, I was chasing after her friend Amy and she was chasing after my friend Andy. We considered each other to be in the way of one another and had a tense relationship based on resentment. We eventually bonded over our mutual quest and commiserated in our failures. Wally tried to encourage me not to give up on Amy and coached me on what I should say.

"Well, if you know so much about how to woo a woman, then get over here and tell me exactly what to say." Wally followed me over to Amy at the other end of the bar, both of us swaggering under the weight of more than a few drinks.

Wally whispered into my ear and I repeated: "Amy, you look really beautiful tonight, your hair looks really nice."

"Thank you, Jeffrey," she smiled and flipped her hair.

Wally whispered in my ear again.

"You know, I have always really like you. I would love to spend more time with you and learn more about you."

"Why is Wally whispering in your ear?"

Wally whispered again.

"Wally may be helping me with the words, but they are my feelings." I gave Wally a thumbs up for the quick recovery.

"Really? You have so little clue what to say to a girl you have to bring a consultant along with you?"

I gave Wally an urgent glare and she whispered again.

"Your shoes are really cool, they really go with your hand bag."

"So you think cheap compliments are going to get me into bed? Is that it?"

"I'm sorry, I've never hit on a girl before. I thought this would be easier."

"I'm sorry, I've never hit on a girl before. I thought this would be easier," I repeated.

"You weren't supposed to repeat that, you idiot," Wally and I fell onto each other laughing. Amy grabbed her handbag and stomped out on her matching shoes and never spoke to either of us again.

"Alright smart guy, you think you can do better telling me what to say to Andy?"

"If I told you what to say to pick up a guy, I think you'd smack me right in the face."

Neither of us ever landed our respective prey and when the pursuit was over, there was just me and Wally left to drown our sorrows and laugh it all off. We never went through a stage of flirtation or sexual tension, just a sibling-like friendship replete with a touch of resentment – and a shared interest in drinking too much too often.

Wally's real name was Danielle Wallenberg and there were too many Danielles in our social circle, so Wally just stuck. Her father was in the Navy and everyone called him Wally too. He once told me: "My father was Wally, I was Wally in the Navy. It's an infectious name, I get it. I like it. I always assumed one of my kids would be called Wally too. It just *never* occurred to me it would be my daughter."

"Did you come alone, Wally? Where's the Beave?" Of course, the downside of being called Wally is that it will be equally infectious to refer to you and your sidekick as Wally and the Beave by anyone who ever heard of Leave it to Beaver. And if the duo are a pair of females it will be even more infectious – a downright pandemic of immature snickering.

"I told you to stop calling her that! She's in the hallway with Nichole, she'll hear you." She gave another punch with a little less mock in it.

"I didn't call her that, I referred to her as that. What she doesn't hear won't hurt her."

"Well she has heard it now that you have everyone in the bar calling her that."

"So sensitive." I said with a light mock poke of my finger. "Don't worry, I told her it's because she has the juvenile humor of Beavis from Beavis and Butthead. She likes it now."

"Stop teasing me, I'm really upset." Wally's face grew all red and puffy. "Look at you. Are you okay? How do you feel."

"Like I could get used to these pain meds. Pretty groovy. The only sensation these pain meds don't mask is the itchy hair growing back on my chest. And the nether regions, Wally, they shaved the damn nether regions."

Nichole and the Beave caught the tail end of this exchange as they came into the room. "Hah!" Exclaimed the Beave. "I hear that's all hip and trendy nowadays, Jeff. There's even a barber in the village where you can get it sculpted."

"No thanks, so far it's like having a cactus in my drawers."

"Oh, that can get pretty uncomfortable, but it gets better after…" Wally interjected.

"Whoa, whoa, whoa, shut the fuck up, stop right there, I do *NOT* want to know how you know this. We are *NOT* comparing prickly panty notes."

Wally always put on a sheepish grin when she knew she could exercise the power of embarrassment over me. It was her effective defense to my reveling in boy-teasing her for being a wussy.

"Ok, how are you doing otherwise," asked Wally. "You look like a mess."

"It's pretty uncomfortable, I have to admit. I can't sit up or lie down on my own. I can't slouch. I can't sit erect."

"Uh-oh, does Nichole know you can't get erect?" the Beave interrupted with a giggle. "Maybe you could sit erect if they gave you a Viagra suppository."

"Uh, settle down Beavis, I do *NOT* want to

know how you know that either," I said in my best Butthead voice, giving Wally an I-told-you-so smile.

"Well since you'll be laid up for a while, maybe we could take your wife out for a stiff one?" The Beave suggested. Nichole's eyes grew wide at the suggestion.

"It looks like it'll be a while before I can give my wife a stiff one or a drink. If you ladies would do the honors, I'm sure she could use one – a drink I mean."

Nichole nodded frantically with her tongue drooping out like a puppy hearing the words 'go for a walk.' And they left me to get some rest.

## 9. Late-Night Nurse of Death

Any medical professional, or medical amateur for that matter, will tell you to get lots of rest and eat well to recover from any and all ailments. It is ironic, then, that in any hospital, they feed you absolute crap and wake you up throughout the night if you're lucky enough to fall asleep in the first place amidst all the beeping monitors and late-night interlopers who come to take out or put in fluids into your body like vampires in the night. The better I got at squeezing in some snippets of sound dreaming the more often I was awoken by the prick of a needle and a night nurse hovering over me like one of those angel of death nurses that kills patients in their sleep. After a few days, I was getting more comfortable in my new environment and more ambivalent about the angels of death and managed to get in a few solid hours here and there. Until, that is, they assigned Cheri to my night shift.

"Good evening Mr. Hornbull, it's me Cheri again. How are you feeling tonight? Have you gotten any sleep? Did you eat your dinner? Been walking? Doing your breathing exercises? Any pain in your legs? Had a bowel movement today? Let's get your meds sorted, take some samples, and get some readings."

Cheri was a very young, very eager night nurse who was very insistent on demonstrably proving her knowledge and ability to perform and thoroughly explain in intricate detail every medication, test and procedure in the book. She was Asian and probably studied very hard in nursing school and had a deep emotional need to ensure that anybody who would listen, no matter how captive, knew how knowledgeable she was. This is probably how she got assigned night shift in the first place. One might think that having been relegated to night shift might have humbled her into not giving so much of a shit but it apparently only hardened her resolve. Too bad for her, I don't think displaying her pharmaceutical knowledge and bodily fluid extraction skills to half-sleeping patients in the middle of the night was going to get her promoted back off the night shift.

"Cheri, please let me get some sleep." I begged her in a drooling, overmedicated half-dream state. "After the week I've had, do you think I give a shit what bodily fluid, reading or tissue you want to extricate from my body in the middle of the night? Have some blood, please; a left foot, come on take another piece of my heart now baby! Just *pleeease* let me sleep through it."

"We'll make sure you get plenty of sleep. But first you need to take your meds, ok? I have pain meds for you. Do you want your pain meds?" She asked with a chipper dimpled grin like she was offering me a dog treat. "Good, we'll give you those as soon as you cooperate and let me do what I need to do for you tonight. Okay? Are you familiar with all your meds and dosages?

"Yes, I know the doctor explained what all those prescriptions were for, and I know it was important, but ten minutes later someone came in and explained they were going to rip a Foley catheter out of my penis and that other shit went right out the other ear and out the fucking window, alright? Can you just tell me again? Or better yet, not explain it again? Please?"

We have an absurd unspoken myth in our national discourse on health care and health insurance: the myth of the patient as a discerning customer. Don't get me wrong, patients need to educate themselves and take responsibility for major decisions regarding their health and their medical care. But we often speak as if we have the knowledge or ability to shop around for better deals and seek more effective treatments. When was I supposed to go shopping? When the cardiologist made it clear the only alternative to immediate, emergency open-heart surgery was to fall flat on my face dead of a heart attack as I tried to walk out of the hospital? Should I have called an ambulance and gone from hospital to hospital seeing who's got a bargain on open-heart surgery? Maybe I could have gotten a bulk discount if I had my knee taken care of at the same hospital. Maybe one emergency room was offering a free Starbucks coupons that day. When are you supposed to question procedures? In the middle of the night when Cheri is babbling to half comatose patients? When was I supposed to educate myself on my meds? In the middle of the night when the angels of death are administering God-knows-what into my veins in my sleep?

I educated myself over time, but this hospital stay will account for approximately all the medical expenses I have incurred in my life thus far and likely the majority over my entire lifetime. There is no 'free market' for health care when patients are rightfully expected to follow doctors' orders. And having a system that pretends there is sets up a medical-industrial complex that is ripe for waste, abuse and even rampant fraud. A parade of doctors breezes in and out of the hospital room every day. Many do not even ask "How are you?" much less take readings or administer tests. But they all sign the chart. Those signatures are what appear on the hospital bill in the end. I have never heard anybody, with the exception of my father, the medical school professor and seriously semi-pro smart ass, call bullshit and ask them to explain themselves. And the only hospitals I have seen that do not have a parade of doctors stealthily signing charts are in England and here in the U.S. in a Veterans' Administration hospital – in both instances, the doctors are salaried and rated according to their patients' outcome, not rewarded according to how many charts they sign.

I received good care and I am grateful, but only by having trust in my care providers and going along for the ride and being confronted by financial costs later. Many are not so lucky and the finances interfere with or even abruptly disrupt their care.

## 10. Ass-Gown Races

I was awoken in the early morning by my now-normal routine of nurses, meds and tests. Dr. Surya came for an early-morning visit. "The surgery went extremely well and there was no heart attack, no damage to or scarring of the heart tissue. We tested your arterial walls in other parts of your body to ensure you do not have a systemic problem with the lining of your arteries that might foretell continued cardiovascular risks and found nothing wrong with any other arteries and no long-term damage of any kind. The sonogram revealed you have an excellent robust ventricular flow."

"Thank you?" I offered, unsure how to respond to a ventricular flow complement.

"Once you recover from the trauma of the surgery, you will have a whole new lease on cardiac health."

"But what caused all this?"

"Well, the known contributing risk factors include the lifestyle behaviors. Your history of smoking, probably a poor diet, obesity, your body weight is 306.4 pounds."

"That's not even close. I compulsively weigh myself all the time, I am more like 270."

"You weigh 306.4 pounds."

"But I weigh myself every day. And I know it's accurate because I monkey with the scale until it gives me an accurate reading that I can believe in. It can't have been over 30 pounds off all this time."

As soon as Dr. Surya left and I had a moment without nurses hovering, I collected my tubes, wires and IV poles, snuck out of the room and set out into the hospital corridor to find a scale that was functioning properly so I could dispel this slanderous accusation that I weighed over 300 pounds. I tried them in the exam rooms, I tried them in the hallways. I intruded into other patients' rooms: "excuse me and my ass gown, I just need to find a scale that works around here."

It took around ten tries and ten readings of 306.4 pounds before it really sank in. I finally got busted by a nurse for roaming the corridors unattended and skulked back to my room.

How the hell was that possible? I have weighed myself every day for years and years. I knew I had been gaining in the months leading up so I meticulously weighed myself every day and adjusted the scale spring and experimented with moving it around the floor and shifting my weight around on my feet until I got an 'accurate' reading. Had my scale been telling me sweet little lies all that time? Once home, a little further experimentation revealed I could get my weight to vary by twenty pounds just by moving it around from spot to spot on the floor, and much more if I tinkered with the spring.

\*\*

I diligently tended to my breathing exercises and quickly settled into a routine of medication administrations, meals and walks. Several times a day an orderly would show up and escort me up and down the hallway a few times just to get me moving.

My rolling out of bed skills and abilities were improving quickly. Elizabeth helped me up for a walk and slipped a pair of red extra-grip anti-slip socks on my feet "We don't want any accidents, these are important."

We gathered up my tubes and wires into bundles I could carry while pulling my IV poles along with me as we headed for the hallway. The corridor of the cardiac ICU was always busy with recovering cardiac surgery patients waddling and shuffling up and down the corridor with their rear ends hanging out of those God-awful ass gowns they make you wear in the hospital. I was always told they made you wear those so you would stay in bed, a practice that harkens back to the days of forcing patients to lay immobile in bed in the name of rest. But now that medical science has deemed lying in bed to be the cause of bed sores, muscle deterioration, circulatory problems, blood clots and much worse, they want us out of bed and walking around at the earliest and every opportunity, so why do we still wear these damn ass gowns?

It was a disconcerting but not unfamiliar feeling of simply being out of shape – getting winded from rigorous exercise except that now the rigorous exercise was walking across the room.

I was panting by the time Elizabeth and I got to the door. I stepped into the hallway and came face to face with another patient, a woman in her seventies, flush from exhaustion and panting from her struggles to walk down the hallway. "Want to race?" I asked her with a smile. She gasped a chuckle and let out a smile. I beat that one-liner like a dead horse with every patient I passed and always got a chuckle out of my fellow patients – not so much out of the orderlies and nurses.

Surveying my fellow patients in the cardiac ICU, I quickly realized that however dire my situation may feel, I was the luckiest guy in the ward. Almost everyone else was in their seventies and had a host of other serious health problems – diabetes, kidney disease, lung diseases and worse. The only other patient who looked to be in his forties was tremendously obese. He was the only one who actually took me up my offer of an ass-gown race down the hallway. Our respective orderlies were amused but not pleased. "Whoa, slow down there fellas this ain't no race track."

Since it was made clear that ass-gown racing was verboten in the corridors of the cardiac ICU, me and the obese guy took to passive ass-gown wagering – betting on which of the old folks would make it down the hallway first. "OK, I've got gray-haired Granny in the diaper, you can take the old geezer with the oxygen tank for two-to-one odds."

Once we introduced odds it got way too complicated for two guys on serious pain meds to keep track of who had won what and owed who how much so we just did it for the sport of it. But the orderlies lost amusement with this joke when we started drawing the old folks into the action: "This ain't no damn ass-gown race track, no ass-gown wagering allowed here neither."

"Come on it's all good old-fashioned fun." One of the old guys protested. "Ass-gown races all day long, doo-dah, doo dah!"

## 11. Nathan and the Pool of Blood

I began to settle into a routine of poking, prodding, meals, medications, more poking and more prodding. Dr. Surya came for his daily visit and gave me my daily reassurance that everything was going well.

"But how did this happen?" was the constant question on my mind.

"Lifestyle factors." Was his perennial answer. "Would you say you have a stressful job?"

My job was with the Federal Emergency Management Agency (FEMA) as team lead of an advance team that is first to respond to an incident or deploy ahead of events with advanced notice like hurricanes. We would deploy to a coast or an island, ride it out and report back afterwards – worrying all the while not just about myself and my team, but about how we are going to put a whole state back together. I lost track of how many hurricanes I had sat through, but a few stood out:

- The Mississippi coast after Katrina, when a county emergency manager told us not to approach dead bodies because they may be guarded by a pack of domestic dogs turned feral or an alligator.
- Sleeping in a wet bed under a leaky roof with no power and no running water in a heavily damaged resort in Puerto Rico.
- The New Jersey State Emergency Operations Center the day of Superstorm

Sandy when the head of New Jersey State Police pointing his finger in my face called FEMA a "clown show" and said "Tell your leadership we have a very large, very loud governor" gesturing to Chris Christy behind him "who has no problem taking this shit to the airwaves."

"No. I wouldn't say that." I lied. Although actually I really wouldn't *say* that. I knew it, and it was true I had a stressful job, but I wouldn't *say* it because I had already stewed over the thought that my work and career may never be the same again after all this. How would I make adjustments to my responsibilities without permanently benching myself?

Work had been calling to see when it was ok to visit and I had been stalling them. I didn't mean to keep them in suspense, I just didn't want to explain the situation before I knew enough to dictate my own time frame and terms of my return. I didn't even know enough yet to know when I would be back to work much less in what capacity – traveling would be out of the question for the indefinite future.

My old colleague, friend and now boss Nathan, my favorite after-work drinking buddy called to bug me into a visit and I acquiesced, he's fun after all. Sometimes too fun, he took the opportunity of his excused absence to visit me to hit Maxwell's Bar on the way to pound a few in my honor and showed up boisterously intoxicated.

"Dude, what's with all the tubes and wires and shit? You look like one of those Borg cyborgs from Star

Trek," asked Nathan.

"I am Jeffutius of Borg. Prepare to be assimilated. Resistance is futile." I hammed it up stiffly moving my arms and head like a cyborg until I cracked myself up and Nathan laughed along with me.

"When are you coming back to work?" Nathan asked.

"I honestly don't know yet. My doctors say a minimum of eight weeks would be normal, but normal also seems to be having this surgery at age 75 with a host of other health issues. I can't imagine that I won't recover faster than normal."

"We need you back Dude, hurricane season is just getting started."

"Oh, Nathan, I don't think advanced team lead is in my immediate future, or my medium-term future. Maybe not in my future at all. It's going to have to be someone else's turn to fly down to the islands and get hit by every tropical storm that passes by."

"It's alright, I got you covered for now," Nathan said with a devious smile.

"Who do you have covering?" I asked.

"I got Ashley to cover," Nathan said. "Is she qualified?" I asked rhetorically.

"She's very eager," Nathan said with a smile.

'Seriously, Dude, when are you gonna be

back?" Nathan asked in a more serious tone.

I recounted everything that had happened and what little I knew about what was to come going forward, but tried to paint as rosy a picture as I could. I didn't want to scare them into thinking I needed to be on permanent restricted duty.

Nathan's eyes were drifting a bit after so much serious talk. "Dude, I got to take a wicked piss, is there a bathroom I could use?"

"Yeah my roommate sounds like he is having trouble in mine, I'll walk you down the hall." And I began the ritual of rolling over, sitting up and gathering my tubes and wires.

"Whoa, are you supposed to get out of bed?" Nathan reached out unsure whether to hold my arm or tubes or get out of the way.

"Yeah, they make me get up and walk every hour or so. The nurse is late, you can escort me."

I shuffled down the hall with Nathan and tried to explain the rules of wagering on the ass-gown races but his bladder was involved in its own race against the clock to get to the men's room.

"Dude, are you sure this is alright? Are you okay to wait out here in the hall on your own?"

"Yeah, no problem, I'll be right here. Go ahead."

As soon as Nathan shut the door a nurse barked,

"Excuse me! You are not supposed to be walking unescorted."

"I'm not unescorted, Nathan is with me and I'm just showing him the bathroom." As I turned to point at the bathroom door the IV tube in my arm got caught on my heart pillow and pulled the pick out of my arm. Blood squirted out of my arm in 24-inch squirts in rhythm with my heart beat and spilled all over the floor and wall in streaks of splatter worthy of a murderous crime scene. I flailed at the freely swinging tube. I caught it after a few tries but had no idea what to do with it once I had it in hand and the vascular gusher continued to spew. Elizabeth marched briskly from the nurses' station and squashed my heart pillow on the erupting vein and said: "Just keep pressure on it and come with me back to the nurses' station. We'll get you fixed up."

Elizabeth fixed the pick and line in a minute at the nurses' station and the excitement was over – for me, anyway. Nathan, on the other hand, emerged from the men's room to find me missing and a pool of blood and splatter all over the floor and walls in my place. He froze for a moment unsure whether to step cautiously around the blood puddles or just run. He tiptoed though the scene of the massacre being careful not to touch the splatter on the walls, found his way back to the room and came slinking in looking over his shoulder for the murderer. "What the hell happened out there?"

I tried calmly explaining it was really nothing to worry about as Elizabeth tried to swab a streak of blood out my hair and off my forehead but Nathan face fell blank as they looked again at my bandages, tubes and bloody heart pillow.

"Don't recover too fast, Jeff," Nathan said "Milk this shit for all it's worth. Take a leave of absence and hang out in Hornbullonia all summer. When are you ever going to have another opportunity to take a summer off?"

I felt very lucky to be in a very different situation than the average American. Not only was my health insurance comprehensive, the federal government has very flexible sick leave policies: generous sick leave, advanced leave you can pay back, medical telework from home, unpaid absence and even leave donations from your colleagues. None of these options cost the taxpayer anything and an organization the size of the federal government can easily temporarily reshuffle to compensate for the absence of one employee. Perhaps most importantly, this flexibility leads to an underlying culture of simply trying to work the system to the advantage of the sick employee unlike many private-sector entities that would gladly fire a sick employee, stripping him of his health insurance in the interest of the quarterly bottom line.

I wouldn't "milk it" as Nathan phrased it, I was too leery of the health and mental risks of stagnating at home to do that, but I am eternally grateful to have been treated with dignity out of concern for my welfare. I wouldn't 'milk it' as Nathan suggested, quite the opposite. In the end, I would grow concerned about my state of mind and my physical and mental activity level while sitting at home so I returned to work far before my doctor suggested and far, far before I could have stretched out the flexibility granted me as a federal employee. I suspect anyone would have done the same. It makes me wonder why the non-government side of the economy has such difficulty finding ways to simply treat the sick with dignity.

## 12. Fat, Drunk and Stupid

"How are you feeling today Mr. Hornbull" Dr. Surya gleefully asked on his morning visit.

"Great, the surgery must have been a success. Every day I get stronger and the days get shorter."

"Days get shorter?" asked Dr. Surya with a puzzled look, proving yet again cardiologists have no sense of humor.

"Open heart surgery on the solstice?" I was met with a blank stare. "Cardiologists really have the sense of humor as Edgar Allen Poe, don't they?"

He didn't get it.

"Never mind. Doctor," I continued." What have you learned about what led up to the blockages?"

"Well, the common contributing factors are the lifestyle factors such as fatty diet, high cholesterol, smoking, high blood pressure…"

"Yeah, you keep telling me that, but what about my particular case? Is there anything about my blockages that indicates exactly what caused them?"

"What we can tell you is how to avoid having the condition recur, which is the lifestyle factors I mentioned."

"You mean: 'fat, drunk and stupid is no way to go through life' is the only diagnostic revelation I am going to get?"

"Let's just say it is best to focus on your diet and lifestyle going forward." He took a breath: "Now, let's get the rest of these tubes out of you."

The doctor and Elizabeth removed the last of my IV tubes, swabbed the needle holes and band-aided them up. Elizabeth added: "Oh, one more thing, new socks."

She peeled off my red anti-slip socks and slid on some new gray ones. "You are now free to roam the halls. Get as much exercise as you can."

"You mean?" I began to puzzle, "The socks? The red socks? That's how the nurses always knew I wasn't supposed to be walking around unattended? I was so impressed they seemed to know every patient and what their walking restrictions were. All the while it was those sneaky little color-coded socks. I can't believe you bamboozled me like that."

"Well if we told you, you might have changed socks and slipped right past the nurses' station and off the ward." Elizabeth said with a mischievous grin.

"Slip off the ward? Screw that, I could have cleaned up on ass-gown race wagering if I knew the code of the socks! How many of those red-socked tortoises did you let me bet on? Did the fat guy know the sock color-code? That's so unfair."

"We didn't want to encourage that behavior either. Just keep the sock color code our little secret, we don't want the other patients getting any ideas – especially your ideas."

## 13. Check Me Out

Before I could be discharged from the hospital and sent on my way, only one hurdle remained: I was required to poop. All the oxy-opioids they had me on constipated the crap factory something fierce. I was not ungrateful for this. It now looked as though I would escape the hospital without having to succumb to the bed pan. After six days on the inside, I think my poop was about as eager to get outside and get some fresh air as I was. But after six days, it is not that simple. I waited, I tried, I waited some more. I felt the occasional twitching cramp and thought for sure this time it is coming. I was beginning to feel like an expectant mother, distended belly and all. I could feel it kick from time to time.

Under Elizabeth's threat of an enema, I retreated to the bathroom with final determination. Nichole stood by the door and acted as my birthing coach: "Push, sweetie pie, push!" she shouted. "Breathe! And push!"

"Oh my God, It's prairie dogging – in and out, in and out." And then in my best Amityville Horror gravelly, ghostly scream: "*GET OUT!!! GET OOOUUUT!!!*"

"Do I need to fetch the apparatus?" Elizabeth threateningly interrupted our antics with little appreciation of the humor.

"No, I'm crowning. I swear. *I'M CROWNING!*" And with a final prolonged growling grunt the bathroom fell silent. I turned to lay eyes on the beautiful bouncing baby turd I had brought into this world: perfectly formed, dark, coiled up, the length and girth of a whiffle ball bat.

"Oh my God. Does anyone want to see this before I flush?"

"Noooooo," replied Nichole and Elizabeth in unison.

I flung the open the door.

"Elizabeth," I said clutching my abdomen, the other arm extended "*THAT* was the big one!"

"With that out of the way, let's get you discharged," Elizabeth suggested. "Ordinarily we refer patients to a rehab facility, but you are young and strong and you have support at home. Nichole, will you be able to help Jeff with some basic needs for a time after he gets home?"

"Of course, I'm taking at least a week off, more if I need to. What do I need to do?" Nichole asked.

"Just help him in and out of bed, make sure he eats properly, does his breathing exercises and walks as much as he can." Elizabeth explained. "Not more than you can, Jeff, don't push it. But do as much as you can. And we'll provide you with a physical therapy referral to make sure you can take care of some basics like getting out of bed and getting dressed, and so you can help him, Nichole. And we'll refer you for physical therapy home care to get you back to being able to do all the little things you need to do to take care of yourself. In the meantime, no running, no biking, no driving, no sex, no saunas, no exertion. Just regular, incrementally increasing mild exercise and your breathing exercises."

"And if you have any problems, come back here to see me," Dr. Surya interjected from behind the desk at the discharge station. "Do not go to the emergency room. They will have to run you through every test in the book only to tell us what we already know. Your heart has suffered quite a strain. You will have good days and set-back days. But every day will get a little better."

"Can you think of anything else you might need," asked Elizabeth.

"Maybe some alarm clocks," I thought out loud. "I don't know how I'll ever be able to fall asleep without the constant ringing, pinging and clanging of alarms going off all night every night. I've gotten so used to my ICU routine I don't know how I'll sleep without them. And some wires and tubes to tie myself up with so I can't get to the bathroom that would really make me feel like I am home in the hospital."

They wheeled me to the door and waved farewell.

# Homeward-Bound and Home-Bound

## 14. Homebound

Getting in and out of a taxi was the first hurdle in getting home. It is impossible to get into an average sedan without scrunching your thorax – not an option for me at that juncture. I had to abandon one and wave off others until we found one of those box-shaped ones I could sit up straight in. Even so, turning sideways to get out was another yogic exercise.

Nichole helped me into the elevator and into the apartment, and I plopped on the couch. My abdomen scrunched and I jolted in pain to get up but was incapable. Nichole had to pull me up by the hands and I sat in the straight-backed wing chair I had always hated. It was my new best friend and part-time home for the next few weeks.

"Honey, wouldn't you feel better if you showered?" Nichole asked.

"Do you want me to shower? " I asked. "Are you telling me I stink?"

"Well, you were in there for six days, I mean, don't take it the wrong way."

"Not at all, SweetiePie. Only those who love you tell you when you stink."

"Well I wouldn't want a total stranger to tell you you stink."

"A total stranger that tells you you stink is just an asshole," I retorted. "Two kinds of people tell you

you stink: those that love you and total assholes."

"And flies." Nichole added "Flies will tell you you stink too."

"Those that love you most, total assholes and flies, which one are you?"

"I love you and I want to cuddle you, not your flies. Go take a shower."

Showering presented a whole new set of gymnastic challenges. My chest muscles still severed, my range of motion was extremely limited. Getting my arms over my head or around my back felt like convoluted yoga positions. Reaching down to my feet seemed unthinkably dangerous. Post-heart-surgery showering could be a gymnastic event. It ought to be in the damn Olympics – several categories, in fact: Speed showering, figure showering, singles, doubles, judges holding up score placards.

Taking a shower, however, also meant confronting a grizzly sight I had thus far very consciously managed to avoid: the scar. I hadn't even looked down at the bandages since just after I awoke from the surgery. I kept the bandages on in the shower to prevent dirt getting washed into the wound. When I got out they were wet and peeling off on their own. I peeled off the wet bandages and turned toward the mirror, a ten-inch incision the length of my chest stared back. "It will be there forever," I thought and it would not fade away over time like I was told commonly occurs.

I was hoping for an impressive number of stitches to brag about but they don't use them anymore – not tape or staples either. They use glue. And the scar is supposed to fade to a thin near-invisible line. But for now, it was an angry looking incision, not even quite a scar yet. I stared at it, confronting it, and resigned myself to owning it, showing it off whenever I could.

I crept out of the bathroom unsure if I should lay the scar on Nichole's eyes just yet.

"Are you OK?" Nichole asked as I peered out from the bathroom.

"Yeah, I didn't think to bring clothes to change into and I didn't know if you wanted to see 'it' yet."

"Well, it's been six days but I have seen 'it' before you know."

Not that 'it', the scar 'it'. Do you want to see it" I asked. Nichole nodded and I stepped out from behind the bathroom door.

"Wow! That is a doozy."

"It is, certainly, the most macho thing I have ever had to show for myself."

"Well I don't know about that," Nichole said with her eyes glancing down and her eyebrows wriggled up.

"I want to post a picture of it on Facebook," I said. "I mean the scar 'it'."

"Don't you dare!" Nichole retorted. "That would really freak some people out. Some people don't even know about the surgery yet."

We came to a compromise. I would post a description of it on Facebook with the qualifier: 'too gruesome to share publicly but anyone who wants to see it privately, comment with your cell number and I'll text it to you.' Surprisingly to me, I only got a couple takers.

Getting dressed was another gymnastic activity I would practice over the coming weeks. I had really taken my dressing range of motion for granted thus far in life and had no idea how get dressed without stretching chest muscles. Button-down shirts only, and those only with assistance. I diligently practiced the Karate Kid technique of donning underpants but eventually decided my physical limitations simply warranted going commando until I could manage on my own. Bending over to put socks on my feet would have to be Nichole's job for the foreseeable future. Bending yourself in half and pulling upward is a cruel and painful motion to inflict upon a post-operative cardiac patient. Whoever invented socks was a senseless, sadistic maniac. I vaguely recall a medieval drawing of a dungeon torture device designed to achieve the same effect.

Getting in and out of bed was another athletic skill I would train for for some time. You can't move in anything resembling a sit-up motion that uses upper abdominal muscles. The preferred technique for lying down is to sit sideways on the bed arrange the pillow and without offering any resistance from your chest muscles to slow yourself, just flop down aiming my head at the pillow, then roll your lower half onto the bed. A head shot at the pillow requires wriggling out of bed sideways and trying again. A wrongly-place pillow or even a thick wrinkle in the sheet can tense the chest muscles and evoke the axe-blade-protruding-from-the-chest sensation I had become all too familiar with.

I can't lie on my side without contorting my slashed-open chest, I can't roll over and I breathe sleeping on my back without gagging on my own uvula. I have long been told by those sleeping next to me that I gag in my sleep while I snore like an angry gorilla. If that wasn't bad enough, I also had no lateral strength in my chest with which to yank the blankets back onto myself whenever Nichole rolled and yanked them off me. In Nichole's defense, every night in our bed we apparently engage in a comatose tug of war with our blankets in our sleep. Her subconscious simply had no warning to adjust to my weakened state.

"Are you suggesting I would steal the blankies right off my sleeping crippled husband?"

"No, I'm suggesting the world-famous blankie-thief cat burglar obviously crept into our bedroom and stole my half of the blankies. I think we should call the police."

"Well maybe you were lying on your stomach and farted your half of the blankies right off of yourself. In which case, you can keep your blankies and your farts all too yourself, thank you very much."

**

I have long desensitized myself to the sounds and noises that emanate from Manhattan streets while I sleep. We had been in the same third-floor, street-facing apartment for ten years and it had been about eight and half since the street noises bothered me at night. But trying to sleep in in the morning on a weekday is an entirely different affair. The sounds of the garbage trucks, sirens, jack hammers, horns honking and assholes shouting at each other all blend in the half-asleep mind's eye to form an image. It's the image of an evil nemesis to Wee-Willy-Winkie, who tip-toes from bedroom window to bedroom window sprinkling dream dust and making sure everyone comfortably falls asleep. His evil arch-nemesis, I will call him Bombastic-Bobby-Bazooka. Starting at about 7:00am, just after Wee Willie Winkie heads to bed after a long night's work, Bobby-Bazooka starts driving around Manhattan in a Dr. Seuss-esque vehicle that is a weird amalgamation of garbage truck, fire engine and party bus manned by garbagemen clanging garbage can lids like symbols in a symphony, jack-hammering, buzz-sawing utility crews and vociferous cast members of the Jersey Shore shouting profane obscenities through megaphones. All the while, Bombastic-Bobby-Bazooka stands atop a podium waving a conductor's wand and basking in delight of all the growls and groans emanating from the bedroom windows of all the late risers. In the half-asleep mind's eye, the acoustic evidence for the actual existence of Bombastic-Bobby-Bazooka appears incontrovertible.

The ear-piercing screeching of the hydraulic

trash compactors on the backs of the garbage trucks, whir and whine and gurgle and bellow like urban whale songs. Maybe that's what whale songs are, the whales are trying to communicate with New York City garbage trucks that they hear from under the sea thousands of miles away. Maybe that's what whale songs mean: "Knock off the fucking racket, we're trying to sleep out here!"

"What, is it garbage truck mating season out there?" I grumble from under the pillow I have pressed over my head like I'm trying to smother myself in my sleep.

"What is that God-awful clanging? Are they rutting and wrestling in the streets like horny elk vying for the favor of female garbage trucks?"

I reluctantly remove the pillow from my head and peek out from under my blinders. No matter how deserving I am of a sleep-in, it is simply not going to happen.

I rock myself over sideways, fling my feet over and slide off the bed. I am beginning to master the debedification process. I shuffled into the living room and gazed longingly at the couch, knowing it would be some time before I could flop on it and curl up.

There is simply no position to sit, stand or lie around in comfortably with your sternum cracked open – not without a lot of Percocet anyway. With enough Percocet one can make one's self quite comfortable with a cracked-open sternum in any position or social situation. Nichole, with the mercy of Florence

Nightingale, came up with two other pain-saving items: A wedge pillow and a hospital tray table. The wedge pillow allowed me to get in and out of bed by myself and even roll and reposition myself a bit and started sleeping nearly adequately. The tray table allowed me to sit up right in the straight-backed arm chair. I could eat, watch TV, and dick around on my computer all in a sitting-up-right position. Slouching on the couch and hunching over the coffee table was out of the question. I was relegated to Nichole's fancy antique wing chair. Nice fancy chair but upright and stiff. I thought it would never be used unless Edith Bunker popped in to have a seat. Now it was my best friend and home away from bed.

I wiled away a few days in my armchair, reading, writing, watching TV and blowing into my breathing-exercise machine, occasionally wincing and clutching my heart pillow to my chest to cough. I took walks in the hallway of my apartment building in my boxers, clutching my heart pillow and exercising my gray-sock privileges, pacing laps in the 50-foot-long hallway. People kept holding the elevator door for me.

"Going down?"

"No, thanks. I'm just going for a walk." And I continued my slow shuffle up and down the hallway.

## 15. Out and About

Nichole needed to get downtown to her family antique store having been away for two full weeks. She was worried what matters her parents may have taken back into their own hands while she was away and I, frankly, needed some alone naptime.

"Are you going to be able to get up by yourself if I leave you?" she asked as she tucked me in for a nap.

"Yeah, I think I have mastered the art of the roll-and-twist technique of getting out of bed. Anyway, the physical therapist is coming over in a couple hours. Leave the door unlocked so I can just yell for her to come in if I can't get up."

"I turned off the ringers on all the phones," Nichole assured me.

"Thank you. I don't know how the world knows when I am trying to nap, but they find out, and that's when everyone calls." I whined. "It's a conspiracy. They won't tolerate me napping."

"I know, Sweetie. And I'll pull down the blinds, so you can sleep a little."

"No, please, no more blinds. Christ, we've been holed up in here with the blinds down for so long we're like Sid and Nancy. Please leave the blinds up or things might turn ugly," I implored.

"Alright my little Sid Vicious, go to sleep. Mwah." And she pecked me on the forehead and left.

About two hours later I was jolted awake by a pounding on my door, a male voice yelling in my living room and my front door slamming. "Hello! Jeff! Are you ok?!" I jolted awake and scrambled through my roll-and-twist maneuver into a half-sitting half-sliding-onto-the-floor position.

"Mr. Hornbull!" shouted a female voice entering my bedroom. "Stop! Don't try to get up. It's okay. I'm Monica, your physical therapist."

"It's me, Fred the super and Carlos the doorman," shouted Fred. "I'm so sorry, Monica said she was your physical therapist and you weren't answering the door."

"We're so sorry, Mr. Hornbull," said Monica as she helped me on my feet and up off the bed, "But I am required to alert my agency when there is no answer at a door and they looked up your medical case. Sometimes when someone with your medical condition doesn't answer the door, it's for a very bad reason. We have to do that for any client."

"I'm fine, I'm fine," I stammered. "Except for the heart attack you almost gave me. Christ. I always complain the world beats a path to my door every time I try to nap, but the whole world never came crashing right through the door before."

"Ok, you okay? We get going. So sorry, but I know what you been through. We don't know what happening inside." Carlos apologized as he showed himself out.

"Thank you, guys. I appreciate it. At least you proved that not only can I sit up in bed on my own, I can now leap out of bed like there is a flaming rattle snake under the covers. Good to know," I said rubbing the sleep out of my eyes.

"So how are you doing, Mr. Hornbull," asked Monica as she helped me out of bed and led me by the arm into the wing chair in the living room. "How can I help you?"

"Well, when we scheduled the appointment, it was so you could show my wife Nichole how to help me up and down and in and out of bed. But she figured that out by the next day and we thought you could help me get up and down and in and out unaided. But I guess I got the hang of that."

"And your breathing exercises?"

"Great, I can keep the little ball hovering in the tube for a good twenty seconds at a pop. And I hug my heart pillow and cough several times a day, although it is still quite painful."

"Have you been active?"

"I walk as much as I can but that's not much. I've worked my way up from the hallway to getting outside and walking to the corner. But I spend a lot of time sitting. I have to sit upright in this stiff-backed arm chair."

"It's not good to spend too much time sitting."

"I know, it doesn't feel good either. Nichole and

I spend so much time playing Scrabble we coined a new medical condition we call 'Scrabble Ass.' Then we binge-watched Breaking Bad and developed 'Breaking Bad Ass,' And in season three of Orange is the New Black we both got an acute case of 'Orange is the New Black Ass.'"

"That doesn't sound good," Monica chuckled "You need to get up periodically and walk as much as you can. Take it at your own pace, but a little more each day. "I was getting a little better every day. I had apparently out-recovered the physical therapist and didn't have much use for her by the time she came. I was on the right track and just had to slowly, steadily keep doing what I could.

**

Soon I was getting outside and walking to the corner, sans-boxers, having graduated to the more-distinguished look of pajama bottoms, un-showered and clutching my blood-stained heart pillow. It was good to get outdoors but strange to see the day-to-day, daytime routines of my neighborhood. I had lived on he same block for ten years but had always been too wrapped up in my own routines of job, travel and social life to learn the faces and routines of my neighbors out and about on my block. In the course of a week, I met and learned more of my neighbors than I had in last ten years – the old English woman who walks her corgis to the benches in the plaza on the corner, every day, the super who I give a thank-you nod to when he redirects his hose from my path when he cleans the sidewalk as I walk to the subway every morning, and Sharif, the Pakistani fruit-cart vendor on the corner. Sharif's cart was well stocked and highly trafficked. The high traffic kept his produce fresh and varied. He had recently expanded to have separate carts for fruits and vegetables. The cart even took on a social street-corner character when his Pakistani compatriot taxi drivers congregated.

One morning I shuffled down to the corner and mingled among the cab drivers scoping out some healthy fruit for breakfast.

"How long have these mangos been here, Sharif?"

"All fresh, everything very fresh," he always replied.

"What about ripe? Have they been here long enough to be ripe?"

"All very fresh and ripe, boss. Everything always fresh and ripe."

"Hey! Quit holding up the line you deranged Hungarian!" a booming voice rang out. It was Big Hans, an old partner in crime of mine from the depths of my partying past. Big Hans was a relic from the old German-Town character and Hungarian flavor of Yorkville – American-born of a Hungarian and German parents – but never call him German, he is Bavarian. He also speaks Hungarian and gets a kick out of my broken Hungarian. He likes to say I speak as fluently as a deranged Hungarian, which you may think is purely a joke, but being the only foreigner who speaks Hungarian that most Hungarians are likely to meet, that's exactly what Hungarians always think: I speak Hungarian, therefore I must be Hungarian, I speak it the way I do, therefore, I must be a deranged Hungarian. It is a logical assumption.

Big Hans and I bonded through shared common adversity during our partying days, we didn't have much in common, but we had been in some proverbial foxholes together. I like to say I at one time dallied in cocaine, not too often and not for too long, but on those all-night-all-day-all-night benders with Big Hans there was nothing dallying about it. Big Hans still lived in his mother's basement and sold pot on the side but had otherwise cleaned up his act the earlier that year, following a near-fatal, late-night drunken bike accident after celebrating his recent release from jail. We swapped stories of recuperation and advice on healthy living and treated each other to rounds of hand fruit from Sharif's cart.

"Hey Sharif, let me get a round of these Japanese plums for the house," Hans offered. "For all your friends here too." The cab drivers raised their plums as if they were raising glasses in thanks.

"Holy shit, Big Hans!" I exclaimed. "We are in the future! Look at us, telling war stories and talking about our health over fruit at a street-corner cart. Feels like we just stepped through a time portal, doesn't it?"

"Did you ever think you'd see the day?" he laughed. "I guess we're both very lucky to have made it here."

"Lucky indeed, it may have been one of those

coke-fueled nights that damaged a couple spots on my coronary arteries that started the build-up of blood crud and caused the blockages."

"Really? Is that possible?"

"Sure. The blockages were localized, not part of a broader systemic condition throughout my circulatory system, I suppose it could have been," I said.

"Is that what caused it?" he asked. "What did the doctor say?"

"He said 'fat, drunk and stupid is no way to go through life.' Other than that, they don't know. I'll probably never know."

"Wow," said Big Hans. "I am going to have to get myself checked out. If that could happen to you, I am lucky to be walking around."

"You should, while you're on a healthy kick. One of the dangers of partying is you blame what ails you on the partying and don't get it checked out. Remember what happened to Nicky Nines? He didn't get his lungs checked out because he figured the doctor would just tell him to quit smoking and partying, turned out he had a lung infection that almost killed him."

"Shit man, you're right. Now's the time for me to get checked out, now that I'm mostly healthy."

"To our health," I raised my plum and Hans bumped it with his like we were raising beer steins. "To our health!"

We sighed and parted on that sober note.

## 16. The Demon Barber of Eighty-Second Street

My feet were getting itchy to walk a little farther, I was getting itchy for a shave and a haircut, and I was getting literally itchy from the hair growing back on my chest, and through the scar, the nether regions and other places where they had shaved my body hair. I was going to ask for advice on Facebook about mitigating all the itching from the hair growing back in all the surgically-shaved places, but I decided I really didn't want to know who of my Facebook friends have had what experience in this regard or where on their body or why. It is apparently so hip and trendy nowadays to be shaved in all the wrong places there are bound to be some real shockers out there and I really didn't want to hear them. I don't want to hear it from you either, whoever you are reading this, not from anyone, ever. So, keep it to yourself and just forget the whole damn thing, okay?

I had a casual acquaintanceship with Boris, my local barber. Boris is ethnically Russian from Uzbekistan, like every barber in New York nowadays. Take it from me, if you have a Russian barber in New York, odds are you have an Uzbekistani Russian barber and they will be thoroughly touched by your thoughtfulness if you ask them about Uzbekistan rather than Russia for a change. I walked the two and a half blocks to Boris' Barbershop and arrived a little winded. I paused at the entrance to catch my breath and tease the cockatiel in the cage by the door. There was a sign that read 'Don't poke the bird. He bites," which I took as a personal challenge. Ordinarily, Boris and his colleague Alex ignored me while I tormented their bird, but my appearance drew their attention away from the customers they were working on.

"Come in my friend," Boris eyed me in my pajama bottoms holding my heart pillow. "You alright?"

"I've been worse," I answered.

"Five-minute wait," said Boris. "Please to have a seat."

"No, thanks. I'm more comfortable standing," I sidled away from the birdcage and waited my turn.

"Clean me up and make it all short please," I requested as I carefully slid into the chair. "Summer is here and it's too hot for all this shag."

The barber chair kept me upright and seated fairly comfortably while Boris snipped away at my head and neck. But then came the beard. He gestured me to lean forward as he reclined the chair. He held my shoulder and leaned me back into the reclined chair. I tried to keep my back, and chest, straight but in so doing my head dangled back over the top of the head rest apparently triggering a spear to spring out of chair back and stick through my chest – or so it felt. I tried to sit back up but my ability to move in a sit-up motion still eluded me and caused more pain, and I was helpless to get myself up or explain to the now panicky barber what on Earth was wrong. I struggled and winced and tried to get him to help me up.

"Please help me sit up," I grimaced in pain.

"No, no, you slide down," he retorted as he pushed me downward in the chair. I finally understood what he was getting at and tried sliding further down into the chair and slipped all the way out of the chair, onto the floor and landed on my knees, arms braced against the counter. Boris, his colleague Alex and the other customers all looked on in shock and concern as I tried to use my arms against the counter to lift myself up, but it required more chest strength than I had. The two barbers helped me to my feet and looked at me with utter confusion on their faces.

"I'm so sorry, I should have explained. I had a major surgery a couple weeks ago." And I pulled my shirt collar down to reveal the top of the angry red scar.

Their eyes popped wide. "Oh, I am so sorry, I didn't know," Boris apologized.

"No, I'm sorry I didn't say anything first," I apologized back.

"Please, sit. We take care of you." Alex said with conviction.

"Thanks, but I was traumatized by Sweeney Todd as a child, I don't think this is a good idea," I resisted.

But they insisted and demonstrated what he was trying to tell me the first time. I slid my butt forward and my back down so the headrest would support my head. It suddenly made sense to me and I sat, but when he reclined the chair I winced in pain again and tried haplessly to get back up.

I screeched in pain and the barber called in for back-up. The two barbers argued in Russian about how to lift me up, waving their arms, one with a razor in his hand, and getting red in the face yelling at each other.

"Alright guys, let's not get too pissed off while you've got a razor at my throat."

"No, no" he insisted. And held my back and neck as his partner adjusted the headrest and chair, I was suddenly un-scrunched and pain free. We all smiled in relief and he went about his business giving my beard a trim. When he was done he called Alex over and they locked arms under my back and aided me up out of the chair like trained barber-EMTs.

"You alright, sir?"

"I guess so. It's shorter than when I came in, anyway," I looked myself over in the mirror.

I wouldn't dare go to any other barber after that. At first because I was deathly afraid of barber chairs and I knew they understood how to get me in and out of it. But as I healed over the next two to three months and this became unnecessary, they always still insisted on maneuvering me in and out of the chair like nurses transferring me from hospital gurney to operating table. It took me over a year to convince them they didn't need to fuss over me anymore. And now I never get my hair cut anywhere else.

## 17. Ladies Who Lunch

My next major excursion beyond the corner was to meet Wally and the Beave for lunch at the Drum, a gastro pub owned by an older English gent who insisted on a few details of English pub ambiance like upholstered barstools and saw dust on the floor. "I've always wanted to be a lady who lunches," I said as I slid carefully upright into the booth holding my heart pillow. Wally and the Beave put on cheery faces to mask their pity.

"So how are you doing?" Asked Wally.

"A little better every day," I answered with an optimistic smile. "It's tough, but I've got a lot to be thankful for."

"Like what?" asked Wally, her head tilted with curiosity. "What's there to like about recovering from open-heart surgery? What are a few of your favorite things?"

"Little brown boxes tied up with string?" asked the Beave, smiling.

"A few of my favorite things," I mock sang, "are: My coughing pillow. It helps lessen the sensation that my sternum is being cracked open like a lobster when I cough, and I cough a lot.

My wedge pillow, which helps alleviate the alien-erupting-from-my-chest sensation when I lie down or sit up. Oxy. Helps alleviate the sensation that I have had surgery at all or that there is anything wrong anywhere in the world. Time. Lots of free time to spend with friends and family, on Oxy.

"And being a lady who lunches," injected the Beave.

"I'm glad we're getting you out of the house, at last," Wally added, stirring her ice water with her straw.

"Yeah I'm walking all the way around the block nowadays. Yesterday when it rained, I took a cab over to the Met and walked around in there to get some exercise."

"Good idea, you can get some culture with your exercise," said the Beave.

"It's amazing how much of the Metropolitan Museum you can see when you are walking as fast as you can. It's weird though," I said. "Every time I wander the halls of the Met I go through the Roman world, the Medieval world and I always expect to turn a corner and bump into a gunfighter in West World."

"Ha! Look out for those gun fighters," the Beave giggled.

A waitress appeared with her pad, tapping it with her pencil. "Ready to order?"

"Yeah, I'd better have a cheeseburger and fries before some cardiologist tells me not to," I said smiling and handing her my menu.

"Fish and chips," said Wally.

"Just a small green salad for me," said the Beave, her voice high and girlish. "I am dieting, and setting a better example for you, Jeff."

"Yeah, right," I said, pushing her menu back to her. "I know your dating diet deception: scarf down two slices of pizza on your way out so your date thinks your delicate when you order a salad. We know you better than that, eat what you want."

"No!" objected the Beave, "We are going to set a good example and take care of you!"

I felt a surge of surprise, the Beave seemed serious for once.

"We got you a present," said Wally looking over at the Beave who handed me a small giftwrapped, bow-tied box.

"A FitBit!" I exclaimed as I unwrapped the gift. "Just like yours, Wally." She took it from the box and started putting it around my wrist. "You realize this means you are now my personal FitBit helpline until I figure this thing out, right?"

"This thing is perfect for you," said Wally. "It keeps track of how much you walk every day, your heart rate, how many calories you burn. If you use the app on your phone you can set weight loss goals, log your calorie intake …"

"Wow! Thanks Wally." I held up my arm to admire it, the glossy face reflecting the neon diner lights. "This thing is perfect. Let's take it for a walk."

Wally and the Beave patiently kept my slow pace as I shuffled around the block with a couple rest stops for some gossiping and clowning around.

"One o'clock, two o'clock, three o'clock, walk," I sang. "Four o'clock, five o'clock, six o'clock, walk. I'm gonna walk … around … the block tonight..."

"You're doing great Jeff," said the Beave.

"Yeah, so good to see you on the road to recovery," said Wally.

"The *sidewalk* to recovery," the Beave said, kicking a wad of trash out of my way.

They walked me all the way to my door and we stood under the awning, out of the sun. "This was great, guys. Don't you worry. I'll be leaping tall buildings in a single bound in no time."

"Whoa, you might want to take it easy and start off with a few town houses, there Superman." The Beave said laughing and giving me one of her signature little dainty high-fives.

"You know, I'm still out of work." Wally reminded me. "We can go on some more adventurous walks when you're up for it."

"I'd like that," I said hoping she understood my idea of adventurous wasn't going to keep up with her idea of adventurous for a while to come. We nodded at each other in agreement and I headed upstairs to rest-up from my two-block walk.

## 18. Good Days and Set-Back Days

The FitBit got me to be competitive with myself to do a little more every day. Soon I was up for real walks. Wally and I set off on an adventure to the southern tip of Roosevelt Island to see the new FDR memorial overlooking the UN on a summer day. It is a strangely remote place for the middle of New York City and a farther walk from the Roosevelt Island Tram than I had realized. It was a hot day and my biological cooling pump was still not up to snuff. I was quickly getting winded and overheated. We stopped at a park bench in the shade for me to pant and cool.

"There's an ambulance over there," Wally pointed toward a park concession stand. "Should I just ask them to check you out."

"God no. I just need to rest a bit and I'll be fine."

"Isn't that what you kept telling people before you went to the emergency room?" Wally was beginning to fidget and look around nervously.

"Don't be such a…"

"Don't call me that." Wally interrupted with a glare.

"Look. They told me to go back to the hospital and see Dr. Surya if there was any complications. They warned me not to wind up in an emergency room. They'll run me through every wringer to cover their own liability ass and tell me nothing new. I'm recovering from open-heart surgery. Of course, I'm struggling. I just overdid it, that's all. We'll head back."

We slowly made our way back to the tram, me stopping to rest and clutch my heart pillow and occasionally excruciatingly cough. Wally was getting more and more visibly concerned. And the harder I tried and the more difficult it got for me to walk, the farther the tram platform seemed to get. I suddenly realized how quickly I had gotten so far from help right in the middle of the New York City. Thank goodness I wasn't hiking in the woods or back to work and working some small-town flood in a remote health-care desert somewhere.

"I'll go back to the hospital and see Dr. Surya, Wally. Let's just get to the tram. We'll take a taxi when we're back to Manhattan."

"Townhouses, Jeff. I'm sorry, this was a skyscraper." She said putting her head on my shoulder.

Wally folded me into a taxi on the Manhattan side of the tram and delivered me home where Nichole met us, folded me into another taxi and took me to the hospital to see Dr. Surya.

I was truly scared by the time we got to the hospital. Nichole and I had trouble figuring out which entrance to go in to find Dr. Surya's office and I was tempted to go into the emergency room entrance. If there was one thing I learned from that fateful day I last went in that entrance it was to not dick around when feeling the feelings I was having right then. But Dr. Surya had warned me not to bother letting an emergency room run me through the litany of tests just to tell me what I already know: that my heart has been weakened by a serious trauma. So, we found our way to Dr. Surya's office entrance off to the side of the emergency room.

"What brings you back here Mr. Hornbull?" Dr. Surya greeted me.

"I just came to let you know I finally understand what they mean when they say it feels like an elephant sitting on your chest. I may have been overdoing the walking. It started to feel just like the day I came into the hospital. Something is wrong. Really wrong," I said with sincere concern.

"Your heart has been through a serious trauma and it will take some time to heal. You will have good days and some days will be set-back days. But you will continue to get a little better every day until you make a full recovery," he said with sincere assurance. "How is it going otherwise? When you are not overdoing the exercise?"

"I have pains all the time. Not from burping, hiccupping or yawning but coughing is still a completely other story, but all in all, I guess it is progress."

"That's normal post-surgical discomfort and today you just overdid the exercise. We'll run you through a few tests to be sure and let you go home. You did the right thing by coming here. You wouldn't be going home tonight if you went back to the emergency room."

Sure enough, the tests told us what we already knew: my heart was weakened from the trauma of the surgery but is on the mend, and the incisions are causing 'post-surgical discomfort' to put it mildly – the gaping gash on my chest is 'fucking killing me' to put it not so mildly.

"I'm going to refer you to a cardiologist for continued follow-ups from now on," Dr. Surya told me.

"Are you breaking up with me?" I asked. I felt a little rejected, like I was being kicked out of the cardiology nest. But it was a good sign, a graduation from surgical recovery to long-term cardiac care.

## 19. First Cardiologist

Dr. Gina Grinstein was an attractive, but homely little science geek of a doctor. Hair pulled back, glasses and a very quiet demeanor. She didn't have much to say as the nurse took a blood sample, blood pressure and an EKG. She just asked me to fill out a questionnaire.

"What symptoms did you have and for how long before you went to the emergency room?" she asked as she reviewed the questionnaire.

"Well, in the weeks leading up to the ER, I had a series of really acute episodes of shortness of breath and chest pains. But for at least six months, maybe even the better part of a year, I was having a harder and harder time with my exercise routine of biking to work and walking home. I was still doing it or trying up until recently. It just got harder and harder. And my weight got out of control."

"How recently did you gain weight and how much?"

"It crept up and up for years. I just figured I was getting old and fat, what else is new? And then when I wasn't getting exercise and felt so out of shape it really skyrocketed in those last six months. It seems to me now that obesity and heart disease is not a one-way street of cause and effect. I mean, how much weight can your metabolism lose if you are squeezing your circulatory system through the width of a human hair?"

Dr. Grinstein nodded. "Well yes, it could be more like a downward spiral. The obesity contributing to the heart disease and the heart disease contributing to the obesity, sure,"

"I'm also still having difficulty breathing, they have me on this inhaler but my lungs are inflamed and I have this wheezy cough," I gave a deep wheezy exhale as an example.

She placed her stethoscope on my chest and asked for another breath. "You seem to have bronchitis tussiculosus."

The most useless diagnoses doctors often give me is to just say back to me exactly what I said to them translated into Latin. Other than that, she apparently has no earthly clue ad it will cost three-hundred dollars from my insurance company and a seventy-five-dollar co-payment from me. Expensive goddamn Latin lesson. How much would that be in ancient Greek, I wonder?

"So, what do I have to do going forward to maintain my health?"

"Well, I'll prescribe some standard meds for blood pressure and cholesterol. We'll keep monitoring your bloodwork and adjust meds accordingly."

"How about alcohol?" I asked in absolute fear of some of the possible answers, notably: '*YOU CAN NEVER DRINK AGAIN!!!*'.

"In moderation is fine," she answered matter-of-factly. "As long as it's not daily."

"You see on the questionnaire there is the little matter of how much I drink the other six days a week."

"Some studies say it can have long-term benefits in small amounts," she interrupted and looked away.

Her defensiveness was not instilling confidence in me. I decided to cut my losses and not volunteer how much I might drink on those other six days of the week. "What about diet and exercise?" I asked.

"Oh yes, those are very important," she stated and turned her head and focus back to me..

"But, I've heard a lot of conflicting things about heart-healthy diets. What diet should I follow?"

"Well, I could give you a referral to a dietician if you like," she said looking down and away and losing eye contact again, "it's really the exercise that will be important."

"What kind of exercise would be appropriate? I am still having difficulty walking around the block. Should we do a stress test?"

"We can do a stress test if you like, but I don't think there is any point. I mean we already know your heart suffered a serious trauma from the episodes and then from the surgery and it will take some time to recover. Let's give it a year and if there is still a problem, we can do a stress test. It is going to take time for your heart to heal."

I could sense concern was beginning to show on my face.

"But don't worry. We caught it in time, you didn't have damage to the heart tissue from the incident and patients who undergo this procedure are usually good to go for seven years or so."

"Seven years?" I asked in a soft voice. "Seven years ... and then what?"

I'm just saying that patients ordinarily don't present with symptoms within seven years of this particular surgery."

"Yeah, but what happens after seven years? Dr. Surya said he thought I should live to a ripe old age," I said growing confused and a little angry. "The whole point of the invasive surgery was that it should never be a problem again."

"And it shouldn't be. It shouldn't be," she backpedaled swiftly. "You just never know, and you need to be diligent about monitoring your own health. If in seven years you present with symptoms, that you will now recognize, we will treat it accordingly with meds or stents."

I was shocked and it showed. Nobody had mentioned any other possibility to me other than I was cured.

"You are going to be fine. None of us ever know how much time we have left. You just have to take extra care of yourself and you'll be fine." She looked me squarely in the eye. "But you can never erase a history of heart disease. That is something you will always carry with you."

I left her office deeply upset at the realization

that my longevity would forever be in question. It should have been obvious without Dr. Grinstein tripping over her bedside manner, but I had been focusing so hard on the positive I hadn't really given myself that reality check. It was also being hit by the weight of the responsibility to take care of myself – not just for a time while I heal, but forever. And not just dieting and exercising but a whole education on cardiovascular health. The one thing Dr. Grinstein's dysfunctional interpersonal skills made clear was that I can't rely solely on doctors to be straight-forward with me or even truthful, much less right all the time.

It seems pretentious to say Western medicine is not holistic until you encounter the likes of Dr. Grinstein. She had no interest in anything outside of lab tests and pharmaceuticals. Not diet, not exercise, not apparent alcohol abuse. She never asked about my job stress or lifestyle. She was a science geek with a bad bedside manner. I would come to learn that the difference between a good doctor and a bad doctor is primarily in their communication skills.

"Why don't you try my mother's cardiologist, Dr. Freeman?" Nichole squeezed my hand and looked up at me in the cab on the way home. "I don't like that she upset you like that."

"She was upsetting. She made me want a freaking drink." I paused and had a minor epiphany. "Then again, she did say that might be alright," I gave Nichole a guilty smile, she rolled her eyes and slunk down in the seat shaking her head.

## 20. Cameo Appearance

With tacit permission from the cardiologist, I thought it would be a good idea to make an appearance at our local watering hole in the wall pub. Reif's is a quintessential neighborhood bar and a quintessential shithole in the wall. It's dark, run-down and full of character, owned by the third generation of the same family since 1941 and *everybody* knows everyone and everyone they ever slept with.

"I don't care what that doctor said, I don't think it's a good idea for you to drink so soon after the surgery." Nichole stopped walking and scowled. "You're still recovering."

"Everybody has to have a vice. I don't do drugs, I quit smoking, I quit caffeine, I don't gamble, I don't dance and now I haven't had a drink in a month. For crying out loud, I don't do anything a Mormon doesn't do – but at least they have polygamy. If I can't drink I want more wives. Either buy me a drink or get to work picking out your sister wives."

"Just take it easy, please," Nichole said, rolling her eyes.

"I'll just make a cameo appearance. I'm not going to drink more than a couple. I just want to get out and see everybody," I explained. "Besides, you said yourself it would ease everybody's worrying to see me."

"They want to see you getting better not getting wasted."

Word had gotten out that I might stop by and there was a good crowd to greet us. Joe the Cop, Nicky Nines, Snake, Boston Brian and Tom and Jamie, the Newman brothers, sometimes referred to as the Newmi – Newmi being plural for Newman in Latin, of course. Wally and the Beave were there too, along with Wally's husband Dan. Those in the know that Wally's real given name was Danielle referred to the couple as Dan-Dan,

"Holy shit, it's alive, it's alive!" Shouted Joe the Cop as I swung the door open. "Long live the Emperor, Jeffonius Hornbullonius Maximus the First!"

The crowd gathered around me for handshakes and hugs. Nichole was like a referee in a boxing ring keeping people from hugging me any more tightly than a hand on the shoulder.

"Careful! Don't squeeze him, his chest is still healing!" she yelled as she wedged her arms between me and the would-be huggers.

"Dude, how do you feel?" asked Wally's husband Dan.

"Like some guy cut my chest open and pulled my heart out."

"Some guy? What was this a back-alley by-pass?"

"Well, sure, he said he was a cardiologist and he was dressed like a surgeon, but was it really just a coincidence that it was the summer solstice? I mean he just *HAD TO* cut my chest open right away on *THAT*

*VERY* day? Why the urgency? Can you prove that after I went under the surgical gown didn't come off to reveal the ceremonial golden loin cloth? And the Aztec headdresses didn't come out?"

"Yeah they probably took turns taking a bite out of your heart before they sewed it back in too," cracked one of the Newmi.

"Classic! He's an Aztec Sun God now," cracked Dan. We all laughed.

"You may now address me as Jeffreyetzl Hornbullatl, the immortal Aztec Sun God," I proclaimed with a wave of my arm.

I bellied up to the bar and greeted Ray the bartender with a smile. Ray is an older rotund Puerto Rican man with a walrus moustache and a beaming smile. He is as crass as bartenders come but friendly and funny and very welcoming. He tolerates me practicing my bad Spanish. My Spanish used to be pretty good until I lived in Hungary and Hungarian words and grammar began finding their way into my Spanish – now I speak Spanish like a deranged Hungarian too.

"Hey Ray," I called out to the bartender. "Con permisso, una cerveza por favor."

"Hey fuck you, buddy," he replied with a shit-eating grin and arms extended in welcome. Ray was the embodiment of the maxim: Midwesterners can say 'so nice to see you' and mean 'fuck you' and New Yorkers can say 'fuck you' and mean 'so nice to see you.'

"Fuck you too, my kind sir. You are a gentleman and a raving asshole," I replied in kind. "What do you say to a beer?"

"A beer?" Ray replied with a raised eyebrow. "Are you supposed to be drinking?"

"Yeah, it's ok, the cardiologist wasn't too worried about it. It's been almost a month. Besides I won't drink more than a couple. I popped a double dose of oxi-opioid things to loosen me up a little."

"You're still on those after a month?"

"No, I weaned myself off of those within a week of being out of the hospital. I didn't want to mess around with that stuff. I just took a couple of the leftovers tonight to take the edge off."

"Oh, well as long as you're just taking oxy recreationally, I guess it's ok," Ray said rolling his eyes and shaking his head as he popped my beer open and slammed it on the bar.

"What about Nichole? You're not getting me in trouble with her, are you?"

"C'mon Ray, you know I'm no fool, I married my drinking buddy. I don't get calls at the bar saying, 'where are you, you drunken idiot?' I get calls *from* the bar saying, 'where are you, you drunken idiot?'"

Joe the cop slid his drink over to offer me the corner barstool, the most coveted piece of real estate in the bar. I held court recalling the events that led me into the hospital and all that transpired afterwards. Kenny the horse-track aficionado took delight in the ass-gown racing racket I had going. "I got to get some of that action down at the ICU," laughed Kenny.

"Man, you are so lucky you caught it in time," Joe the cop shook his head in disbelief.

"Damn right, I'm not gonna call a mis-deal. I'll take the hand I was dealt, thank you very much. No cards for me. I'll check," as I rapped my knuckles on the bar. "I drew a twenty and I'll stick."

"No way, Dude. You drew a black jack – unbeatable," said Nicky Nines, a proud Italian with slicked back hair and a missing index finger. Nicky Nines reached out to shake my hand, which always freaked me out a little. His stubby right index finger felt like that school yard prank when a kid would tickle your palm with a curled-up index finger when you shook hands. It gave me the heebie-jeebies and I had to stop myself from making a quivering body shiver like he shook my hand with a joy buzzer.

Irish Brian raised his glass to the crowd: "Jeff, after what happened to you, I decided to get some things that felt wrong checked out. The diagnosis was not a healthy one, I have some blockages in my coronary arteries. I'm on meds and a diet plan. But thankfully I caught it in time. And that's thanks to you for the wake-up call, buddy."

The crowd raised glasses and toasted each others' health.

"Yeah and Big Hans too," said Kenny. "He's

going around saying he owes you his life. He got himself checked out because of you and they're putting in stents into his heart."

"Thanks to Shakey," I added. "If it weren't for him, I might not have gone to get checked out on time either. I thought of him. He led me there."

We all raised glasses and bottles in silence.

"Jeffrey, you're drinking?" observed Tom Newman.

"Hey, I just spent thirty days in the hole – that's a long stretch in the no-alcohol hole. Besides, I won't drink much, I took a couple oxy-opioid things before I came out, I can't drink much on those."

"You're not supposed to drink on those!" Tom exclaimed.

"Have you been seeking a medical degree in between substitute teaching gigs there, Tom?" quipped his brother Jamie.

"Hey, my wife is a doctor, you know," Tom pushed his thick glasses to the bridge of his nose.

"Yeah, a gynecologist," I said, pointing at him with my bottle. "So, what is your professional gynecological opinion as to how I should get fucked up, Doctor Newman?"

"Dr. Mook prescribes medical marijuana, actually," interjected Mook, a small, scrawny but muscular construction worker in a high-visibility lime green hi-viz hooded sweatshirt.

"You know I don't really do that, Mook," I said.

"If you're feeling the need for some sort of intoxicant, I highly recommend it for your condition – chronic pain treatment, stress relief, sleep aid, and it might just improve your social skills. It's certainly better for you than alcohol and oxy. Step outside to my office and allow me to administer your medication." Mook stepped back toward the door, swung it open with one arm and waived the other across his waist in a right-this-way gesture.

"Wait a minute, wait a minute," Tom Newman interrupted in a whisper. "We can't just all march out together at the same time to smoke dope, it's too obvious. Go one at a time and give some sort of subtle signal for the next guy."

"Okay, a subtle signal?" Mook replied. "How about I cup my hands over my mouth like this and go: 'CA-CAW, CA-CAW!!!'" he shrieked on the top of his lungs with his head tilted upwards.

With the entire bar now staring at us, Dan, the Newmi and I left the ladies to chat at the far end of the bar and indiscreetly fumbled past each other out the door behind Mook onto the sidewalk and sidled a couple doors down the block.

"Step into my office for a safety meeting," said Mook as he stepped into the darkness of a recessed doorway.

"Safety meeting?"

"That's what we call it on job sites. If some foreman asks 'hey what are you guys doing standing off over there?' you just say 'safety meeting.' Or you can call the guys into the office for a 'safety meeting.' They can't deny you a safety meeting."

"Even if it involves drugs on an active construction site?" asked one of the Newmi.

"Well, that's why we call it a safety meeting and not a drug meeting, dumbass. Take this." Mook drew a vape pen out of his shirt pocket and handed it to me.

"Really, I have to take it like that?" I balked.

"Well, if Mr. Hornbull doesn't want to take his medication orally, I'm sure we can arrange that he have it some other way," said Mook doing his best Nurse Ratchet impression.

"Stop blowing smoke up my ass, Mook." I gave a half smile and took the pen.

Mook gave me some simple instruction on proper vape pen usage and we passed it around a couple times. I drew one puff and let out a small cough which caused me to hold my chest and wince in pain. Coughing was still painful and uncomfortable for me, but to those unfamiliar it looked far worse.

"Are you ok?" asked Dan as his eyes went wide and he placed his hand on my shoulder.

"I'm fine Dan, I'm fine," I gasped and pointed

to my chest. "It's just the surgical healing. Coughing can be painful."

Dan looked relieved and smiled as I passed him the vape pen. Nichole and Wally emerged from the bar and peered around the edge of the door to see me passing Dan the pen and him drawing a drag.

"What is that?" asked Wally as her husband drew a puff.

"It's a nicotine pen," Dan sputtered. "I'm, uh, trying to quit smoking."

"And what were you doing with it, SweetiePie?" asked Nichole with a furrowed brow.

"Uh, I'm trying to start?" I said. And Dan, the Newmi and I erupted into stoned giddy laughter. "It's alright, my gynecologist Doctor Newman prescribed it for me."

Nichole and Wally both folded their arms and glared at me and Dan.

"Looks like Dan-Dan gonna go bam-bam," whispered Mook as Wally led Dan away from us bad influences.

The tension of the moment was cut by a large hulking figure swaggering around the corner and toward the bar. It was Big Hans.

"Dude, you saved my fucking life!" he yelled as he came toward me.

"He's drunk as a skunk," muttered Nichole as Big Hans came toward me. "Hans, no hugging!" she shouted.

Big Hans came at me for one of his signature bear hugs, oblivious to Nichole's plea. Hans was exceptionally muscular from pumping iron during his recent stay in prison. His arms gripped my whole body and squeezed, lifting my feet off the ground and crushing my healing chest. He *was* drunk as a skunk and I was squirming like the cat in the Pepe LePew cartoons trying to wrest myself free of his embrace as he tried to kiss my cheek.

"You saved my fucking life, Dude!"

"Hans, put him down, you're hurting him!" Nichole cried.

He released and I staggered clutching my chest in pain.

"Oh my God what's wrong?" asked a panicked Wally. "Are you having a heart attack? Should I call an ambulance?"

"No!" I stammered and staggered back toward the door of the bar.

"Oh my God, Dude, I'm so sorry, I didn't think," Hans apologized loudly. Too loudly for Wally to hear me try to stop her from running into the bar crying to call an ambulance. By the time I followed her to the door clutching my chest, everyone was convinced that I was having a heart attack.

"Stop it, everyone calm down," I said, my hands up in front of my chest. "It's just the scar, I'm fine." I straightened up, stretched my arms back and swung them across my chest a couple times. I lifted my head and smiled broadly. "I can breathe!" And I took a deep, expansive, pain-free breath. "Oh my God. I think my gynecologist just cured my chest pain."

"Are you sure you're alright?" Nichole asked as she guided me by the arm to a barstool.

"Yeah, I'm fine," I said with a growing giddy smile, gazing up at the sky and taking in the fresh air. "*Everything* is just fine."

"You okay, Jeff?" asked the Newmi.

"Yeah, I think I just discovered the cure for open-heart surgery," I replied. "Poking smot cured me of post-surgical pain and might just cure me from excessive drinking to boot. I mean smoking pot."

**

The vape pen had clearly done a far better job at pain relief than the dangerously addictive oxy pain meds the doctors so freely foisted upon me. Even the next day I felt better than I had since the surgery for having stretched upright and breathed deeper. My lungs felt better. Marijuana never really took off as an alcohol substitute for me. But I never could handle the combination of alcohol and pot, so it did serve the purpose of stopping me from drinking for a while.

And it was growing apparent that cutting out

drinking would be a good idea. The two and a half beers I had made me light-headed and made my heart feel weak. It was subtle, but I had learned a hard lesson in paying attention to subtle signs from my heart. I felt light-headed and there was a strange little pitter patter I hadn't felt since my heart began to recover shortly after the surgery and it made me uncomfortable.

Although Dr. Surya had assured me I had no signs of weakened heart muscle or other sign of alcohol damage, the more I thought back over the previous months, it was apparent that my straining heart was not helped along by alcohol.

"The alcohol is not hitting me right," I confessed to Nichole as we sat in the corner barstools. "I got to lay off the booze for a while longer."

"That cardiologist is an insensitive quack," snapped Nichole. "I want you to see Mom's cardiologist, Dr. Freeman."

"Thank you, ThweetiePie." I slurred as I laid my intoxicated head on her shoulder and closed my eyes for a moment of affection immersion.

The other reason not to go out drinking also quickly became apparent: my friends get really annoying and repetitive when they get shit-faced and I am nursing my second beer. The upside is that the temptation to drink fades at this point as I have no desire to join in the act.

I laid off the alcohol and sat in the corner of the bar, observing the crowd drift off into intoxication without me. I wondered to myself if I would be able to maintain my social station with the gang without drinking. Did I even want to? Just as I was posing these questions to myself, Wally opened the women's room door and out fell Snake, having passed out leaning against the door of the small, single-occupancy bathroom with Snake Junior in his hand. He awoke to the sensation of hitting the wall of the corridor, which from his perception he he could only assume to be someone hitting him. He fought back against his imaginary assailant ferociously, lying on his side on the floor, the shoulder of his leather jacket in a puddle of his own piddle, kicking the wall with his steel-toed construction boots and punching the women's room door, the floor and anyone who tried to stop him.

"Whoa, whoa, whoa, break it up, break it up," shouted Ray as Wally ran out of the corridor with her hand over her mouth and he raced from behind the bar to break up Snake's own personal bar melee of one. Joe the Cop joined to calm him down and they both helped him up.

"Where is he? Where did he go? The mother fucker!" shouted Snake.

"Where'd who go? You got in a fight with yourself you idiot!" Ray shouted back.

"Jesus Christ!" exclaimed Joe. "Twenty-five years on the job; I've never broken up a fight between one guy before."

"I'll walk you home, Snake," said Joe as he helped him to the door with one arm on his shoulder, until he realized his arm was on the wet shoulder and tucked around his other side and they shuffled out the door together.

It is important to me to maintain my close-knit social circle of friends. I have a lot of fun drinking with them. But I realized I think I like my friends better when we're not drinking. For some months to come I would pop in early and see people. Nichole would mull berries for me and Ray would add seltzer and make me virgin mocktails, but I'd head out early.

"I really shouldn't go out drinking even if I am not drinking." I confessed to Nichole in the taxi home that night. "I'll try that cardiologist of your mother's. You get to work on the sister wives – some hot ones. There must be a dating app for that."

## 21. First Visit to Second Cardiologist

Dr. Freeman was old-school. He was wearing a white lab coat, stethoscope, thick glasses and David Niven's mustache. He was congenial but serious with a touch of formality. He looked like a 1950's doctor that might have told a television audience to smoke cigarettes to reduce stress, except that he was clearly too straight-laced to suggest such a thing even in the 1950's. He probably had never worn a pair of jeans in his life.

His waiting room was homey and comfortable, but it struck me as odd that a cardiologist would have arm chairs so comfortable they are difficult for the infirm to get out of. Hi aide helped me up and showed me into the Dr. Freeman's office.

"So, you're Miriam's son in-law?" he greeted me with a smile. "You've had quite an ordeal."

I shrugged and sighed in agreement as we shook hands across his wide oak desk. I slunk into the leather armchair making one of those leather-arm-chair fart noises as I slid. I looked behind me as if to signal to Dr. Freeman it was the chair. But it's his chair, he must know that. I can't be the first one to make one of those reverberating vibrations. My eyes gazed around the room at his collections of memorabilia. His shelves were covered in little gag gifts his patients had given him over the years, his walls covered in framed New Yorker cartoons about doctors. The environment was anything but sterile – in the most positive way.

"Tell me about what happened. How long would

you say you had symptoms leading up to the event?"

"I had a series of episodes of shortness of breath and chest pains in the weeks leading up to the trip to the ER, but really I guess it was six months to a year before that my weight was getting out of control and I was getting in worse and worse shape. I kept trying to stick to my exercise routines: biking to work, walking home; but it just getting harder and harder."

"Did you know something was wrong then?" asked Dr. Freeman.

"Honestly, I just thought I was getting old and fat. I was concerned, but I didn't think it spelled impending doom by any stretch."

"Didn't you ever seek out medical attention?" He looked at me from under his reading glasses.

It suddenly struck me as astounding that I hadn't been far more alarmed by my symptoms far earlier. I thought back before the acute episodes to all the huffing and panting and minor chest pains – and some that weren't so minor now that I think about it. I had simply grown acquiescent that I was getting old and fat. But not too long before, I was so fit.

About three years earlier, some friends and I entered a trail-running marathon – hardcore hills, clamoring over boulder fields and down streams. It was the third year in a row we did it. My goal was always to hike half. The first year I was the last guy on the trail before the half-way mark and got swept by the safety crew on an ATV. I came in last among about 3,000 people.

The second year I wanted to run the first three miles through town, so I wouldn't have to relive the indignity of huffing it out of town in last place. I was so far behind everybody else the spectators were packing up their lawn chairs and coolers when I came around each bend and someone would shout: 'Wait, there's one more. Go! Go! You can do it!' They waved flags at me and looked at me with the most horrid pity. They must have thought I was the token disabled vet or Special Olympics athlete or something. I didn't have the heart or the courage to tell them I was just a fat out-of-shape bastard and they didn't need to wave flags at me and cheer about it. It was embarrassing. I did a little better the second year, but the third year I really put in a lot of effort. I wanted to run at least parts of it, but it was just getting harder and harder.

"I did go to a doctor," I explained to Dr. Freeman, "a young little twerp doing his residency at a primary care doctor's practice – and tried to explain I was concerned about not being able to get into shape, that I was getting winded so easily and I felt like there was something wrong with my heart. But when I explained I was training for a trail marathon, walking ten miles and climbing up to 100 flights of stairs at a pop, he was totally dismissive. 'If you can do all that, there is nothing wrong with your heart' he said. I asked if I should do a stress test, an EKG, or any other test and just threw the questions back at me: 'would you like to do an EKG? Do you think you would like to have an EKG?'"

"These young doctors," said Dr. Freeman, "We train them to be more attentive and responsive to their patients, but now they put the patient in charge. It's that Millennial generation, they're so overly sensitive. And they're all terrified of getting sued for malpractice for telling a patient what to do, so they turn the decision back on them."

"I know. What the hell ever happened to doctor's orders? How the hell am I supposed to know what tests I need? I didn't go to medical school."

Dr. Freeman showed me down the hall to the exam room. "Strip to your shorts, gown open in the back." He tossed a folded paper ass gown at me and left me alone for a minute to change in privacy.

"Who took care of you over at Murray Hill?" He asked as he prodded my chest with his stethoscope.

"Dr. Surya."

"Dr. Surya? I suppose he did that off-line surgery of his?" Dr. Freeman said in a gruff voice and with a stern look.

"Yeah, he said off-line was hip and trendy and all the rage. He said the surgery went really well, all things considered." I wondered why he was seemed so disapproving of Dr. Surya.

He rubbed the sonogram gel on my chest and began sliding the probe across my chest in back-and-forth sweeping motions. A fuzzy image began to appear on the screen, but not much to look at to my un-trained eye.

"Is it a boy or a girl?" I quipped to no reaction at all from Dr. Freeman.

Then I saw a gentle rhythmic flapping. "Oh, I see something moving," I said. "What's that?"

"That's the valve." His congeniality faded into seriousness when he looked at the screen and he excused himself from the room.

I watched the echocardiogram image run in a loop like a gif image. "Funny," I thought. "I would have thought a beating heart would have more obvious throbbing motion than that. All I could see was the valve gently flapping in the flow of the blood. Dr. Freeman came back in a few minutes later.

"What did they mention to you about alcohol-related deterioration of your heart muscle at the hospital?" He asked.

"Nothing," I answered. I was shocked he asked. If there was an obvious problem why didn't Dr. Surya say anything? Why was Dr. Grinstein so dismissive about alcohol Did I bring all this upon myself after all? My head was spinning with confusion and dread that he might tell me I can never drink again. "Why do you ask? Dr. Surya said I had a very strong heart. He even said I had a robust ventricular flow. I don't know what that means exactly, but I thanked him for the compliment."

"And Grinstein? Did she mention damage to

your heart? Or alcohol?"

"She said I could go back to drinking in moderation."

"What?!" he exclaimed. "You *cannot* drink alcohol with a heart as weakened as yours. I just called the hospital when I stepped out to request the test results from before and after the surgery. If the damage wasn't there before the surgery, then it was caused by the surgery. You could sue them and I would back you up on that if you want."

"No, I don't want to sue them. Even if things went less well than they could have, they still saved my life." I was shocked at the suggestion. Is Dr. Freeman just sue happy? Was there something Dr. Surya wasn't telling me? Was Grinstein incompetent or covering up for Surya? My head was swimming with confusion. "What exactly is wrong?"

"None of the four major heart-wall muscles are beating. You see those flaps?" asked Dr. Freeman, tracing his finger around the outline of the image of my heart on the monitor. "That's the valve. But I don't see your heart-wall muscles moving at all. You look like you're dead."

"They said my heart went through a good deal of trauma from the surgery and it would take some time to recover, but that it was normal." I recalled.

"Some degree is normal, sure. But I'd say you are in the bottom two percent, which is even more unusual considering you're relatively young and fit for this procedure. I guess you just drew the short straw," said Dr. Freeman, shaking his head. "It's that damn off-line surgery. That young doctor is trying to make a name for himself performing as many of those procedures as he can get his hands on. And it is still risky. And unnecessary on a young, strong guy like you."

"The surgery was unnecessary?" I asked. What now? Was his all for nothing? Was I taken for a chump? Was my father biting his tongue this whole time that I had made a rash decision at the suggestion of some medical huckster?

"No, the surgery was absolutely necessary," Dr. Freeman said to my relief. "I am just not a fan of that off-line business, without the heart lung machine. I mean, how can you perform surgery while dancing around to the rhythm of a beating heart like that?" Dr. Freeman said with a shuffle of his feet.

"He really dances like that?" I looked at him quizzically.

"No, of course not, or uh, I don't think so," he quickly regained his composure "I'm just not a fan. It's asking for something to go wrong. The benefit is for older people who have a higher incidence of dementia following open-heart surgery, they call it pump head. But a young guy like you shouldn't be struggling like this. Have you had any problems?"

"Yeah, I went for a long walk and felt like I was having a heart attack, literally. What should I do about exercise? Should I push myself to get into shape?"

"No. Walking is fine. Walk as much as you can as often as you can but don't overdo it, don't strain yourself. And no weight-lifting. Aside from your healing bifurcated sternum, you don't want to gain muscle mass. Every pound of flesh contains something like a mile of blood vessels, whether it's a blob of fat or a denser pound of muscle it still represents that much more work your heart has to do."

This was all coming back into the realm of common-sense advice and I was relieved. "And what about weight loss? Should I be on a specific diet?"

"I will refer you to a dietician, but to give you a general idea: this is lunch." He held up a take-out container of tuna salad on a bed of lettuce. "This is my lunch and I might not even eat all of it today. Sometimes I save half for tomorrow. Breakfast is a cup of oatmeal – only a cup. Oatmeal every day might do more than any cholesterol medication. Keep your portions small, you'll get used to it, and cut out the fatty stuff and that's all you really need to do."

"Okay, great. I can do this. How much should I set out to lose?"

"Worry about eating healthy and the weight will follow. Don't worry about numbers, worry about lifestyle change that will affect your long-term health. You need to eat reasonable portions and very low saturated fat. And no alcohol at least for thirty days until I see you again."

"No alcohol?" I asked. Another thirty days? I thought. I just did thirty days. . "That's fine, but what about medical marijuana? Is that something you can prescribe? For my condition?"

"Medical marijuana? To treat what symptom? Pain? I can prescribe something for pain."

"No, not pain. And I don't want any more oxy anything."

"Then for what medical reason?"

"Well, you said no alcohol, for medical reasons. I mean, what, am I supposed to do? Just walk around sober? Like, all the time?"

Dr. Freeman exhaled a small huff as he looked down at me. "I wouldn't consider your adversity to 'walking around sober' a medical condition. If you have trouble 'walking around sober'," he said with air quotes and a scowl, "I can refer you to a support program."

"No, no, It's not even me, really. I just happen to have a wife and several bartenders depending on me to get back on the drinking horse eventually."

"Well give me thirty more days off that horse, please?"

"Aw man! Another thirty days in the hole? That's a long stretch in the no-alco-hole." I sighed. But I dropped my protests of abstinence and requests for medical marijuana lest I wind up in a program. And I didn't even bother asking about medical Mormon sister wives.

## 22. Pills, Pills, Pills!!!

Dr. Freeman greatly simplified my medication regimen. He knocked back my metoprolol to half what it was, since it was probably contributing to my drowsiness. He eliminated superfluous meds like stool softener to counteract the oxy I was no longer on. And he added baby aspirin, 81 milligrams daily. It may sound innocuous, but it might be the drug most likely to save my life if I had another cardiac event, he explained.

The number of pills I was taking daily dropped significantly, but the routine of it started to blur and I had trouble remembering whether or not I took the damn things on any given day. I tried putting them in another room so I would remember if I went in there to get them. I tried putting them on the coffee table where I can't miss them, but then I couldn't remember if I took them or just thought about taking them. Then I tried putting them on the top shelf of the medicine cabinet and asking Nichole to get them for me. She was too short to reach and made a memorable effort of reaching, stretching, jumping or looking for a step stool. This helped me tremendously, and annoyed Nichole to no end.

"Why don't you get one of those weekly pill boxes, like my Mom has?" Nichole suggested.

"I beg your pardon. Do I look like some senile old fart who needs an Alzheimer box?"

I used to feel sorry for old decrepit people who were so demented they needed those pill boxes with those compartments with the days of the week and AM, PM, lunch and dinner written on them. "Really? They can't even remember if they took their pills today. How pathetic." Now, however, I would suggest taking pills on a regular routine day after day for months if not years on end before passing judgement on the dementia box.

At first, I started second guessing whether I took the pills the night before. It didn't take me long to start second guessing whether I just took my pills ten minutes ago, or had I just thought about it ten minutes ago. I know I thought about it: Nichole reminded me, I went and got them, and I even remember taking them, but was that yesterday? This little pill routine is the same every day and the days easily blend and blur.

Of course, point of pride prevents me from getting one of those senility boxes at my tender young age of forty-nine so I had to develop my own mental mechanisms for being sure I remembered taking my pills. Saying what I was taking out loud to Nichole was a good start but when you begin to do that every day, day after day, that can get blurry too. So, I started saying it more forcibly, waving my finger at her: "I took my pills!" then shouting it three times; then saying it in a funny voice: "I took-a-da-pills, I took-a-da pills, I took-a-da, took-a-da, took-a-da pills." Soon, in order to be sure I'd remember it clearly, there was a song and dance that went along with it. I even lose track of which pills I have taken in one sitting. If I have six pills to take, by the time I get to pill number four, I'm like: shit, did I take one of the yellow ones already? So I came up with a special silly voice I'd say out loud for each pill:

the mellow yelllllooooow, ala Donovan; the little pinky,
in a high-pitched little piggy voice; the wee little white
one; the *Biiiig* white mother fucker; etc..

It started getting silly but still it was a lesser
assault on my pride than buying one of those old-people
boxes. I will dance down the street in my own personal
naked conga line singing: "I took-a, took-a, da PILLS! I
took-a, took-a, da PILLS! I took the melllllooooow
yelllllooow" before I disgrace myself by owning a
weekly pill box. Fortunately for everyone, it didn't
come to that. After a few months of ever-increasing
singing, dancing, pill-popping performances in our
living room reaching new heights of absurdity every
night, I realized that I could keep my pill bottles in a
basket and place each bottle in a second basket as I took
them thus avoiding the whole song and dance, but it
hasn't been nearly as much fun ever since. I still might
yet form my own personal naked conga line of one,
dancing down East 82nd Street using my pill bottles as
maracas just to be really sure I remember if I took-a-da-
pills. Then if I forget whether or not I took my pills, I
can just ask anyone in the neighborhood or pop by the
local police precinct, they'd be sure to have a record of
it.

## 23. The Nutri-Nazi

Dr. Withers' office was in her apartment on Central Park West. Her desk was in her dining area next to her kitchen. She was a tall slender woman in a body worthy of a dietician, skinny as a rail, which made me wonder just how much effort she puts into not eating.

She greeted me at the door and seated me at her dining table next to her desk in her cramped but organized apartment. It must be a disadvantage of working from home that you have to keep the place orderly enough to pass for a workplace. Or maybe she's just really anal.

"I've read your diet questionnaire and medical history that you submitted online, I guess you have quite a dietary reckoning to consider," she began. What would you say to setting an initial goal of getting you down to 185 pounds?"

My eyes widened at the suggestion and my stomach sank with disappointment. I was willing and eager to do a lot for my health, but not to chase the unrealistic ideal of skinny, anal dietician. If I was going to make a go of this it would have to be on realistic terms.

"I'd say that doesn't sound the slightest bit realistic or even necessarily healthy, to be honest," I replied. "My cardiologist says I should focus on eating heart-healthy not on a number of pounds lost – 'eat healthy and the pounds will follow' he says."

"That is certainly true," she said, nodding. "And

please, don't ever allow me to contradict in any way what your doctor tells you to do.

"How about an initial goal of losing 30 pounds?" I counter offered. "I've lost 20 since I was in the hospital, that would get me to 50 pounds lighter and within reach of 240, my pre-quitting smoking weight. That's been my goal for the last ten years."

"And you have some experience dieting to try to achieve that?"

"Yeah, I set short-term goals from time to time to knock off 20 pounds here or there. I had a couple periods where I stuck with it longer term, six months or so. One time, about four years ago I lost fifty pounds and was at just about the pre-quitting-smoking-weight goal."

"Ok good, so you have experience with dieting. What kind of diet strategy did you employ?" she leaned forward and clasped her hands.

"I did low-carbohydrate dieting."

Her face and shoulders dropped: "Ok, that is about the opposite of what you need to do and may have contributed heavily to your cardiac health problems."

"But I didn't do low-carb the way some people do," I began back-peddling I didn't worship at the altar of the reverend Atkins like some people do, I read Doctor Atkins book and eliminated the unhealthy refined carbohydrates and reintroduced the healthy ones like he says in the book."

"I need you to forget everything you ever thought you knew about eating healthy," she snapped, then took a breath and paused. "The dietary advice I'll give you is for you and your medical history. If you were diabetic I would give you radically different guidance. If you had Crohn's disease or gluten intolerance it would be different again. But you need to get your blood cholesterol and weight down really low and keep it there."

"I actually had some good habits," I looked her in the eye and pled my case, "I read labels, I eat a lot of vegetables."

"Vegetables are fine. But with your condition, there are things you must entirely avoid: nothing deep fried, nothing baked, no processed meats, no sausages or processed deli meats, no fatty pork products, No duck or goose, keep red meat to a minimum, very little cheese."

'Oh my God, no wonder this woman's so skinny, she really fucking hates food,' I thought. I was beginning to think my nutritionist thinks food is really, really bad for you. She doesn't just hate food, she finds anyone who eats it to be morally repugnant. My life has fallen under the grip of a nutri-Nazi. If the definition of puritanism is the irrational fear that someone, somewhere is having fun, then she is a nutri-Nazi puritan who lives in mortal fear that someone, somewhere is enjoying their food.

I could sense that she could see the fear on my face, and she shifted to a more compassionate tone. "There is no such thing as 'good food' and 'bad food,'" she said wagging her finger in mock disapproval "There are balanced diets and imbalanced diets. What we have grown up thinking of as normal is really unbalanced – way too much fat, sugar and processed foods. Our ancestors evolved to be rewarded by rare treats that are high in fat or sugar. But our bodies didn't evolve to eat that all the time.

"A balanced diet is high in soluble fiber and healthy grains. Soluble fiber is found in things like eggplant, squash, cantaloupe – anything with a thick skin and a fleshy center. White bread is not a healthy grain. Healthy whole grains are quinoa, wheat berry, barley, farro – things we are not normally accustomed to. These foods will help lower blood cholesterol and coupled with consuming less saturated fat will comprise a balanced diet and a healthy blood-cholesterol level.

"And be careful with cooking oils. If you want to get a sense for what oils and fats are more or less healthy, think about what it looks like at room temperature and then picture it in your blood stream. Do you want solidified bacon fat in your arteries?"

I wrinkled my face and shook my head in the negative.

"Or olive oil?" She asked "Olive oil is kind of silky smooth, right?

"And you can go too far in another direction," the Nutri-Nazi continued. "Vegans have their own health issues. In fact, you can eat a lot of sugar and things baked or deep fried in unhealthy oils and still be vegan. Your body needs protein, it needs fat. Don't consume zero fat. And don't deprive yourself of the things you like, you can eat anything sometimes. If you want ice cream, you can have a small portion once a month. If you want red meat, you can have a small, six-ounce, portion once a week – or a burger once a month. You like cheese? I'll give you an ounce of cheese a day."

I listened intently and my mood took a dramatic turn for the better as she laid out a fairly common-sense approach. This was all sounding doable and achievable.

"Make cheat dates. Once a week go out to dinner and have whatever you want, or pick a day a month where you eat anything you want for a whole day. If you get right back on the diet, one day won't hurt you. It's all about consistency in the long-term.

"It's not about depriving, it's about change. You'll have to learn to read labels, and read them always. Keep the saturated fat down to nine grams a day and your calories down to 2,000.

"You're not going to starve. I don't want you to go around hungry, it's counterproductive. Your body will go into starvation mode and start storing everything into fat if it 'thinks' it is not getting enough food. Let me show you what you can eat."

She took out a bunch of plasticized rubber foods. And asked: "show me what things you like. You can have any two of these proteins."

I picked out two rubberized scrambled eggs and a plastic piece of fish, wiggled them a little and placed them on my plate.

"You can have any four of these vegetables, one of these healthy grains, two fruits," she continued.

Together we assembled an average days' worth of food, a substantial amount of food when all put together. "Alright," I smiled, "I can do this."

Dr. Withers proceeded to do the one thing that changed my diet and lifestyle more than anything else had done for me. She told me to take a picture of it. Every day I would pull up the picture on my phone and ask myself: "what have I not had yet today?"

In the weeks and months to come, eating healthy would become my new hobby. I discovered all manner of healthy things I didn't even know I liked: farro, quinoa, bar-b-que tofu, curried cauliflower, grilled eggplant. Not all good food is healthy food, but all healthy food is good food. And if you're not eating much, you can afford to eat well. Pricey restaurants aren't so pricey if you have a salad and an appetizer for dinner. Factor out all the alcohol I would have otherwise drank and they're almost paying me to eat.

The license to occasionally cheat had a huge psychological effect. Knowing I could cheat once in a while not only softened the sharp edge off the prospect of never enjoying burgers and ice cream again, it made me selective in when I would have one – so selective I never ate it. I wasn't going to blow my monthly burger on a mediocre burger. So I became so finicky I only found two cheat-worthy burgers over the course of the next two years.

**

Reading labels is tremendously important for one simple reason: we do not ban anything from the food supply for its long-term health risks. The FDA bans things that cause acute sickness and labels the rest for you to figure out. The processed food lobby has managed to thus far prevent even trans-fats from being restricted. If terrorists put something in the food supply that killed as many people as the number of preventable deaths trans-fats likely cause in a given year, we'd be at global war. But that many deaths resulting from corporate profits – well, that's just freedom. And you are free to learn some chemistry and squint at the labels. But beware, the processed food lobby not only spreads their own vested information about what is and what is not healthy, they lobby to disguise unhealthy ingredients in the labeling. They fought for the right, for example, to list the trans-fat content as zero percent if it is below one percent. So, you have to know to look for the word 'hydrogenated' in the ingredients to see if it really has zero trans fats. And then they lobbied to change the names of trans-fat ingredients we learn to recognize as unhealthy, such words other than hydrogenated to describe trans fats.

Even if you learn to recognize the unhealthy dietary landmines, they can be so prolific they are impossible to avoid without relegating yourself to the produce section of the organic health food store. Think I'm exaggerating? Try going a week without consuming trans-fats or high-fructose corn syrup. Then read up on how natural "natural" flavors and colors are, and what you have to do to avoid consuming potentially dangerous pesticides. While I was going through reacclimating myself to my new dietary habits, my wife Nichole broke out in an all-over body rash. The only thing we were told was it came from an ingested chemical – no clue as to what. If it showed signs of continuous exposure, they could have tried narrowing in on what exactly it was. But she was relatively fortunate, it recurred in lessening degrees for a year before it worked its way out of her system. And we never had any idea if came from pesticides, contaminated shellfish, preservatives or whatever else could have led to a chemical exposure and reaction like she had. No wonder the Nutri-Nazi hates food so much – scary stuff. She really put the fear of Cheezus in me.

**

I had to learn to be careful of some 'healthy' things like vegan cheeses that are made of palm oil, vegan ice cream might as well be sugar-flavored Crisco. You don't want to picture sticky, sugary Crisco in your coronary arteries. And who knows what evil lurks in the heart of a vegan cookie.

When reading labels and keeping a running tally of my fat and calories got tiresome, I learned to just fall back on the safe foods. Other than a few vegan landmines, however, my diet became more and more vegan-like. Not because I necessarily had to for health reasons and not for moral reasons, but just because I wanted to eat what I can eat with impunity without thinking too much and that usually turned out to be the immediate vegan option. In fact people began to mistake me for a vegan all the time and I'd reply: "No, I am not vegan, I am just too lazy and stupid to do math at every meal. Give me the salad, hold the math, arithmetic on the side and stick the multiplication in a doggie bag please."

Cutting out bread and other refined carbohydrates from my diet gave me control over short-term weight loss and unexpectedly alleviated other long-standing symptoms I had come to take for granted. Bread in particular, I learned, was actually responsible for all the digestive ills I had long blamed on my heavy beer intake. I thought I got gas because I was a fat beer-swilling slob and never thought to seek medical of dietary advice on the issue. Turns out the gas and bloating goes away when I cut out the refined carbs. My bulbous belly made so many squeaky, gurgling, groaning noises I thought I was pregnant with a fetal humpback whale singing in my belly. But the low-carb diet cured me of that, so I guess it was just digestion after all. I should have figured that the gestation period of a humpback whale couldn't have lasted the fifteen or twenty years I was walking around with a distended, gurgling, whale-singing belly, and I think I would have remembered being inseminated by a whale no matter how drunk I was, and not being female really should have clued me in that I wasn't pregnant, but I was relieved all the same when the noises and the girth both subsided without me bringing a bouncing baby humpback into the world.

Going forward, I took Dr. Withers advice and ate all the heart-healthy things she told me to eat and cut out the heart-unhealthy ones. I attacked the calories from both ends of the dieting ideological spectrum at the same time and kept the big-ticket carbs out of my diet too. Both high-fat and high-carb foods are high calorie, so why not. Both dieting approaches would have you eat more fruit and vegetables and healthy grains. On top of that, I just kept the protein down to small, healthy portions of fish, tofu, beans, and occasional meat and, voila, I was low-carb, low-fat, low-calorie compliant.

Beyond a diet of whole grains, vegetables, fruits and small portions of healthy proteins, it's not really worth getting into the nitty-gritty of the latest fad diet or latest study about a particular food being good or bad. As my dad says: "Wait long enough, it'll be good for you again."

My dieting advice: keep your fat low, your carbs, your sugar low and your calories low. No, this does not mean you will eat nothing but lettuce and Styrofoam. Have fun exploring all the new things you can eat. You'll enjoy it all the more, full in the knowledge that it's good for you.

The biggest difference in how I dieted going forward was simply a heavy dose of stick-to-it-ed-ness. I wasn't in it for the short term to lose 20 pounds and then fall off it. If I had a moment of weakness, had a cheeseburger emergency or had pizza thrust upon me, I didn't throw up my arms and say 'oh well, I'm off the diet. Maybe I'll start again next week.' And I didn't hide in a closet and flagellate my sinful flesh for enjoying a meatball. I would say: 'oh well, I had a moment, I enjoyed it, now I'm right back on it.' And I had a commitment that I was on it forever, and it felt good and I felt in control. Don't tell yourself you're on a diet for two weeks, tell yourself you're on it for a year.

I read about a study that showed that reduced calorie intake over the course of a year resulted in the same amount of weight loss whether it was done in spurts or spread out, In periods of intensive dieting or small changes over a longer period – just stick to it and keep adding to your really good dieting year and you will keep getting results, slowly but surely. Just pick some manageable dietary changes, stick to them and plan on losing weight at a slow pace and seeing substantial results only over a long period. For me, I had to make serious changes toward a heart-healthy diet, I had to stick to it and the weight loss followed as Dr. Freeman and the Nutri-Nazi said it would. I would lose nearly 100 pounds in the following 18 months. The Nutri-Nazi's far-off goals were attainable after all.

## 24. I Quit

I sat in Dr. Freeman's waiting room leafing through magazines and eyeing my watch. Half an hour behind schedule, I noticed. The healthier I get the less attention lavished on me. Not a bad problem to have in the grand scheme of things. The other patients ahead of me were all older and clearly on the down swing. I guess I'll take the upswing even if means the odd half hour in the waiting room. The aide held an elderly woman by the arm as he escorted her out of Dr. Freeman's office and toward the front door. He popped his head into the waiting room on his way past.

"Dr. Freeman will see you now," he said and continued out to help the woman into a taxi. I guess I don't need to be shown in, I certainly don't need to be helped out of my chair any more. I pushed the office door open and peered in for permission to enter.

"Come on in. Wow, look at you." Dr. Freeman greeted me.. "You look like a new man."

"Yeah, I've lost a bit of weight in the last month."

"A bit? I could see that as soon as you came through the door," he looked me up and down. "How's your energy level? Your mood?"

"I'm glad to have lost the weight. If that what is you mean?"

Dr. Freeman leaned in across his desk. "Sometimes people suffer emotionally after heart surgery, or any trauma for that matter. How's your state of mind?"

I was confused by the question. I was beginning to feel better than I had in years. "Feeling lucky to be doing so well – and fit and slim." I patted myself on the abs.

"Good. Let's get you in the exam room and take a look how many pounds you knocked off. Down to your shorts, gown open in the back."

I stood on the scale and slid the weights back and forth. It didn't look right to me unless I had lost another thirty pounds in the last few weeks.

"You've lost another thirty pounds," Dr Freeman said with surprise as he tapped the weights into balance "You saw Dr. Whithers?"

"Yeah, I've been eating healthy and enjoying it – feeling great."

"Good, but I want another thirty days without alcohol as well."

"Oh man, another thirty days in the no-alco-hole? That's a long stretch in the hole. And so unfair, it's not like this was caused by alcohol – alcohol didn't clog my arteries."

"No, but it can contribute to the obesity and hypertension, and more importantly it can weaken your heart muscle when we really need you to re-strengthen your heart."

"That first cardiologist had her distinct advantages," I grumbled.

"How are you doing on the smoking front?" asked Dr. Freeman.

"Smoking?" I replied with a touch of indignation, "I quit over ten years ago, never had a puff since."

"No relapses?" he asked. "A lot of smokers say never again, but then after a few drinks…"

"Other smokers didn't go through what *I* went through to quit. I exercised the nuclear option, I ain't doing *that* again."

"What? What did you do? How did you quit?" Dr. Freeman asked, removing his reading glasses and looking at me in anticipation.

I began to explain to Dr. Freeman that just over ten years earlier, I went to Alaska and paid a bush pilot to drop me a hundred miles from anywhere with a map, a compass, a backpack and no goddamn cigarettes.

I figured I didn't want anyone near me, and certainly nobody wanted to be near me when I was going through the maddening mood swings of nicotine withdrawal. I figured it would actually take an edge off of the withdrawal if I knew there was no chance of getting any cigarettes. That's the hardest part of quitting for me, the constant internal bartering: 'Ok, this is it, now I can't take it anymore. I'll buy a pack, but I'll only smoke two today. And I'll throw the other half away.'

It's maddening. I figured, out there I would just say to myself: 'you don't have any cigarettes, you ain't gonna get no cigarettes, so just get over it. Or die.' The 'or die' part actually wound up adding an unexpectedly more massive amount of stress than I bargained for.

I had been there before. Three trips in the previous three years, each with three backpacking trips into the bush. And I put a lot of planning into it – researching several areas and several possible trips, studying the maps for weeks. The place I went was actually my third choice, but the first two bush pilots said: "Are you crazy? I'm not taking responsibility for you." So, I didn't tell the third one I was planning on losing my marbles on nicotine withdrawal alone in the bush. Not until I got there, anyway, and I realized I had been studying the wrong place on the map for all those weeks. I had the drop off spot wrong.

I confessed my plan to the bush pilot and admitted that the added challenge of losing my marbles might complicate navigating my way cross country. He took it in stride and didn't refuse to drop me off. He talked me into a toned-down version. I would hike a twenty-five-mile loop and get picked up at the drop-off spot rather than the planned 25-mile hike to find the pick-up spot. It seemed easier and safer. The area was high in the Wrangel Mountains near the border with the Yukon Territory – high alpine tundra, easy to navigate long distances. And spectacular mountain and glacier views. I was supposed to be able to see Mt. Logan from there, the highest peak in Canada, but I never did figure out which one it was.

It should have been doable, but things started going wrong from the start. FIrstly, I grossly underestimated the nicotine withdrawals. I had quit before, but I always caved eventually and didn't realize how much worse it would get on day two or three. And I didn't realize how much worse my addiction had gotten since I last attempted a break-up with nicotine. It quickly deteriorated into a five-day screaming argument with the sky. Every time something went wrong, I'd throw my head back, scream in frustration and shake my clenched fists. "Damn you to hell, can't *anything* go right?" I started a list in my head of all the things that if taken away from my situation, I would be fine:

Take away the fact that I was in a situation dependent on my wits and I had thrown my wits away with my cigarettes, and I'd be fine.

Take away the fact that I was alone, and I'd be fine. I grossly underestimated how weird it is to be alone for five days. I would have felt sorry for anyone who had to be near me, but have you ever gone five days without talking? It gets to you.

Take away the fact that I lost a contact lens and I'd be fine. I was fiddling with my stove trying to make lunch on the first day and I accidently shot a stream of camp gas in my face. I washed my eye out with contact lens solution and the lens slid out. For the rest of the trip, I had to hold one hand over one eye to see anything clearly.

If it weren't for the mosquitoes eating my pecker alive every time I peed, I'd be fine. I swear those fuckers were mainlining off my penis veins. I was afraid they were going to collapse my penis veins like a bunch of penile junkies. I peed with one hand and waved the other back and forth around my junk to shoo the swarm away, attempting not to swat the family jewels or my own pee stream in the process. Not having a free hand to cover one eye with I had no depth perception and a less than one-hundred-percent success rate at those attempts.

Take away the fact that I forgot the poles and stakes for my tent, and I'd be fine. After I was through grabbing my head, pulling my hair and jumping up and down screaming at the sky: "Holy shit! Holy shit!" I headed back to a ravine I had crossed earlier that first day. There were some small trees with low branches there and I jury-rigged my tent from a low branch and duct-taped a poncho on the front. It was pretty good for a withdrawal-crazed brain. I decided to stay put there near the drop-off/pick-up spot and abandon the hike. I gazed upon my make-shift shelter with pride and said to myself: "as long as it doesn't snow in July, I'll be fine."

Take away the fact that it snowed in July every night and sagged my sopping wet jury-rigged tent onto my sleeping bag and clothes in my sleep every night and I would have been fine. Take away the grizzly bear stalking my camp site and I would have been fine. I heard it the first night grunting and crashing through the bushes while I was trying to fall asleep, but I convinced myself it was the imagination of my overactive, emotionally unstable, nicotine-deprived brain. But when I woke up – got up, I should say, I didn't really sleep between the bear grunts and the drooping snow-laden tent – I found a steaming pile of bear poop melted into the snow right where I had eaten the night before. I set up a cook spot about a hundred yards from my tent spot so as not to attract bears. I guess that paid off.

The bear was back every day. But he never figured out my food stash, bungee-corded to a tree in a Kevlar bag. I only actually saw him on the way out. I was hiking back to the pick-up spot on the flat hard-gravel-packed mesa where I was dropped off, and I nearly stepped over the edge of a sudden drop off, about five feet down into a depression with a spring in it. The bear was in there sipping from the spring and had no idea I was there right above it.

I had bear spray – a highly pressurized aerosol can that in two one-second blasts discharges a 30-foot cloud of highly concentrated pepper spray much stronger than what they sell for spraying at people – strong enough to knock an angry grizzly bear on his ass as he charges at you. It's so concentrated and pressurized, the bush pilot asked me, as a matter of routine, if I had it in my back pack. He asked me to remove it and he duct-taped it to the wing of the airplane in case the pressure change of the short flight made it leak, it would have blinded us both, unable to even see the instruments much less the mountains all around.

I also had small explosive bear-bangers, a flare gun and an air horn – all of which were only intended to give the bear something to think about other than me for a quick second while I sidle away. Bears are usually very skittish. The real danger in a bear encounter is surprising it. Guides had always told Nichole and I that

you really just need to let the bear know you are there
and let him know you are human, and they will choose
not to stick around. You let them know you are there
and human by doing things only a human can do: wave
your hands over your head, clap, and talk. Don't shout,
singing can make you sound calm. And I was wearing
bear bells on my belt so I'm always making noise. So, I
figured if I'm going to clap my hands over my head and
sing while wearing bells it only made sense to me to
sing Hare Krishna. So, I un-holstered and took the
safety off my bear spray and flare gun but left them
hanging loosely on my belt. I clapped my hands over
my head, swiveled my bell-laden hips and sang out:
"Hare Krishna, mother fucker!"

The bear looked up at me and I swear it gasped
and bulged its eyes. If that poor animal could have
screamed like a little girl, it would have. And it ran as
fast as a race horse away from me and kept going as far
as the eye could see.

I set up camp at the pick-up spot that last night.
I had spent the last few days fashioning poles and stakes
for my tent out of branches with my hand saw and
carried them, slung over my shoulder back to the open,
wind-swept pick-up spot. But it wasn't a free-standing
tent, it needs to be staked into the ground to give it
tension. But the ground on the rocky mesa was way too
hard to get a stake in, except for some mossy patches of
lichen. I had to walk around looking for four mossy
lichen patches in the shape of the footprint of my tent
before I could pitch it.

While I was walking around looking for a tent

spot, some ugly clouds rolled in. I looked up and around
to survey the weather and realized ugly clouds were
rolling in from every direction at once. When they
converged directly over my head and the last blue patch
was blotted out from the sky, it suddenly grew dark and
with a clap of thunder, golf-ball-sized hail stones came
raining down, pummeling me all over like a sitting duck
on the driving range of hell. I crouched and held my
backpack over my head but couldn't hold it there for
long. I grappled for my foam ground mat and unravel it
over my head and crouched underneath it. It worked
except for my knuckles that were taking regular
thwacks from the golf balls whizzing out of the sky.

It lasted about twenty minutes. When it cleared,
a thick fog took its place and I couldn't see five feet, but
I put my pack on, slung my branch-poles over my
shoulder and trudged on looking for a tent spot until I
got totally disoriented in the fog and looked for a spot to
sit. I thought I saw a bright white rock or sun-bleached
log I might be able to sit on. I wondered what a log was
doing in this treeless high-alpine tundra. I walked over
to it and realized it was a bloody ram skull. I had seen
mountain goats and Dahl sheep in the distance and once
I saw a group moving quickly and sleekly on a distant
mountainside. They were spaced out farther than a flock
and I thought at the time maybe it was a pack of wolves.
Now I thought maybe I was right.

I found four patches of mossy lichen in the
shape of my tent floor and rigged up my tent with my
pole branches, duct tape and bungee cords and
hammered the hand-carved stakes into the ground with
a flat rock.

The fog lifted like a veil off my face, and the spectacular mountain views reappeared. At the same instant, I realized the nicotine-withdrawal haze had lifted as well. Suddenly everything was clear in sight and mind. I was going to be fine. Even with the bloody ram head, the rock hard ground, the bruised knuckles from the hail, my collapsed penis veins and the bear still lurking out there somewhere, I would be fine. I finally had one thing going for me, one thing taken away: the insanity of the nicotine withdrawal. But in that moment of clarity, I had a sinking feeling that I was too late to stem the tide of declining health. All those years of heavy smoking, drinking, lethargy and gluttony, and all the years and uphill struggle since then to reclaim my health and fitness. I felt, out of shape and overweight and wondered if I had quit too late, or just in time. It was probably both – just in time to prevent my future heart disease from killing me but too late to prevent it from happening; too late to get out of the downward spiral, but soon enough to beat the odds.

The timing of my quitting was very calculated. My father, the medical school professor, used to give me articles about the effects of smoking that were coming out in the nineties in an attempt to get me to quit. He'd ask me: "did you read the article I sent you? What do you think?" And I'd answer: "I think it says nobody dies of lung cancer in their twenties, and I have the data to prove it, thanks." And that was true, there was lots of evidence that if you quit before you smoke twenty pack-years – a pack a day for twenty years, half a pack for forty years or two packs for ten years – you would fall back into nearly the same risk groups as those who never smoked. And the health risks only really started picking up after age forty. I smoked about a pack a day for nineteen years and quit when I was thirty-nine, that was no coincidence, it was a long-calculated risk.

"How did you feel after you quit?" asked Dr. Freeman. "A lot better, I'm sure."

"Not really. Certainly not immediately." I answered. "Everyone always asked me: 'Don't you feel great now that you quit?' But I didn't. I was still winded and wheezy all the time. My cough lasted until I was in the hospital. They gave me a steroid inhaler for the cough and it worked wonders to alleviate the coughing. But it made me wonder: 'Why the hell didn't someone give me this ten years ago?' Until the coughing was an issue following the open-heart surgery, the only thing doctors had to say about it was: "Well, you shouldn't have smoked all those years. Told you so. Pfffth (raspberry tongue fart)."

I spent ten years trying to regain some semblance of cardio-vascular fitness, and just grew resigned to the fact that my quitting calculations only calculated probabilities of death and didn't factor in the long-term damage. And, in the six months after I quit, I gained fifty pounds. I joked all the time: "Great now instead of dying of lung cancer at sixty I'll die of a heart attack before I'm fifty." And at the age of forty-nine, look what happened!

"I think you should be grateful you quit when you did," said Dr. Freeman, digesting my fantastical tale while reclining back in his chair with the fingertips of each hand gently touching in front of his chest.

"I am. I can't imagine having gone through what I went through with the weakened lung capacity and chronic coughing of a smoker. I don't think I could have survived it."

"And how's your physical shape now?"

"Now I'm in the best shape since before I started smoking, thirty years ago. But it took all that to quit, and all this to clear up my lungs with the inhaler and the surgery to clear out my coronary arteries. And now, finally, after all that, I am starting to feel pretty fit."

"And after all that I guess I don't have to worry about you going back to smoking," said Dr. Freeman.

"And I don't think you have to worry about my approach becoming the next fad fitness plan."

# Getting Better

## 25. The Great FitBit Wars

I was finally feeling back to normal and then some and able to keep pace with Wally on what were now regular walks around Central Park. It was a beautiful late summer day – a bit warm, but I wasn't overheating like I used to. The circadian cooling pump was once again performing to specs. Wally and I were doing so much walking lately my knee was chronically swelling. I insisted on walking on the bridle paths, the horse trails, which were a softer, lower impact surface for my knee than the paved paths.

"How many steps are we up to, Wally?"

"You mean how many times have I stepped in horse shit?"

"I mean FitBit steps."

"I've got about 9,000," Wally answered, peering at the small screen on her wrist Keep going?"

"I don't even have 8,000. What kind of crap is that? We both started out at just about 1,500."

"Well, you probably take longer steps than I do." She said glancing down at my longer legs and stride.

"Yeah, but I'm getting shafted out of my steps. We walked the same distance."

"You don't have to get competitive about it."

"Moi? Competitive?"

"No, certainly not" Wally said. "The guy who knocked down three bridesmaids to catch my bouquet at my wedding would never be overly competitive."

"Bouquet catching is not for the faint of heart, Wally! I warned all those bridesmaids of that before they decided to take me on in that arena."

"Well, if you want to get competitive about it, there are challenges in the app we can do."

"Challenges?" I said, raising an eyebrow.

"Yeah, look." Wally held my phone out and began navigating the FitBit app. "The Work-Week Hustle. I'll friend you on FitBit, you accept. Now accept the challenge. And we can invite other friends to join. Let's invite Joe and Ro, I'm already FitBit friends with them. And now we can see each other's step count for the week. You try to keep up with each other and whoever has the most steps by Friday at midnight wins."

"You're on, Wally." And I quickened my pace and started to pull away from her.

"Hey! Where are you going?"

"Well, I'm never going to get more steps than you walking along side you and your dainty stride."

"You're ditching me? I'm not getting into this with you Hornbull, if it helps you motivate to exercise to keep up with me you go ahead, but I'm not getting into it with you" Wally shouted, her voice fading as I pulled farther ahead. "You prick!"

I had one distinct advantage in the up-coming all-out FitBit combat that had been initiated: sheer pig-headed stupidity that resulted in an absolute unwillingness to stay within the bounds of reason. I walked an extra lap around the reservoir for an extra 2,000 steps and headed home with a total of 12,000 for the day – a new record. Nichole was home by the time I got home. I was suspiciously pleased with myself and she quickly extracted the day's events out of me in a gentle wifely interrogation.

"Sweetie, don't get competitive with Wally." She said shaking her head. "This won't end well for either of you. Don't poke a sleeping Wally, let her be."

"It's fine." I said waving a hand. "She doesn't have the resolve to make a thing out of it. But it'll keep me motivated. Besides, she doesn't have the heart to beat the poor little cardiac boy." I held out my phone and showed her the app. "Look, I'm already 2,000 steps ahead for the day."

"Actually, it looks like you're only a couple hundred ahead."

"What?" I snatched the phone back from Nichole. "She stopped. I saw her step count stop an hour ago."

"I guess she started again," Nichole shrugged. "So what?"

"Fuck that, I'm not starting out behind on the first day." And I jumped of the couch.

"What are you doing? Where are you going?" Nichole sat up on the couch, her eyes following me in disbelief as I walked toward the door and started lacing my shoes.

"I'll be right back. Just going around the block real quick."

I held my own with Wally day-by-day but she was showing no mercy. Every time I skipped ahead in the step count, she would retaliate. She was clearly doing the same thing I was: jumping up and walking whenever falling behind in the step count. By Thursday night I was 1,500 steps behind and concerned about going into Friday with a deficit. I called Dan, Wally's husband, on his cell at 10:30 at night: "Is she in for the night? I need to go into the final Friday stretch in the lead."

"Would you please stop antagonizing my wife with this shit?" he answered incredulously. "We were out to dinner with old friends last night and she left the restaurant to walk around the block because of this stupidity."

"I knew it! I knew she was plotting against me."

"Then she made us walk all the way from Midtown to "get some air." Leave this alone and let us get to sleep, please? We're already in bed."

"So she's in for the night and in bed? Perfect." And I headed out the door as Nichole stood shaking her head in disbelief.

I came back in about twenty minutes and 1,500 steps later.

"Well I hope you're quite pleased with yourself," said Nichole her jaw slacked in disbelief.

"I am." I said looking at the FitBit app. "I am now ahead by… wait. What the? How did she? Oh my God. She must have run out the door as soon as I got off the phone with Dan. That bitch. She's got 500 steps on me."

"Don't even think about it. You're not bothering Dan-Dan again at this hour and you're not leaving the house. Get to bed right this instant."

"This is *so* unfair, I ruined my favorite walking socks over this, this week. Look, I got a hole in my toe," I said with a pouty face.

"I'll darn your socks for you tomorrow, SweetiePie."

"I wonder why they call it that: darning socks. Is it because it is a really annoying thing to have to do? Do you suppose that's where the word darn comes from? From people getting aggravated because they had to darn their socks by candlelight in the nineteenth century?"

"Sure, I'll bet if you lived in the nineteenth century we'd be calling it 'holy fucking shitting' our socks to this very day. Good night."

The following day started out wet and rainy with a forecast of from bad to worse.

"Perfect!" I said to Nichole. "Wally will never get out in this slop. She's way too smart to go out trekking around in the rain over a FitBit challenge."

"So, your strategy is to outsmart her with sheer stupidity?"

I paused in contemplation, eyes rolled up toward the ceiling. "Cunning stupidity and didactic buffoonery. It will go down in the annals of FitBit history as the Rainy-Day Sneak. Only the truly shrewd would venture out in the wind and the rain where others fear to tread. Coming around the final stretch of the FitBit challenge: I'm a mudder, my mudder was a mudder. I love the slop, love it, I tell you!"

Nichole hung her head in despair as I strutted out the door and into the rain. But it worked. I trod across town in the rain for the better part of the day and ended a few thousand steps ahead. Joe and Ro however pulled out of nowhere late in the day to rejoin the pack. I ran into them in front of the bar that evening sipping frozen drinks out of to-go cups under the awning in front of the bar, taking shelter from the rain.

"On your way in or out?" I asked.

"In" they replied. "Just finishing off our daiquiris."

"So, I've been watching you on the FitBit app. How the heck did you guys pull ahead of the pack on a day like today, anyway?"

"Treadmill at the gym," Ro said between sips.

Friday evening came upon us and all the FitBit competitors had arranged to meet in the bar to celebrate the effort. I was ahead by a couple thousand but taking no chances. I left the apartment and headed to Central Park for a quick topper-offer lap around the reservoir to put any thoughts of a last-minute comeback out of anybody's mind. I was last to arrive at the bar, feeling like a conquering hero. Ro and Joe were out front sipping frozen drinks again, Wally was out smoking on the sidewalk.

"Ladies and Gentlemen, the victor." I announced. "While you were all here licking your wounds and sipping your frozen drinks, I was out pulling the Friday-Night Sneak – another of my personal cunning strategic additions to Art of FitBit War."

"Sorry, bud" said Joe shaking his head with curled lips. "Ro and I pulled way ahead earlier. We just didn't synch our FitBits with our phones, so you never saw what you were really up against."

I whipped my phone out of my pocket and checked the app. I had maintained my lead over Wally but way behind Joe and Ro. "How the hell did you guys get three thousand steps ahead? I've been duped! The Friday-Night Synch Sneak! Foiled again."

We all had lots to celebrate all the same. We each had our best week ever in steps, calories and active minutes. We all topped our personal best during both the next two weeks with more of the same strategic FitBit tactics: the Rainy-Day Sneak, the Friday-Night Synch Sneak et cetera. Wally and I continued our tit-for-tat rivalry but Ro and Joe always snuck up from behind to win the week. They ended every week sipping their frozen drinks on their way into the bar while Wally and I developed repetitive stress ailments from over-doing it. Wally had a painful bone spur on her heel and I had an old knee problem flaring up.

"Can't we go back to non-competitive walks like we used to?" She pleaded. "How about something a little less hard on our bodies, say Australian Rules Football next week?"

"You caving, Wally?" I grinned.

"I just don't like the idea of everyone watching me on the FitBit app. It knows when I've been sleeping, it knows when I have been bad or good, it's like fucking Santa Claus."

"Oh, cut it out you two" said Ro. "You know the only way Joe and I keep beating you is by strapping our FitBits to the blender and racking up thousands of 'steps' per daquiri, right?"

Joe gave a shrug and an apologetic smirk of confirmation. Wally and I glanced at each other with furrowed brows and gripped our drinks and motioned to throw them at Joe and Ro.

"Truce!" Ro pleaded with her palms facing outward in front of her chest.

Wally and I lowered our shoulders and raised our glasses.

"Truce," Wally conceded.

"Well played, sir and madame," I said shaking my head. "Well played."

## 26. The Bronx Zoo and the Monkey Poo

Joe and Ro's blender, despite its history of FitBit duplicity, became my new favorite toy for virgin mocktail making. It was a way to keep me busy while socializing in the bar. Ray let me keep the blender on the bar while I manufactured my virgin concoctions: virgin banana-blueberry daquiris were a favorite. But I still had to curtail the cocktails, virgin or not to control the calories.

Nichole and I met Wally and the Beave for drinks around happy-hour time on a Thursday. We arrived early to commandeer the valuable bar-front real estate in the corner and set up the blender and fruity picnic. Ray was gracious about letting me bring in my own ingredients and concoct my own concoctions. He couldn't be bothered anyway.

"I don't care. If it ain't got no active ingredient in it, it ain't in my contract," he'd say. He wouldn't charge me and I wouldn't sit there and not tip, so it worked out for both of us. Besides, between Nichole, Wally and the Beave, the group of us were putting plenty of money in the register. We settled in and loosened up. And in walked Sammy.

"Oh Christ, someone open a window. Here comes Stinky Sammy," Wally whispered under her breath.

Sammy had a well-deserved reputation for having the meanest case of perpetual beer farts you ever heard or smelled.

"There's something wrong with that boy," the Beave whispered back with a crinkled nose.

"You guys are really rushing to judgement here," I protested.

Wally held the collar of her blouse over her nose. "What? Are you going to tell us he just overly generous with his intestinal gasses?"

"Personally, I don't believe that much stink can possibly come out of one man's ass," I argued. "I think his reputation has actually given everyone else license to fart when he walks into the bar. Like: 'Oh look, her comes Stinky Sammy, I can finally let this one loose.'"

"I don't think any of the guys who hang around in here are ever holding anything back in that regard," the Beave said..

"Neither do I. I think it's the women," I said to looks of scorn from the three women facing me, but opted to dig myself in deeper. "Think about it. Women are too mortified to fart in public, but everyone has to fart eventually. So, women hold onto their farts like Charlton Heston holding onto his gun with his cold dead hands until Sammy walks in. They have the perfect scapegoat! I put forth that every time poor hapless Sammy walks in the bar there's a giant communal exhalation of female flatulence," I proclaimed with a raised accusatory finger.

"Besides, girl farts do *not* smell like *that*," Wally objected from behind her blouse collar.

"Yeah, I fart rainbows and poop jelly beans like a unicorn," the Beave giggled to herself.

"But I can hear them too," Wally replied. "What? Sammy walks in and suddenly everyone is a fart-triliquist?"

Mook eyed the wave of looks and sneers passing down the bar as Stinky Sammy walked by and spotted his own opportunity to stink up the joint incognito. He cupped his hands in front of his mouth and shouted: "Ca-caw!!! Ca-caw!!!"

"What does that mean?" Nichole asked.

"That means we're going outside for some fresh air," I replied. The ladies gathered their coats, purses and cigarettes. "I think Mook wants to poke smot."

"Yeah, poke'em if you smot'em," Mook shouted. Nichole, Wally, the Beave and I slid out the door behind him. "I love Stinky Sammy, he's the perfect cover."

"Oh, don't you dare. We just came out here to escape that," Nichole shook her head and finger at Mook.

"No, I mean for smoking stinky pot," Mook clarified. "No one can smell my skunk weed inside when I smoke out here once Stinky Sammy walks through crop dusting the place."

"No officer, there's no problem here. Stinky Sammy just walked by, that's all," I said. "I'm sure they'd just scurry back to the squad car holding their ties over their noses. The perfect alibi."

"That boy is an animal," Wally lit her cigarette. "He might as well throw his poo around the room like a zoo monkey."

"Oh-ho, you want to see a monkey throw poo?" Mook asked. "I know how to make that happen."

"Will it make Stinky Sammy go away? Sounds like it might be worth the trade," said the Beave.

"I'm telling you, I met a guy in a bar in midtown who was a tiger trainer in the circus, and he told me how to really make a monkey freak out and throw poo at you," Mook flailed his arms like a monkey. "You find the dominant male and show him your teeth. Apparently, this is an affront to his masculinity, and he'll freak out and throw poo at you to defend his honor."

"We *must* try this," I stated emphatically as I exhaled the Mook's vapor.

"You *must* stop vaping with Mook," Nichole retorted. "Let's get you back inside to your bananas my little monkey."

"Yes, I need another banana daquiri," my tongue started tripping over my syllables .

"I think you've had enough," Nichole replied. "When you lose track of how many syllables there are in banana, you've had enough banananana daquiris, virgin or not.

"Well how the hell am I supposed to keep track of how many syllables there are in my banananananas? There could be any number of them. That's like asking me how many syllables there are in cinnamonin. Do you think Ray has any cinnamonamonimin? For my banananana and bluedababerry daquiris?"

"Let's get you back inside and on your bar stool," Nichole led me by the arm away from Mook and his vape pen. "You can show Stinky Sammy your teeth and see if he throws poo at you."

\*\*

The next day Wally and I returned to our non-competitive walking routine; our first destination: the Bronx Zoo to determine the veracity of Mook's poo-flinging claims. We approached the baboon habitat and slowed to a cautious pace.

"So how does this work exactly?" she asked, looking across the railing and moat at the troop of baboons. "How do you know which is the dominant male?"

"That's why we are going to the baboons. According to my internet research, they are the easiest to spot. The males have bright red, white and blue noses and butts."

"He doesn't throw red, white and blue poo from his red, white and blue butt does he?"

"There's only one way to find out, Wally." I

answered, raising my eyebrow.

We ambled and navigated our way through the zoo to the baboon habitat. There was a large and obvious sign in front of the baboon display that read: Please do Not Annoy the Animals. "I guess we are not the first ones to think of this" Wally said gently biting her index fingernail. "Can we get in trouble?"

"Nah, we'll be subtle. Look at that guy with the big nose and butt, he must be our man."

I flashed a toothy grin at him but he didn't seem to take much notice.

"I think you have to look more threatening than that, like you are going to bite him." Wally made a more chomping gesture at the baboon, and he seemed to take an interest in us.

"Wait, wait, hang back. We don't want to get caught annoying the animals." We tried being subtle for a while, like we were flashing secret baboon gang signals with our faces, and the dominant male was definitely interested but not visibly annoyed and certainly not flailing his feces around.

"Alright, there is nobody here. Let's pull out the stops" I suggested. "Put your finger in your mouth, pry your lips wide open like this and really show him all your teeth."

Wally and I pried back our lips to expose our teeth in evil grins. The baboons all got excited and the dominant male rushed forward. "Oh my God, it's working, do it again" Wally said excitedly.

The male baboon opened his jaw wide and his lips peeled themselves back to reveal a fearsome, fang-filled mouth.

"Do it again, quick, before anyone comes over here." I said, and we both stuck our fingers in our mouths and made the offending facial gesture.

The baboon was not about to tolerate this affront to his dominance and made threatening yelps and growls. The females scattered like they knew some bad shit was about to get thrown around. The dominant male rushed toward the front of the enclosure and began, well, shall we say 'spanking the monkey.' Wally screamed and ran.

"I am *not* getting *that* thrown at me," she called back over her shoulder as she ran.

I was a little slower on the uptake on what was soon coming our way, but once the light bulb went off over my head I turned to run and took one sideways step in a half-turned running motion and my knee made an almighty pop. I fell to the ground. Wally jumped behind a bush and began frantically frisking herself: "Oh my God, did I get it on me? Did he throw it?" she screamed as she ran her fingers through her hair and patted herself down in a frenetic self-frisk.

"No, damn it, would you help me up please?" I pleaded.

"I'm not going anywhere near you until you

thoroughly certify yourself to be monkey-spunk-free."

All the commotion attracted the attention of a couple of zoo attendants who began to approach us. "Are you alright?" they asked.

"I'm fine." I said as I slowly got myself into a standing position. "I just twisted my knee, it's OK."

The zoo attendants had an awfully contemptuous look about them for someone coming to help an injured man. I suspect they had seen this scenario before and suspected juvenile foul play. I also suspect the baboon had through years of trial and error learned the reaction he could get from his auto-erotic actions and knew full well how to dispense with another couple of clowns who reckoned themselves smarter that the average monkey. It certainly does make one feel foolish to get caught in the act of losing a poo-flinging battle of wills and wits with a baboon. But considering the baboon's behavior, I don't quite see why I was the one to be made to feel that I was the one caught with my pants down. Doesn't the baboon bear any responsibility for this little encounter turning south?

"Just please don't annoy the animals," one of the rangers warned, pointing at the sign.

Wally and I headed for the exit. "I can't believe I let you talk me into that," Wally called back over her shoulder, then swished her pony tail as she turned her head away from me as I hobbled three paces behind.

"I can't believe you wouldn't help me up," I yelled after her. "I could have been having a heart attack for all you knew."

"You could have been having a heart attack for all I care," as she added another stride between us, her long ponytail swaying back at me.

We walked past the rhinoceros habitat just in time to witness a large male rhinoceros unload a freshly baked, steaming loaf of rhino dung onto the ground with a dull thud.

"Oh my God, rhinos don't throw their poo, do they?" asked Wally as she siddled behind me for cover. Then she skipped ahead leaving me to hobble after her all the way to the exit.

**

Dr. Freeman was concerned that the baboon incident pushed my knee problems over the top and pushed me to finally seek out an orthopedist. "If you can't walk, you can't exercise, you can't keep up the weight loss and your heart won't continue to recover as well as it has been. This could have serious long-term consequences," he insisted.

He put the fear of Kneezus into me enough to agree to go see an orthopedist named Dr. Mallard, but only reluctantly, putting my relationship with her on a rocky setting from the get-go. I sat impatiently on the exam table waiting for her to find time for me. I looked none too pleased when she finally arrived.

"So how did you injure your knee?" asked Dr. Mallard. She was a stiff-looking woman with hair tightly pulled back, thick glasses and conspicuously good posture.

"Uh, it's kind of a long story. I twisted it turning to run."

"What were you doing when you twisted it?"

"Turning, just turning, nothing out of the ordinary." I stuttered defensively. "Never mind what I was doing, I turned this way," I said reenacting the twisting motion, "and put my weight on it funny, like this."

"Alright, alright" she responded obviously confused at my elusive defensiveness, "You made what's called a chord step, a sideways step, that puts a certain pressure on the joint. Sit up on the exam table and extend your leg, please."

"How would you rate your pain on a scale of one to ten?" she asked with her hands wrapped around my extended knee measuring the circumference of the swelling.

"A two, I guess. It's not the pain, it's just so swollen I can't fully extend it or bend it."

"Well, we'll reduce the swelling with a draining and a cortisone shot and I'll give you something for the pain." She said as she drew a syringe with a frighteningly long thick needle.

"You seem like an intelligent, professional man," she began for no reason. "What do you think of all this hysteria over Trump?"

I was in no position to get in a political argument with a woman pointing a joint-penetrating needle at my knee. I nodded blankly.

"I mean, all these young people are getting all hysterical about political correctness and the rest of us just want our taxes to go down. Don't you agree?" she asked rhetorically as she broke skin with the needle.

This would be a bad time to offend so I grimaced and bit my tongue, figuratively and my lip literally. She slowly, forcefully inserted the needle directly into my right knee joint. It was painful and horridly uncomfortable to feel the needle continue so far into my body, but I could feel some pressure being relieved.

"I mean what do they expect when you see what's going on all around us. My elderly 90-year-old mother had to move out of the town where she raised a family because of the way it is changing. She had a man from India or somewhere living on one side of her and I guess we are calling them 'Africans' now on the other. I mean, I'm sure there are very nice ones, but they are not people she can pop over and have a cup of tea with."

"Well, there's a good chance the Indian gentleman might have a taste for tea," I quipped.

"Oh, I know that, but imagine my poor mother," she said laughing, "It was just so much easier for people like us when we were all the same, don't you think?"

"When were we all the same?" I couldn't help asking.

She looked noticeably disappointed she had not recruited a kindred spirit. I slid tepidly off the exam table and took a few cautious steps. I could move more normally and walk more naturally and nodded with a grin of approval.

"I'll schedule you for an MRI and x-ray for this afternoon so we can see what's going on in there and I'll give you some sample meds to help with the pain until we see the results and determine how to move forward from there."

"I really don't need anything for pain," I repeated.

"Well, high-dose ibuprofen will help with the swelling primarily," she replied.

**

I spent the afternoon and early evening in an imaging clinic getting x-rays and an MRI and losing my patience with avoiding questions about how I injured my knee. "What difference does it make? Does it affect how you take an MRI depending on what I was doing when I twisted it?"

I came home to several voice mails from a pharmacy asking about a delivery. Neither Nichole nor I could figure out what it was about. We were shrugging and scratching our heads and the phone rang.

"Hello?"

"Hello, this is Keene Pharmacy. We need to collect payment information from you for your co-pay for your prescription. How will you be paying?"

"Prescription? What prescription?" I asked.

"Did you visit Dr. Mallard today? She called in a prescription."

"She said we would discuss prescriptions next week after the MRI."

"We cannot deliver your prescription without full payment. The amount is three-hundred-and-fifty-two dollars. How will you be paying, sir?" she said with increased conviction and lessening patience.

"Three-hundred-and-fifty-two dollars? Haven't you contacted my insurance? I gave Dr. Mallard my insurance information."

"Three-hundred-and-fifty-two dollars is your copayment, sir. How will you be paying?"

"What pharmacy did you say this is? I provided my pharmacy information to Dr. Mallard. Who are you?"

"This is common, sir. Your pharmacy probably doesn't handle tightly-controlled pain medications such as the OxyContin prescribed to you by Dr. Mallard. The State of New York requires we verify photo identification and your address upon delivery, and we require payment in full before we can deliver. How will you be paying, sir?"

"Oxy what?! Are you kidding? I rated my pain a two out of ten. I don't need that."

"Your prescription has already been filled, and we are now simply asking for payment and address verification to finalize delivery."
"I'll tell you what, keep the oxy and knock yourself out." Click!

It would seem our entire nation is focused on our growing opioid abuse epidemic, with the notable exception of the medical community. They seem to continue to hand out the oxy-opioids like candy with the hubris that they are doctors, so it is okay. When I left the hospital, I was told pharmacies won't deal in oxy-anything anymore so I should just come back to the hospital for more oxy for as long as I thought I needed it. I took it in decreasing amounts for one week, then took it once before bed to help me sleep for a week, and other than the occasional recreational use, that was it. I had some chronic pain, but I was fine. Every doctor I spoke to offered it up indefinitely.

And Dr. Mallard? Sending it to my house after telling her I don't need or want it and rated my pain as a two out of ten? It gave me suspicions that she was trying to win a cruise from the pharmaceutical industry for collecting the most frequent prescriber points.

My suspicions about her mercenary nature grew when I later got solicitations in the mail from a lawyer saying my case was referred by Dr. Mallard to help determine who is responsible for my injury. Probably like one of those late-night cable commercials – no, not the escort service prostitutes, the personal-injury lawyers – well, yes actually, like the prostitute escorts except they escort you to court to screw anybody they can squeeze a dime out of. Maybe those late-night cable commercials should think about doing combo ads – like when they do action movie merchandising at fast-food chains – they could combine the personal-injury lawyers and the escort-service prostitutes: 'New York's sexiest lawyers will escort you to court, take down your opponent's briefs and make him pay.' They could even offer combo deals: 'the solicitors special, a lawyer and two hookers for the price of one, lose the case and we give you a free blow job!'

By the time the law office called me on the phone, I finally had cause to spill the whole baboon bag of beans: "I injured my knee fleeing a poo-throwing masturbating baboon. Alright? Why don't you slap him with a lawsuit? Be sure to tell the process server to wear a rain coat." Click!

## 27. Sleep Clinic

I explained to Dr. Freeman that if there is one health problem that permeates my entire life it is sleep disorders. I have read from many sources that sleep disorders and heart problems share an association, although the causality of the relationship seems to be murky. But one association in particular – weakened heart muscle after heart surgery – seemed to fit my description.

He shook his head and rolled his eyes a little: "if you want a referral for a sleep study, I'll give you one."

"I'm really asking your opinion as to whether you think I should get one."

"You may be right, there is a relationship and probably a causal one at that, I'm just skeptical about our ability to diagnose and treat these disorders, that's all. I'll give you a referral to the sleep clinic if you want one."

On the one hand, I couldn't remember the last time I felt so fit, but my new-found fitness made my perpetual grogginess stand out all the more. The better I felt the more I reflected back on what bad shape I had been in and for how long leading up to my recent nadir of cardiac health. In the ten years since I quit smoking, I never fully recovered from the previous twenty years of smoking. I put effort into dieting to control my weight in my adult life but in a manner that thumbed its nose at the best available scientific evidence for a heart-healthy living – and my diet in my teenage and childhood years consisted of trans-fatty twinkies, donuts and ice cream.

But more than anything, sleep problems had always had a permeating effect on my overall health for as long as I could remember. Trouble sleeping has been so fundamentally ingrained in every fiber of my being for so long I believe I can firmly trace the origins of my sleep disorders back to the early paleolithic era. Allow me to explain.

People sometimes confuse having a sleep disorder with simply being a natural night owl. I am neither a night owl nor an early riser. I am far more fucked up than that. I might be up until 4:00am on any given morning and a week later I might wake up at 4:00am. I can force myself into a societally-acceptable schedule, but my body clock and my chronic fatigue keep their own schedule regardless of what I do. I can, and usually do, wake up on a prescribed schedule to meet the demands of life but my body clock continues taking laps around the clock and I can palpably feel when my body has its own strong circadian opinions of when I should be asleep or awake. For the most part, I drag my tired ass through life half-asleep.

Night owls have a longer circadian day – a body clock that operates on a cycle of longer than twenty-four hours. Morning people tend to have one just a little bit shorter. It is easy for morning people to extend their body clock by staying up later, but difficult for night people to move it backwards – you can't force yourself to sleep just because there is a compelling external reason like a morning meeting. You can only move the clock back with alcohol, sleeping pills and occasionally a refreshing dose of jet lag. These things can get you to sleep, but none of them help you greet the next day bright-eyed and bushy-tailed in the morning. A solution I have employed through periods of my life is staying up all night one day a week, exhausting myself into getting to bed early the next night.

Morning people have no such internal discord and no conflict between their internal clock and their alarm clock. If they get off schedule, all they have to do is stay up a little later to get back on schedule. They don't get why the rest of us are continually dragging ass through life.

Morning people and night owls have palpably different personality types as well. If you graph out the mental and physical energy levels of morning and night people, the two profiles are discernably different – not just in the time of day but in the intensity and timing of the peaks. Night owls' have higher peaks, and those peaks occur together: mental and physical energy peaks coincide in the evening, explaining night owls' greater creativity and sociability. Morning peoples' graphs are flatter and physical energy occurs earlier in the day than mental energy. Hence morning peoples' preference for going to the gym early and generally being uninspired, uncreative dullards the rest of the day. Yet somehow morning people have invented a narrative in their minds that they are better than the rest of us. They get on their high-horse about how early they get up, and how early they go to the gym and how far that cane stretches up their ass. You never hear a night owl patronizing a morning person for their sleep habits: "Oh yeah, well *I* was out until 4:00 am while *you* were in bed sleeping all night, you lazy sack of shit."

This dynamic can be traced back to the rise of agrarian society in the late Neolithic Bronze Age era. In early agrarian society, it was probably very productive to get up early in the morning. And night owls were probably a bunch of pissy, whiny sticks in the mud.

Which brings us at long last back to the early Paleolithic era. Before agriculture, you see, night owls had a purpose. And that was to keep the camp fire going and stop the leopards from eating the morning people, so they could get up in the morning and go find us some food to cook on the camp fire the next night. Marshmallows were particularly hard to find in the paleolithic era and the night owls were entirely dependent on the morning people to keep the supply of smores ingredients flowing to the campfire. And this symbiotic cycle repeated for hundreds of thousands of years. The night people vigilantly stayed up protecting the morning people and told creative stories around the campfire that became the foundation of oral tradition and human culture – like the age-old epic of the escaped lunatic with a hook for a hand. This is also why musicians are night owls, they had to continuously bang things and yell to keep the saber-toothed tigers and the cave bears away from the morning people while they slept.

Granted, getting up early to sow and harvest the wheat and grind it into gruel came in pretty handy for the first ten thousand years or so of the agricultural revolution, but now, with the advent of electricity and perpetual light, there is nothing inherently unproductive about being a night person. Most jobs can be done any time. And there are, in fact, entire industries reliant on night owls: performing music and serving drinks to all the other night owls, for example. And we need night owls to support those industries by drinking – all that alcohol isn't going to drink itself, now is it? Night people are only (arguably) less productive because we still live in a morning person's social world. Let's see a morning person live and work in a night-owl's world. Sanctimonious fucking morning people, we could have just tip-toed away from the fire and let the tyrannosaurs have their way with them while they slept at the end of the last ice age if we only knew how much shit we would have to put up with from them a few million years later.

**

I have had terrible problems sleeping my entire life. Some of my earliest memories as a young child are of lying awake at night frustrated and scared, alone in the dark. I was tired all day and awake late into the night. My schedule would shift erratically. My parents called me lazy and always tried to stop me from sleeping in or napping, not knowing I had been up through the night. I didn't dare tell them, because I thought I would be in trouble for staying awake late at night. And I suppose I would have been, my teachers and parents scolded me so frequently for falling asleep during the daytime, to this day I lie about having been asleep when woken: "No, no I wasn't sleeping, I swear," I tell Nichole while gagging on my last snore and wiping drool off my shirt. She doesn't argue with me anymore.

I used to make a dummy of myself under the

covers in case my parents checked on me late at night when I would sneak to the living room to watch TV. I knew every floor creek, stair squeak and squeaky couch spring in our Brooklyn apartment by heart. I'd tiptoe and slide my socks across the floor into the living room, turn the volume down and gently switch the TV on.

As a young child I knew what time each station played the National Anthem and went off the air. Yes, that's right you youngsters out there in barely-publishable-memoir-land, TV stations went off the air at night, no repeat of the day's line-up, no infomercials just the National Anthem (don't ask me why) a test pattern (don't ask me why) followed by the snow of dead air. UHF channels would go off at exactly midnight because they would shift their frequency to match changes in the night-time ionosphere – that's right again, kids, I'm talking about actual broadcast TV. In case that is not freaking you young'uns out enough, it was a black and white TV too, with no cable, and it was carved entirely from stone and wood and had elk antler antennae and I had to get up and go to the TV to change channels or adjust the volume. The closest thing to a remote control in the house was me when my older brother would threaten me into getting up and changing the channel for him. Late at night I would sit on the floor to avoid unnecessary movement when fine tuning the volume to compensate for passing cars, shouting drunks and other noises of the Brooklyn streets at night.

In my teen years, my late-night routine was rudely interrupted one summer when my older brother Chris brought home a stray cat. We named her Ester in homage to the senior cat of the household, Sylvester.

Sylvester was a neutered male and Ester was an unneutered female that was perpetually in heat. She went through back-to-back-to-back estrous cycles and screamed her insatiably horny little head off all night every night. She would walk up and down the hallway all night waving its tail, wafting its pheromones and wailing its lungs out: "Meow-WOW, WOW-rear-OW, MeeeWie-MEOW!!!

We normally slept with the bedroom doors open to get a cross breeze because we had no air conditioning. That's right kids, I harken back to the days before everybody had air-conditioning in every room – we didn't even have one of those pterodactyls that would fan you with their wings like the Flintstones had – although we were saving up for one of those guys that fanned Cleopatra with a palm frond.

So, the cat was free to wander into each bedroom howling its horny howls until the room's half-asleep occupant would roll over and throw something at and it would run to the next bedroom without ever taking a break for a breath between groans. Each of us tried to scare the cat out of our respective room's and into someone else's by throwing bigger and heavier things at the cat: clothes, shoes, books, appliances anything in reach. Eventually we had trained her to sit in the hallway and peek its head around the corner for each howl: "Meow-rear-WOW, WOW-rear-OW, Fuck-Meee-NOW-in the-rear-MEOW!!! And we'd throw all kinds of shit at its head as it peeked around the frame of the bedroom doorway. We would wake up in the morning and the hallway would be littered with the detritus of the previous night's flinging frenzy.

Eventually we caved in and slept with the doors closed, but Ester just compensated and screamed louder, only relenting temporarily when one of us would leap out of bed in crazed, sleep-deprived frustration, grab the cat by the scruff of the neck and fling it down the hallway. It would get back to its howling a few minutes later, hopefully in front of someone else's door for a change, but sometimes those few minutes and the soothing gratification of vengeful feline flinging was enough to get back to sleep.

One groggy morning my brother, myself and even my poor, dear Canadian mother fessed up to the number of times we had each flung the cat down the hallway the night before. We all agreed we had to do something to break this absurd routine. We came up with a plan to build a cat barrier wall at the end of the hallway consisting of a piece of plywood propped up by an old steamer trunk. It kept the horny howling cat on the other end of the apartment, but it kept me on the other side of the barrier from the TV. I tried my best but there was no getting through the barrier without the horny cat skirting past me and racing down the hallway howling its head off with me in pursuit on the creaky floor and the plywood falling over.

This drove my poor mother bat-shit crazy. The cat climbing over the barricade one way and me stumbling past it the other: "Why can't you just go to sleep?" she pleaded.

"I can't sleep," I pleaded back. "Please don't make me sit there in the dark with nothing to do."

I argued my case for a new color TV in the

living room and me taking the black and white into my room so I wouldn't have to clamor past the horny-cat barricade in the middle of the night. She bought it. She had no choice. The situation was getting desperate.

Ester, however refused to be silenced. She figured that if she couldn't get past the barricade, she would just have to scream louder to get the attention she craved. The barricade did nothing to drown out the wailing. Chris pulled me aside one morning in a fit of sleep-deprived frustration, pinned me in a corner and laid on his best big-brother bully face: "It's dirty work, Dude, but one of us is gonna have to do it. One of us is going to have to fuck that horny cat," he commanded. "I sure ain't gonna do it and Sylvester has no balls. That leaves you. It's the only thing that'll ever shut it up."

"Yes, but for how long?" I questioned.

"For as long as you have to until it shuts the fuck up!"

"No, I mean how long do you think it would shut up for even if…"

"We're going to have to kill it," he said with tears in his bleary eyes.

My mother came to a similar desperate conclusion. She offered either of us a twenty-dollar reward if we could find a new home for Ester. She insisted on humane parameters, no shelters or abandonment, knowing full-well that a twenty-dollar reward for two teenage boys to find a tortuously horny cat 'a new home' (in sarcastic air quotes) was essentially tantamount to putting a bounty on that cat's head. Chris immediately concocted a cock-and-bull story for my mother about a sweet little bat-shit crazy old lady who took in unwanted cats and cared for them and loved them all forever and sold Mom on the idea of gifting Ester to her.

"If she wants it she can have it, that's a wonderful idea," she exclaimed without believing a word of this nonsense. As far as she knew or cared the cat was destined to be a puss-in-concrete-boots at the bottom of the Gowanas Canal. "I just don't want to hear another word about what you did with it." She might as well have said: "Just make it look like an accident."

Chris put Ester in the kitty carry case and brought her to the far side of Prospect Park. He opened the lid, dumped the cat and ran. The terrified cat ran after him. He ran faster and further but he was no match for the cat. He ran in spurts and bursts all the way across the park with the cat in hot pursuit, mewing and crying. Finally, some fine, upstanding, concerned citizen schmuck-wad came to his aid: "Excuse me son, it that cat chasing you?"

"Yes, I'm very afraid," Chris stammered, out of breath. "I don't know if it has rabies or what. It's been chasing me all the way across the park. Don't let it hurt me."

"Don't worry young man, I think it's just a frightened stray. It's probably lost," and he gently approached Ester and picked her up. "I'll take care of it, you go ahead on home."

It was a happy ending for all, really. We never saw Ester or that incredibly stupid and gullible nice man ever again. Neither Chris nor I ever had to bear the mental scars of having committed felinocide or worse yet felinophelia. Chris went and got himself a dime bag and a six pack with his reward money, I got my own TV in my bedroom, we all got a color TV with a remote in the living room (a modern one cast in bronze), Ester got a new home, some dickhead in Prospect Park got a new cat and everyone but me went back to sleeping at night.

My mother stopped arguing with me at this point about staying up late, sleeping in on weekends or napping after school. Now that I had a TV in my room I wouldn't wake anybody up creeping around the apartment late at night so she let me be.

That summer I had a block of three weeks of downtime with no schedule and no parental meddling in my sleep schedule, so I decided to conduct an experiment on myself. I slept when I felt like it, went to bed when I felt like it, woke up when I felt like it and I kept a journal and plotted a graph of my sleep and wake rhythms. Through my self-experimentation I determined I was on a longer than 24-hour circadian rhythm. I wasn't a night owl per se, I would go to bed later and wake up later and later every day until I went all the way around the clock every ten to fourteen days. Sometimes I would be on a normal schedule, sometimes a completely ass-backward one and all things in between.

In college, every woman I slept with woke me up and asked: "Are you alright? You sound like you can't breathe." Once a college girlfriend startled me awake by leaping out of bed to call an ambulance because I had stopped breathing in my sleep and was audibly gasping for air.

I also learned in college that drinking my face off could reset my biological clock by making me pass out at a prescribed time. This was the one practical lesson I learned in college that I was actually able to apply to my life in a meaningful way. I drank my face off a lot from there on out.

Of course, the more often you apply this method, the groggier you get, the more often you have to 'reset your clock' and into the downward spiral you go. The more you try to control your biological clock with alcohol, the more alcohol controls your biological clock. In my post-college years in Hungary I compensated for this daily downward spiral with obscene amounts of caffeine. I was drinking a dozen double Hungarian weapons-grade espressos a day. The caffeine exacerbated the problems of jolting awake, trouble falling asleep and really messed with my mental schedule. I started jolting awake not just gasping for air but my heart arrhythmically pounding out of my chest as well.

During my semester as an exchange student in Hungary, my friend Agi was a medical student. I kept in touch with her as my informal medical advisor during my years in Hungary. She had become a psychiatrist and I thought maybe she could help with the sleep problems. She prescribed me some sleeping pills and referred me to a cardiologist about the thumping arrhythmic heart pounding. And so it was sleep problems that drove me to my first cardiologist, at the ripe young age of twenty-seven – the same age that Jim Morrison, Janis Joplin, Jimi Hendrix, Kurt Cobain and Amy Winehouse all died from their own downward spirals. That was the nadir I tried to bounce back from for the next twenty years or so, and it all started with sleep disorders.

**

I reported to the sleep clinic at eight o'clock as instructed with an overnight bag packed with my pajamas, pills and reading materials. The door was locked and the lights were out. I walked around the building looking for another entrance and ran into a couple other people with overnight bags, looking into the darkened windows. Once assembled in a group, a nurse approached the door with a set of keys in her hand and introduced herself as Mona. "Sorry folks, we close up between the day time office hours and the night shift. Follow me."

Mona gave us a packet of medical history and insurance forms to fill out. This was my first visit to a medical facility not directly related to heart problems and I had forgotten the common experience of forms and waiting in medical offices. Cardiac clinics are too afraid for their liability and their image if you drop dead in the waiting room to keep you waiting too long. Imagine how many patients would wait very long to see a cardiologist who has dead people in his waiting room. 'Get-em-in, get-em-out before they croak in here' is their patient-care strategy. The sleep clinic has no such urgency about their patients, what are they going to do? Fall asleep in the waiting room? They want you to fall asleep: 'Have some triplicate insurance forms and a brochure about cleaning the mold out of your CPAP, we'll be with you in couple hours' is their mantra.

A couple hours later it was my turn for the pre-test interview at the nurse's station. I recounted the short version of my history of sleep disorders to Mona, the night nurse.

"That's quite a history. Didn't you ever have a sleep study done before?" Mona asked.

"There were no sleep disorders when I was young, Ma'am, only lazy bastards. Teachers called me a lazy bastard for falling asleep in class, sent me to the principal who called me a lazy bastard, my mother still calls me a lazy fucking bastard for being tired all the time. No sleep disorders, just lazy bastards."

"Your mother calls you a 'lazy fucking bastard'?" Mona recoiled in disbelief.

"Well no, not in those exact words, she's from Canada. She says, 'lazy bum,' but I'm from Brooklyn and the 'fucking bastard' is clearly implied."

"Haven't you ever spoken to a doctor about your sleep problems?" asked Mona.

"Yeah, I knew a psychiatrist when I lived in Budapest and I asked her if she could do anything to help. She prescribed some pills for me. I don't know what they were, they were white and really small."

"You had a psychiatrist?" she asked with a raised eyebrow as she jotted a note on my chart.

"No, I *knew* a psychiatrist, an old friend. She prescribed me some pills."

"Were they effective?"

"Oh, they worked alright. I would wake up in the morning feeling like I had never known what it was like to get a good night's sleep in my whole life. I was so awake and aware and full of mental energy I didn't know what to do with it all. Then I would nod off like a heroin addict for a moment, then I was fine again, and that cycle would repeat all day.

"The problem was they worked too well. They made me so comatose I would wake up feeling like I was being smothered. I guess I went from waking up from not breathing to not waking up from not breathing. My heart was pounding. And I swore my heart was struggling when I lay on my left side. My psychiatrist friend took me to a cardiologist, he dismissed the whole thing like a true Hungarian cardiologist with a cigarette dangling out of his mouth as he read the EKG, but I have tried to avoid sleeping on my left ever since."

"And you continued taking these pills?" Mona asked.

I explained how I started breaking the pills in half, and then in quarters but it was hard to get the little tiny pills into even fragments. I used them in small doses and in sparing frequency. I'd use a pill fragment every week or two to reset my biological clock and get back on a normal societally-acceptable schedule.

When I got to grad school in England I went to a doctor and asked if I could get the same pills in a lower dosage. She took one look at them, peered up at me from under her reading glasses with raised eyebrows, and asked: "Did you enter the country with these?"

"Was I not supposed to?" I asked timidly.

"Well, we are going to have to put these right in the rubbish bin." She held them out with two fingers, stepped on the pedal of a waste paper basket on the floor dropped them in and let the lid slam back down with a clang.

I bartended in a late-night club on weekends in grad school in Liverpool. I would go to work Friday night after dark, go home and to bed in the dark, wake up Saturday in the dark, go to bed in the dark, wake up Sunday in the dark and stay up all night every Sunday night to catch up on reading and writing and go straight to class Monday morning in the first daylight I had seen in three days. It had a tremendously depressing effect on my emotions.

"That must have been very difficult." Mona the night nurse leaned forward in rehearsed empathy.

"Not really. The three-day stretches of darkness plunged me into fits of depression, but other than that it was a great schedule for me – around the clock every week, that's exactly what my messed-up inner clock likes."

**

Efrain, the technician escorted me to my room – sort of like a well-kept, cheap motel room with a murphy bed. Much better than the open-ward I envisioned with a dozen of us suspended from the ceiling by wires and tubes like we were in some sort of sci-fi suspended animation. There were wires involved, lots of them – EKG wires on my chest (in my damn chest hair again) and on my legs, EEG wires all over my head, all of them leading to an electronic briefcase that I could unplug from the wall and carry to the bathroom.

I barely got any sleep at all. I was doubtful they could get any meaningful results from under two hours of restless half sleep. But Efrain the tech was cheerfully optimistic: "I'm not really supposed to share results, we'll schedule a consult with one of our sleep specialist MDs for that. But from what I saw, you definitely tested positive for moderate, quite possibly severe, sleep apnea. The doctor will talk to you about a CPAP and get you fitted. And also, when you sleep on your left side, your heart rate gets slow and struggles. Your blood oxygen level dropped down to sixty before you woke up."

"Holy cow!" I slapped my knee. "That's what I said twenty years ago, and to I don't know how many doctors since then. You finally cracked the case, Efrain."

"You're definitely a roller and turner in your sleep. If you can't help rolling onto your left, you can wear a bra with a tennis ball in it on your left side so you can't roll over."

"I'll take my chances with the heart stopping, but thanks Efrain. I feel vindicated after all these years."

I left the sleep clinic at 6:00am and schlepped home through Central Park. I slept all day and royally screwed up my sleep schedule but good.

I never got a call to schedule a consult with the sleep specialist doctor. After a few weeks I called the clinic to ask when I could expect the results and a consultation with the sleep doctor.

"What's your last name again? When were you here?" I could hear the sound fingers tapping on a keyboard. "Which doctor did you speak to?"

"I have never spoken to any doctor, that's the problem."

Who was here the night you were here?"

"Mona the nurse and Efrain the technician. The technician said it looked to him like I was positive for moderate to severe sleep apnea and would need to talk to the doctor about it."

"Ok, I'll look into it and get back to you."

Two days later I got a call back from the sleep clinic: "the doctor was wondering if you could come back for another study and a CPAP fitting."

"A CPAP fitting? I haven't even gotten the results. Can I have the results forwarded to my cardiologist?"

"Honestly, we can't locate your results, but since the tech said you were positive for sleep apnea, we can just redo the testing while we fit you for the CPAP at the same time. That would have been the next step anyway."

**

I showed up at the clinic for my second visit with my overnight bag at eight o'clock again. The door was locked again, but I knew not to be concerned. I found the other patients wandering around the building looking for an entrance. "Sleep clinic? This is the entrance, they're just late again." I assured the other patients.

Five of us waited outside on the steps for half an hour before my cell phone rang. "Mr. Hornbull? This is Efrain the sleep clinic technician. Listen, we are having trouble with the computer system, we can't do the study tonight. Sorry for calling so late but we have been working very hard to correct it, but. You will have to reschedule your study."

"Efrain, a bunch of us are standing outside," I spoke loud enough for the group to hear me. "Do you want to just come out here and tell them all at once? Maybe help us reschedule?"

"Oh, I am not in the clinic, nobody is in the clinic. We can't help you now."

"But you said you were working hard on the computer system."

"That was the day shift, the computer went down during the day, so nobody bothered coming in tonight."

"Actually, five of us came in tonight, Efrain. The patients. We're all standing outside. Didn't anyone think to call the patients and tell them not to come in?" I shrugged at the other patients. They shook their heads and walked away one by one.

**\*\***

On my third visit to the sleep clinic, Efrain fitted a CPAP to my face. One thing I knew right away, I would never be able to sleep with this contraption on my face. I had all the requisite wires all over my chest (in my chest hair again) and all over my head all connected to the electric briefcase. I had an air tube protruding from my mask that connected to a separate air pump briefcase. The tech got me situated in bed and left me to get to sleep at my own pace. I sat up reading for hours. I tried turning out the light and shutting my eyes, but it was impossible. I couldn't roll on my side and I had been unable to sleep on my back for so long it seemed so unnatural. After an hour or two of aggravated, fruitless attempts at sleep I had to go to the bathroom. I knew from last time I was supposed to disconnect the wire briefcase, but I couldn't figure out how and the tech never showed me how to disconnect the air hose. I fumbled around in the dark for the light switch and the call button. I buzzed with increasing frequency and frustration but got no response. I tried ignoring the urge, but my bladder would have none of it, it was not to be ignored. I took my best guess and pulled wires and disconnected the tube from the brief cases. I shuffled down the hallway connected to my briefcases by the wires and tubes like I was boarding an Atlas V rocket on my way to the moon.

I got back to my room and tried to figure out how to reconnect myself. It had stopped getting late and started getting early. I had no sleep and no semblance of the requisite cognitive ability to figure out the wires and tubes. I pressed the call button over and over out of frustration knowing at this point it was as useful as pressing a door close button on an elevator or a pedestrian crosswalk button. I just left it and tried to salvage an hour of sleep before it was time to get up and get out of there. I did not sleep at all.

The tech told me I was positive for sleep apnea. "I'm not really supposed to discuss results, the doctor will have a consultation with you, but I can tell you that you tested positive for moderate to severe sleep apnea."

I was a little befuddled by this. "I'm just wondering, Efrain," my voice grew tense. "How do you know that when I didn't sleep, and my wires were all disconnected?"

Efrain dismissed my derision and handed me my discharge paperwork, including a customer satisfaction form. He handed that to the wrong grump after the wrong sleepless night. I filled in the circles and handed back the clipboard.

"I'm just wondering, if you don't mind," Efrain injected timidly. "I noticed you marked 'poor' on the 'technician's instructions' box, just for my own professional improvement, was there something I could have done better?"

"Sure, I understand, that's fine. You didn't explain to me how to unhook this stuff to go to the bathroom. I almost peed in my pants and then never got to sleep because of that."

"*YOU* said you had been here before," he snapped back. "We get rated on these surveys and I wish you would be a little more thoughtful about your response. This could have consequences on my performance rating."

"Well, the test could have consequences on my health, or life, or death," I snapped back, with all the irritability of a sleepless night. I took my tee shirt off while changing out of my pajamas revealing my full-chest-length scar. "I'm here because my sleep problems may be a major contributor to *this*. I wish you would be more thoughtful about how you administer the damn test. This is my third time here without getting any results out of you people. You want me to amend my answers on the survey? Give it here. I'll rewrite you a new customer God-damn satisfaction survey."

Efrain clenched the customer survey forms and clip board against his chest "We are actually not allowed by policy to return the forms once filled out," he said and left the room in a pissy little huff.

I took my morning pills, packed my bag and ducked out without another word to or from anyone. I had already returned to working fulltime by the time of my third clinic visit and had used all my sick days. But I was so tired, I called in and declared a 'medical telework day,' went home, slept all day and screwed my circadian schedule *real* good.

**

A few weeks later, I called the clinic to see if I needed to schedule a consult with the sleep doctor: "I thought you were supposed to call me, but I haven't heard anything, so…"

"Yes, Mr. Hornbull. We would like to finalize your fitting for a CPAP and place your order. They can cost between a thousand and two thousand dollars with all the necessary accessories. How will you be paying for the device?"

I held the phone away and looked at it crosswise as if it would repeat that for me. "How do you know what CPAP, if any, I need if you don't have any results from my tests and I never spoke to a doctor?"

"Haven't you had a consultation with the doctor?"

"No, that's why I'm calling. Can I schedule a consultation?"

"I'm so sorry. We'll have to get your results to the doctor and call you back to schedule the consult."

A few weeks later I got a call from the clinic saying my bill was past due.

"I don't see how my bill could be past due, seeing that customarily services are provided first, and the bill is sent later. I never received any results, my cardiologist never received any results, I never had a consult with a doctor to discuss any results, and here's the zinger: I never received a bill. *Furthermore*, you are an in-system service provider and I should not be on the hook for a dime, so you need to take the bill up with my insurance provider."

I took the issue up with Dr. Freeman next time I saw him. "Can't you call them and ask for the results? Aren't they affiliated with the same hospital that you are?"

"I could give you the number for the customer service line for the medical center," he said shaking his head and looking away dismissively.

"Aren't you interested in the results?" I was getting aggravated by the whole affair.

"I don't care about their results. You've seen their operation. Do you still care about their results?"

"No, I guess I don't," I finally conceded.

I never heard from them again. They probably got their money from the insurance provider and maybe put a dent in my credit rating to boot – I don't know, I haven't checked in a while.

By the time I had schlepped myself to the sleep clinic for a third time, I had been exercising in ways I was previously unable, I had made big changes in my diet and I had lost a significant amount of weight, I didn't drink anything like I used to, I was keeping to a bedtime schedule even on weekends, I was sleeping better than I had in years, I no longer kept antacids and water by my bedside; and, according to Nichole, I no longer snored.

No doubt I was born with an out-of-whack internal clock compounded by teenage and young adult disruptive circadian rhythms and adult lifestyle adjustments. But how I dealt with that: alcohol and caffeine abuse, staying up all night, succumbing to fatigue and inertia all exacerbated the sleep problems late into adulthood and compounded my downward spiral of broader health problems such as obesity, high blood pressure and eventually, yes, heart disease.

Doing what I could to control the causes and reverse the downward spiral – it is as good as it was going to get. I didn't need medications, medical devices or surgery to treat the symptoms, I needed to take care of myself to treat the cause.

I had been in a rock-star downward spiral of stimulants and alcohol at the same cursed age that all great rock stars die. I wonder how close I was to their fate. Before you sarcastically ask me how much coffee Jimi Hendrix drank, remember this: he died from taking sleeping pills to sleep off an all-night drinking spree. And those symptoms I went to the Hungarian cardiologist for at the age of twenty-seven? They never went away until after the heart surgery twenty-two years later.

Fat, drunk and half asleep is no way to go through life.

## 28. Dentist

There is a well-established link between gum disease and heart disease. This may not seem intuitive at first, but we have all heard of infections entering the blood stream causing blood poisoning. Blood stream infections can cause veins to turn visibly bright red through the skin and if those lines reach the heart: good night. Now hold your index finger on your lower jaw and your thumb on your sternum. An infection need only travel that far to damage the lining of your coronary arteries and create a spot for plaque to begin blocking blood flow to your heart. Add a jigger of trans fats and a splash of Hungarian pig fat, shake well and presto, you have coronary heart disease.

My gums chronically bled for years and years since I was a morose teenager with all the requisite anti-social poor dental hygiene habits. I had come to think of it as normal for gums to bleed every time I brushed my teeth or ate an apple. And in fact, it may not be so unusual, but my situation had worsened a couple years earlier. A couple spaces between crooked teeth regularly bled and one wisdom tooth had come to a tee on a few occasions. The only thing that prevented me from taking care of it sooner was a lapse in insurance followed by the discovery that vodka makes for quite an effective oral disinfectant. You laugh, but answer me this: would you rather go to an oral surgeon for an extraction or go to the nearest bar and repeatedly gargle vodka? Granted it only works for a limited period and then you have to return to the bar and repeat the process often, but this fit neatly into my schedule and was a sacrifice I was willing to make in the name of oral hygiene.

Ray the bartender used to just shake his head in disapproval as I squished the vodka in my cheeks, tilted my head back shaking my head and wincing in pain: "Why the hell don't you just go to the dentist already?"

"Because I'd rather come to see you, Ray," I'd gasp affectionately as I exhaled the vodka fumes.

The insurance lapse had nothing to do with me changing jobs or dropping plans. I have been in the same job for twenty years. It was a provider that dropped my federal government employee union dental plan, followed by the union adapting a new provider who had a most ingenious business model: take all the money and don't provide any services. Quite profitable I'm sure, but I don't suppose the fact that my infections could have killed me had a line on their ledger. Nearly two years of that bullshit left me so skeptical that any major work would be covered in the end, I was hesitant to get it taken care of at all. But now, for all I knew, my seemingly minor dental problems could very well be a critical underlying factor in my heart problems.

I sat in the waiting room filling out insurance and medical history forms. I had forgotten the usual routine of waiting on appointments. Cardiologists seem to have a stronger commitment to punctuality instilled in them than dentists. I suppose it could be deemed negligent and certainly rather embarrassing for a cardiologist if one of their patients dropped dead in the waiting room – a more likely prospect than someone dropping dead while waiting for a cleaning I suppose.

My name was finally called, and a nurse escorted me into an exam room. I spied the dental chair and immediately recoiled in fear remembering the ordeal of the barber chair. Barber chairs and dentist chairs are alike for a reason: way back when, barbers used to treat tooth infections and even pull teeth – a thought that never instills confidence while waiting on a dentist. *Where exactly did you go to school for this?* I decided to sit and wait in the chair in the corner usually reserved for mothers of uneasy children. The dental assistant or technician or hygienist (or whatever the current politically-correct term is nowadays) entered the room and looked shocked the chair was empty and a little startled to see me in the corner. She looked surprisingly young for a dental anything to me, she looked about fourteen.

"Mr. Hornbull?" she queried. "Please have a seat. So why are you here to see us today, Mr. Hornbull?"

"Just a cleaning and a check-up, I guess," I shrugged with a little cagey trepidation about explaining the whole background right off the bat.

"Okay?" She suspiciously eyed my shiftiness. "I am going to need your help to take some x-rays. Use your left thumb to hold this here." She jammed my thumb in my mouth against a hard-plastic sensor. "Then your right index finger here. No, no, here," she corrected my motions.

"Sorry, last time I was in a dentist chair all we had to do was bite on a piece of cardboard. None of this oral Simon says. And you had to wait for the x-rays to get developed in a lab somewhere and come back in week to see them," I said as the images instantly appeared one by one on a monitor.

"That must have been quite some time ago. How long has it been since your last check-up?"

"Thirty years," I answered in a high-pitched voice, fearing being judged. "I lived abroad for a long time, I didn't have insurance for a long time," I continued. "And I never really had any serious problems."

The dentist came in the room and began perusing the x-rays on the monitor. She made the fourteen-year-old technician look like an old hag, she couldn't have been more than twelve.

"Hi, I am Doctor Kaylan," she introduced herself. "If you're ready for your cleaning, you can sit back and open wide."

She inserted that spit-sucking vacuum and began prodding around my gum line.

"You have a significant amount of bone loss and receding gum line."

"Bone loss? That sounds serious. Am I destined for dentures?"

"No, it's normal for your age," she said with contemptuous 'didn't-you-know-you-were-old?' look that only a twelve-year-old can give.

*Does your mother know you play with her lab*

*coat and dental tools when she leaves you alone in the office?* I thought to myself. "When is she coming back?"

"Okay, let's take a look. Well, I see a potentially serious problem or two," she recoiled. "There is a gaping hole in your lower molar and I'm surprised you never had this wisdom tooth removed, it's almost sideways against your cheek. Does this wisdom tooth ever cause you discomfort?"

"Uh, only on and off… for the last thirty years or so," I admitted

I explained that I had lived abroad for a long time and then I had no insurance for a long time, it wasn't easy. Of course, they had dentists in Hungary at that time. My English friend Jonathan went to one once to have a swollen tooth looked at. There was one large room with a couple dozen patients waiting their turn in one of a dozen dental exam chairs and one dentist. The dentist took one quick look and she called over a big burly guy who stood behind him, held one forearm on his forehead and one forearm on his lower jaw forcing his mouth open. The dentist pulled a pair of pliers out of her hip pocket and YANK! Out came the tooth. The dentist went on to the next patient. I opted not to be that next patient.

Jonathan was actually pretty happy in the end. The bleeding stopped after a couple days on some serious painkillers and no more problems with that tooth ever again.

I used to ask my friend Gabor the dentist to

look at it when I ran into him at the bar when it flared up.

It felt safer. I figured the chances of him having a big burly Hungarian and a pair of pliers at the ready were substantially less in the bar. All he could do was give me advice. So, he advised me to go see the big burly Hungarian and get it yanked. And I'd say, "Give me another vodka to swish between my teeth and gargle and I'll stave off the demon Hungarian dentist of Fleet Street for another week" – week after week, year after year."

"How long exactly did you keep up this vodka-gargling therapy of yours before you came to see me?"

"Until my heart surgery, now I can't drink vodka. And my cardiologist says there may be a link between gum disease and heart disease, so…"

"Heart surgery?" she exclaimed. "You have had heart surgery recently? I can't perform any procedures on you without written clearance from your cardiologist." She dropped her cleaning tools on the tray and took two steps back recoiling in fear.

"It's on all the forms I filled out, didn't anybody review those if it's so important?"

"Well I can't accept liability for that kind of thing, you'll have to contact your cardiologist and get us a signed release and schedule another appointment."

"Whoa, hold on. Firstly, I used up my bank of sick time after all this and don't want to take another day. Let's try contacting him right now so I'm sure I'm getting you what you want. Secondly, let's discuss what we can and can't do without the waiver: an exam and a cleaning today, actual work later, perhaps?"

She flatly refused to even look around or offer an opinion on the x-rays she already saw. This is one of those times where it was laid bare that a medical professional was acting not in the interest of my health but in the interest of covering her own liability ass and protect her own insurance ass.

Between my years in Communist and post-Communist eastern Europe and my 20 years in federal government, I learned a thing about dealing with the bureaucratically weak-minded: convince them that I will be a bigger pain in the ass if they do not do what I want than if they do and they will quickly rush to my needs if only to get rid of me. I got Dr. Freeman on the phone with the receptionist and got a letter faxed over. It said: 'No extractions for one year.' It wasn't good enough, it wasn't on letterhead so I got the receptionist and the office manager on the phone and got a second letter. It wasn't signed and wasn't good enough so we got the Dentist, Doctor and all their staff on the phone until we got what they wanted, reviewed by the Dentist's insurance agent and me back in the chair three hours later.

Everyone was pissed at me and I had lost all faith in the dentist's intention to look out for my interests, but I was determined to make her go through with it all out of principle. I was pissed too and I wanted to her to know it.

"So, what caused these holes in your lower molars?" She withdrew her hands and tools from my mouth to answer.

"That's where my braces were attached when I was a teenager. I stopped going to the orthodontist and the brace anchors stayed there until they came loose on their own and I pulled them off with pliers in the bathroom mirror."

"Why on Earth did you do that?"

"Well, I refused to go back to the orthodontist, and he wasn't too hot on seeing me again after I kicked him in the balls as he leaned over me in the exam chair."

"Are you getting combative with me Mr. Hornbull?" she said as she backed away in fear again.

"No, no, I didn't even kick him out of anger or anything, I was choking on the plaster from the mold he jammed in my mouth and he was leaning over me restraining my hands saying 'stop, you'll upset the mold.' I don't remember what he said exactly after I kicked his nuts into the back of his throat, but I remember he sounded like Mickey Mouse when he said it."

In hindsight, if I hadn't kicked my orthodontist in the nuts, and I had finished my orthodontal process, I might not have had chronic gum bleeding and not developed an infection that may have led to heart disease. Maybe heart disease was my bad orthodontal karma coming back to haunt me. I didn't want to be combative, but I think I subconsciously wanted to put the child-dentist on notice not to fuck with me too bad lest she suffer the fate of my now-sterile, childless orthodontist. But she got herself into a hurry after that and began aggressively jamming that sharp little shepherd hook deep beneath the gum line and scraping all manner of ungodly bloody goop out from every nook and cranny – very painfully at times. I wanted to scream "It's safe, it's very safe," but she was clearly too young to catch the Marathon Man Nazi dental torture reference, so I just amused myself in my own head with that thought to distract myself while I rinsed mouthful after mouthful of bloody goop scrapings into the little spit sink.

"I'm going to have to recommend that, as soon as your cardiologist allows, we schedule you for a deep cleaning of these lower front teeth."

"That wasn't deep enough?"

"The deep cleaning I am referring to involves partial extraction of the teeth to clear the particulate matter out from under them. And I would like to refer you to an oral surgeon for extraction of those lower molars with the holes in them and extraction of the inflamed sideways wisdom tooth."

I was roiling from a cleaning turned bloody mess and the thought of all that tooth pulling scared the hell out of me. "Let me take some time to think about that."

"Do you floss, Mr. Hornbull?"

"I never really got the hang of it to tell you the truth. Sometimes I use a thing on a stick that looks like one of those plastic swords they spear fruit with to garnish a cocktail. I figured if I can't wedge floss in those tight spaces the gunk can't wedge itself in there either."

"Something else that's normal with age is that the spaces between your teeth grow as your teeth wear down. It's not unusual that you need to start flossing more aggressively and routinely as you get older."

I was left a little confused about how much of my dental woes should be alarming and how much was normal for my alarmingly advanced age. The bloody goop continued to ooze out from under my gum line for days. I spent the weekend wondering what the heck the pubescent dentist had done to me while chewing on a wad of bloody gauze like a dog that found a bloody tampon in the trash.

The following week I started getting messages saying my insurance had approved the deep cleaning of my lower front teeth and the extraction of my wisdom tooth and wouldn't I like to make an appointment to get all this done. No, not really. I had specifically said I did not want to take any drastic action just yet, so why are they clearing this with my insurance company? I called the dentist and they said they had not called me nor had they contacted my insurance company. I checked the messages and sure enough it was a different name and number than the dentist I had been to. Who the heck was this and why do they have information on me down to the details of which teeth we had discussed?

Someone leaked information. But to who? An underhanded rival dentist? A con man? A dental scam artist? Were they out to relieve me of my my money or my teeth and then my money? The actual dentist assured me they do not share such private information and I welcomed them to the Information Age and assured them they did, knowingly or not. Either way I lost all faith in the teeny-bopper tooth doctor.

I called another dentist to ask what the heck the twelve-year-old had done to me, but they told me it was not unexpected for a guy who hadn't been to the dentist for thirty years to bleed from the gums for a few days following a deep cleaning. I made an appointment with the other dentist all the same, just to get a second opinion on the more extreme of her recommendations. I would have had more trust in asking the barber if he wanted to take a crack at tooth extraction for old time's sake than I had in the twelve-year-old.

The new dentist showed me a different floss-on-a-stick option that was more like a pipe cleaner on a tooth pick and showed me how to get in through the gaps from down at the gum line. It worked. Between mouthwash a couple times a day and the pipe-cleaner flossers, the bleeding became less frequent and less severe over time.

The wisdom tooth still had the occasional period of inflammation, but I learned how to maneuver the pipe cleaner stick way back and way in between and torture myself like a masochistic Nazi dentist. I grew to perfect a one man performance of the torture scenes from Marathon Man with Dustin Hoffman the torture victim and Lawrence Olivier the evil Nazi dentist – both roles being acted out by myself in the bathroom mirror.

The new dentist had the added appeal of not being eager to extract anything unless necessary. This was comforting on the one hand, but on the other, I never was sure she wasn't coddling me like a millennial: "Would you *like* to have your teeth extracted?"

"Obviously not, but do I need to have teeth extracted to prevent infections that could potentially lead to another heart attack?"

I suspect this millennial medical coddling is actually just another liability-ass-covering technique to absolve the dentist or doctor from having told you to do anything. If it goes wrong, I didn't tell you to do it. I don't know. But for lack of knowing and absent any doctor's orders, I opted for a sustained campaign of intensive oral hygiene – and it seems to have worked, who'da thunk?

## 29. All Hail Hornbullonia

It was late August and the summer had almost slipped away without even one trip to Hornbullonia at all – my plan to convalesce there all summer was shot since it was taking so much longer to heal and regain strength than I had hoped, and all the doctors' appointments were hogging up my schedule. And my hope of being able to medical telework from the woods would be shot if I couldn't get some form of communication up there. I was thrilled when we bought the place and I figured out there was no cell reception there. I ran into the realtor who sold us the place in the supermarket after we had bought it and told her: "You know, you really should have told me there is no cell reception up there."

"Oh, I'm sorry," she back-pedaled quickly and nervously. "I didn't think, I mean you could have checked…"

"I would have offered you more money," I said revealing a wry smirk. "You should advertise that feature when you're selling to city people."

As much as I enjoyed being out of reach and out of mind, it became problematic as an upwardly-mobile young FEMA-ite. I listed the phone number for our Wiccan neighbor to the east – the Wiccan Witch of the East's – on our emergency call-down roster with a note: *call for activations or deployments only, this number is for a neighbor who has to ride a half mile on a mule to relay messages*. I failed to mention that it was a Kawasaki Mule ATV I was referring to and let the office scuttlebutt mill have a few whispering giggles at my expense at the thought of me only being reachable by mule train in an emergency.

One summer a couple years earlier, we had an activation of our emergency operations center to start pre-landfall preparations for a hurricane we were monitoring, and the Wiccan Witch got the activation order call. She dispatched Jim on the Mule to relay the message, but I was in town checking messages on my cell already, so I could monitor the monitoring. Jim looked around the camp for something to write a note on, then looked for something to pin it on the gate with. I returned from town to find a note pinned to the gate with a mouse trap that read: 'Jeff, FEMA called. Come to the cabin.' I had already gotten the activation order and replied, having called in just as the order was going out. Just by chance, I was the first to respond to the order. I packed up, headed out and I was the first one to report for duty to the operations center in the City. I framed the mouse-trap and note and hung it on my cubicle wall with a caption: 'The mule-train, the fastest communication plan in FEMA.'

I brought my FEMA satellite phone with me in the hopes I could at least be reachable. But satellite phones need line-of-sight with communications satellites that are in geosynchronous orbits around the equator, so you need a southern view for them to work. Hornbullonia is on the side of a north-facing slop of a mountainside. The thing only worked if I drove out to the corn field behind Sueville on the other side of the pond, which was okay for making a call out (although not a lot more convenient that just driving to town and getting a cell signal). But I needed to be reachable and the only way I could receive a call was if I was standing out in the field when someone was trying to call. Of course, a lot of my colleagues say I am always outstanding in my field, but I am not always out standing in my field. Read that sentence again. Repeat, until you audibly groan. Ok, now you got it.

Nichole and I had purchased Hornbullonia ten years earlier. We got to know each other on group camping parties the bar regulars used to throw. Nichole and I eventually inherited the role of being the usual camping party masterminds. But after a while, we grew weary of being crammed into campgrounds with a greater population density than a refugee camp – it's simply not camping if you can't pee in the woods with impunity, much less if you can't pee in the woods without peeing on your neighbor's tent. And on public land we got too old to be harassed by park rangers like we were a gang of teenage vandals. We had a back-packing faction that would venture out on the trails and up the mountains – mostly centered by the Newmi, the Newman brothers. But the big party groups required staying as close to the trailhead parking area as legally possible, so we could drag coolers and all the unnecessary gear the inexperienced campers bring. The large groups with the all the coolers within shouting distance of the parking lot was usually enough to draw the interest if not the ire of Ranger Dickhead. Finally, one astute drunken camper pointed out that land in upstate New York can be as cheap as a thousand dollars an acre and suggested we all chip in and just buy a party-plot of land. And so Hornbullonia, from its inception was founded on the premise of partying in the woods.

We bought a twenty-acre parcel within a hundred-and-sixty-acre off-grid community that was founded as a commune in the seventies. I guess you could call it a gated community, it has a cattle gate at the head of the community dirt road. There were still a couple founding hippies and four people lived there year-round with solar panels, wood stoves and outhouses – summer, autumn, spring and winter.

Nichole and I and set out to tame the wild frontiers of Hornbullonia, starting with clearing the brush and fallen trees off the remnants of the old logging road that leads from the community road into Hornbullonia. We set up camp in an overgrown clearing with a view of the mountains and started clearing out the dense brush with simple tools and our bare hands. The brush was so dense I occasionally lost Nichole in the bushes. "Dr. Livingstone, I presume," I proclaimed when I finally found her tangled in a thorn bush.

Once camp was established and civilization had taken a firm foothold we dubbed the camp Nicholopolis, the capitol of Greater Hornbullonia and coronated ourselves Emperor Jeffonius Hornbullonius Maximus the First and the Grand Duchess of Nicholopolis, and there was much rejoicing throughout the land. We continued recreating civilization with a series of building projects. The first thing I built was the bar – just a bar, sitting by itself in the woods – of course, I mean you need somewhere to put your beer while you're building everything else, right? The bar has to come first. Duh.

Once I had a fire pit, an outhouse and a bar, I thought I was done building stuff. I mean, what else does anyone really need? But the wife was carrying on about a roof and rain and I don't know what, so I built us a luxury lean-to and named it Hornbull's Grand Erection in homage to the Brooklyn Bridge's original moniker: Roebling's Grand Erection. I objected to traveling all the way from the City to the mountains to be in an enclosed space, so every structure was out door or open-faced: Outdoor kitchen, bar in the woods, and an open-faced lean-to with a view of the mountains from the foot of our bed. The outhouse was also more 'out' than 'house' with a view into the woods and the mountains in the distance from the royal throne.

I got much more skilled in carpentry as I built things over the years. You can date the structures in Nicholopolis by quickly eye-balling how closely it looks like it was built by Homer Simpson – the more out-of-whack the older it is.

Once Nicholopolis had all the necessities of life in the woods, I shifted my focus to the Lower Camp. We made a guest lean-to, fire pit and tent spots for our groups of reveling guests. Once that corner of the wilds of Hornbullonia was tamed, it needed a better name than just the Lower Camp, so in honor of Grand Duchess Nichole's middle name, we named it Lauralopolis. But since everyone already knew it as the Lower Camp, we thought it would be easier for everyone if we just called it Lower Lauralopolis.

I made one exception to the no-enclosed-spaces architectural theme when we built the sauna. My Mom is from an area of northwestern Ontario that was settled in my grandmother's generation by immigrants from Finland who came to northern Ontario for the warmer climes. Needless to say, they brought their saunas with them.

The Newmi began to strenuously object: "You build one more thing and you're not allowed to call this camping anymore," Tom barked.

"Yeah, what are there peacocks roaming the grounds?" Jamie added. "This place is a damn spa now."

They had a point, at the rate we have been recreating civilization in the woods, I figure we'll be flying around Hornbullonia in hand-carved jet-packs in a just few more years.

**

Nichole, Mook and I arrived before noon in Hornbullonia. Mook had slept most of the drive up, his small thin frame and bulbous, bald head made him look like a fetus curled up in the back seat. He was hungover, but he wouldn't have missed the opportunity. He hadn't been to Hornbullonia all summer because of my medical absence from my throne. And, Nichole guilted him into coming along to make sure I didn't hurt myself doing any heavy lifting or otherwise overexerting myself. Mook is a skilled carpenter and all-around handyman, very adept and knowledgeable for such a knucklehead.

"Oh shit, whuh? We're here?" Mook grumbled

himself awake. "What about beer? I thought we were stopping at the supermarket?"

"You slept through it," Nichole replied. "But no need to worry, we got you a twelve-pack of PBR. Isn't that what you usually drink up here?"

"Yeah, I've been known to have more than twelve, however, I mean, in a whole weekend."

"Well, I can't drink and we've got some work to do, anyway," I reminded.

Mook cracked a beer and got to work on his twelve pack. "So why are we taking these trees down? What's the plan here?"

"The plan is to move the mountains a little to the right."

We established Nicholopolis in a clearing on the hillside above where the previous owner had cleared a narrow stretch of forest to create a view of the mountains in the distance. The gap had regrown in by the time we bought the place and I re-cleared the scrubby sapling regrowth to expose the view of the rolling hilly cow pastures and the mountains beyond.

"You like the views of the mountains? I made them myself," I would often brag.

"Wow, it looks great," Nichole exclaimed. "Until somebody builds a shopping mall in that cow pasture in five years."

Five years later, there was no mall, but someone

opened up a gravel-pit quarry just beyond the pasture and slowly ate away at the rolling hills in the foreground of my view.

It is surprising how much encroachment can be legally imposed upon private land. In the ten years since Nichole and I bought the property, natural gas fracking became all the controversy in our corner of upstate New York. The New York Times even datelined a feature article from our little village. Before New York State decided not to allow it, we were ground zero for the whole fracking debacle. Without having sold any rights, the miners could have drilled the gas right out from a thousand feet under our feet, or placed a precarious toxic retaining pond up the hill from our camp. They built a pipeline right alongside the boundary of Hornbullonia. Or as I like to say, the pipeline company was kind enough to install a kick-ass sledding hill for our amusement. Nichole and I saw a work crew clearing a swath through the forest about three miles from Hornbullonia so we pulled over and asked them when they thought they might be working by our place.

"Oh, in about three hours," the foreman replied.

And sure enough, they did. They cleared a 50-yard swath of forest three miles in a matter of hours. The machines looked like they escaped off the screen from a terminator movie: A giant claw with a chain-saw finger would grab, cut and chuck the trees over its shoulder to a machine that stripped the branches and piled the logs aside, a tractor with an enormous hook dragged through the ground behind, yanking the stumps out of the ground and passing them over to a grinder that chewed them up and spit out piles of mulch. Grab, cut, chuck, rip, grind. Grab, cut, chuck, rip, grind as fast as you can read these words they were repeating the cycle of forest destruction. It makes you imagine what is going on in the Amazon where they really have free-reign to rape the environment.

We gave no permission and got no compensation. All we received was a series of notices from an oil and gas corporation saying tough shit, this is what we're going to do, sucks to be you – that and a life-time supply of fire wood and a kick-ass sledding hill.

On the other border of Hornbullonia, lay the disputed frontier with the land of Assholistan. Assholistan is ruled by the Shah of Assholistan, an ornery old local redneck who hates hippy vegans, Wiccans, artists, city people and pretty much everyone else and is simply a stark raving dick. We rarely saw the Shah, he lived in town and had little use for his little wood lot. He bought it to log it (in strict violation of the community rules and deed restrictions). Once a year he would come up the mountain to hunt turkeys, set up a shooting range and make a racket just to intimidate and annoy his neighbors.

I arrived at the entrance to Hornbullonia one fine summer day to find the road blocked with a pile of branches and conspicuously bright-colored survey tape in the trees. I called the Shah and he went into a tirade about how I was trespassing across his property to get onto mine because the communal road meandered out of its right-of-way onto his property and therefore he owns the first five feet of my driveway. He really just wanted to sell his worthless land for an inflated price by using his aggressive intimidation to extort his neighbors into paying an inflated price for it.

There was no reasoning with the Shah, but his wife was an absolute sweetheart who worked at the local grocery store. So Nichole and I fended off the Shah's hostilities by baking a pie for his wife in a gesture of good neighborly relations and she nagged him into ceasing his hostile actions. He resented this treacherous weaponization of neighborly love and loathed us all the more for out-maneuvering him. Alas, while there was a cessation of outward hostilities, the situation in the disputed Hornbullonian-Assholistani neutral zone remained tense.

On our southern border, there was another quarry eating away at the top of our mountain, and now to our north in the valley below our view of hills was being eaten up by a massive gravel pit. A view had been cleared of the hills to the north, but the regrowth of saplings had sprouted back up into adolescent trees and began blocking the view again. I wanted my view back but not looking into the gravel pit, so Mook and I were clearing the trees to the right of the view so I could move my view and the mountains a little bit to the right.

"Ok, that sounds a lot easier than moving the mountains," Mook was relieved to hear.

"Then, we're going to plant low-growing fruit trees in the gap so the view will remain clear."

"Why are we cutting down these trees in front of

the outhouse? What's the plan here? You want a view of the mountains while you're taking a dump?" Mook asked sarcastically.

"Yes," I answered emphatically.

"I love it!" Mook shouted with a fist bump toward the sky. "All hail Hornbullonia!"

"What about the logs? Why are we hauling them up the hill?"

"Yes, the plan is Nichole wants to poop in her slippers."

"Huh? She doesn't like the outhouse?"

"We are going to lay them into the ground to make steps on the trail to the outhouse, so Nichole doesn't have to lace up her hiking boots to go poop. She can go in her slippers."

"Ok. That makes *a lot* more sense than what I was picturing." Mook scratches his bald head. "So, you've got a new outhouse?"

"Yeah, we really built it like a brick shit house. I named it the Fortress of Solitude. You know, like where Superman goes to be alone and think things through?"

"Ha! The Fortress of Solidturd," Mook cracked himself up. "Is it a composting outhouse like the last one?"

"Yes, but the last one was too far from camp. And believe me, it's a lot farther away late at night."

Having never dallied in the art of composting my own bodily waste before, I figured I'd build it far enough from camp that if it all went horribly wrong, I could just bury it and never tell anybody what had happened there. But it worked so well I was pissed that it was so far away.

The composting was simple. Instead of flushing you throw a scoop of rotten sawdust or peat moss down the hole after it, occasionally I rake it flat and cover it in hay, so the bacteria can breathe in there. And it's elevated off the ground to let air through. It rots the 'deposits' into compost in a matter of weeks if you do it right, but I let it sit for two years or so to be sure I never see anything icky. I use the compost to fertilize the fruit trees and one day I'll use the fruit to make moonshine. Then when someone takes a snort and says: "Wow, that is some really good shit," I can say: "Why yes, it is, I made that shit myself."

I have a whole line of brand names I can put on the label for each batch: Good Shit; Strong Shit; Outrageous Shit; The Real Shit.

Shakey helped me build the outhouse. He always wanted something named after him, but I told him he had to help build something if he wanted it named after him. He helped with the wood shed, but it was not worthy. I don't think the outhouse was worthy either, but he was a good sport in helping anyway. But he wasn't much of a carpenter and he got frustrated: "I'm an actor, not a carpenter. Just give me some simple task I can do," I told him to sit, relax and just help me with the math to check for square periodically. "I'm an actor not a mathematician damn it," he implored.

"Ok," I replied. "You can memorize lines, right? Memorize this: The square root of the hypotenuse is equal to the sum of the squares of the other two sides."

"Hah! I know what that is," he exclaimed.

"The Pythagorean Theorem."

"No, it's what the Scarecrow said when he finally got a brain." Shakey leapt to his feet clumsily as if he were falling upwards like the Scarecrow, pointed his index finger up against his temple and in his best Scarecrow voice blurted: "The square of the hypotenuse is equal to the sum of the squares of the other two sides!" Then he'd sit back down and drink beer until I needed to check for square again and up he'd leap, pointing at his temple reciting the Pythagorean Theorem. He loved it, he really hammed it up. And we got the foundation perfectly square. I offered to name it the Shakey Foundation, but it was *not* worthy.

**

Nichole stood on the edge of the hill and directed Mook and I toward the view-offending trees like a Roman empress giving the thumbs up or thumbs down to their fate. We managed to fell them with the chain saw without dropping any on each other's heads and strip the branches off without cutting each other's hands off – no thanks to the amount of beer and pot Mook was consuming.

"Maybe I should handle the chain saw, Mook.

You're not looking too coordinated."

"Nah, it's alright. I'm not drinking any more."

"You can drink if you want, just let me do the sawing."

"Nah, it's not that. I drank it all already."

"You drank the whole twelve-pack?" I did a double take at him. "We've only been here three hours."

"I didn't drink all of them," he balked. "How many did you have?"

"None. The cardiologist gave me another thirty days in the no-alco-hole, remember? I haven't had a drink in two months."

When the Grand Duchess was satisfied with her new mountains, it came time for the muscle work of dragging the logs up the hill. I grabbed the butt end of log and started up the hill.

"Whoa, whoa, whoa," Mook waved his arms like a referee calling a foul. "You're not supposed to be doing the heavy lifting, that's why I'm here. Nichole made me promise."

"Alright Mook, grab an end, I can manage with the two of us on one log. They're not that heavy."

We got to the top of the hill and Mook was panting: "Hang on a minute let me rest."

We got another one up and he was looking weak

in the knees. "Maybe you need to lie down, Mook. Are you alright?"

"It's just a lot of work getting those suckers up here. Aren't you winded?"

It dawned on me that I was not. It wasn't Mook being wasted. Wait. It wasn't *just* Mook being wasted, I was in really good shape. I couldn't walk up that hill much less drag logs up it without getting winded since, well since ever.

Mook made me promise not to do any heavy lifting until he woke up, and I lied and told him I wouldn't. But I had been waiting all summer to spend time up here and I was of the not-so-cautious belief that the exercise was just what the doctor ordered. It wasn't, the actual doctor ordered the opposite of heavy lifting – no heavy lifting. I was referring to that little doctor inside me. He ordered a hefty dose of heavy lifting.

I grabbed the butt ends of two logs and dragged them up the hill behind me, marveling at my cardio-vascular stamina and my upper body strength. I trotted back down the hill and grabbed two more.

"Jeffrey," Nichole stomped her foot. "You were supposed to wait for Mook to do that."

"Mook is a wastoid and I am freaking Superman," I proclaimed.

There was not only light at the end of the recovery tunnel, I was suddenly in the best shape since before I started smoking – thirty years ago. I wore myself ragged and it felt fantastic.

## 30. The Vegan Vegas of the Woods

Nicholopolis has quite the night life scene for an isolated camp in the woods. The neighbors pop over often. One of the vegans pops over when his wife isn't around to sneak some meat, his wife sneaks over when he isn't around to bum cigarettes. Nicholopolis is infamous throughout Greater Hornbullonia for being the vegan Vegas of the woods. Nichole and I arrived unscheduled and unannounced one time to find a neighbor and his visiting brother drinking whiskey at the bar, tipsy, guilty and giggling. Which was fine, I had bought him the whiskey as a thank you for hauling lumber on his Mule, but the Wiccan Witch wouldn't allow it in the house, so we had an understanding that he could stash it at our place and make use of the bar any time.

The usual Hornbullonia happy hour suspects began to assemble by the pond. Jim and his wife, the Wiccan Witch of the East. Little Cindy-Lou Sue who lives in Sueville in the valley past the pond and who I imagine gathers with all the little Sues in Sueville to hold hands and sing every Christmas ala Dr. Suess, with me scowling down at them from the mountainside like the Grinch. Sue is a militant vegan who speaks with an English accent – because she is from across the pond, I assume. Sue complained vocally and emotionally when I stocked the pond with fish because fishing was tantamount to murder – the taking of the life of another sentient being. The fish were Shakey's pet project and he passed away before they grew large enough to eat, so the fish had the last laugh. I was never comfortable pulling a hook out of a fish's mouth, much less gutting it, so I just bought worms and fed them from the dock. They learned quickly that the sounds of footsteps on the dock meant the worm man cometh and came running (well, swimming I guess) from all over the pond to snatch worms out of my fingertips. I could even play tug-of-war with them.

My other highly-trained performance animal is Alvin the chipmunk. Alvin is a very special little chipmunk who will do anything for a nut. I firmly believe he would give his left nut for a nut. He literally sits in the palm of my hand or on my knee and stands and jumps for a nut dangled over his head. I sat at the picnic table hand-feeding Alvin, twirling an almond over his head making him dance around in little circles.

"You're teasing him, Jeffrey," Sue objected.

"I don't think Alvin is objecting to this arrangement. I think he is quite content to shower me with cuteness in exchange for a winter's-worth of nuts."

"But you're exploiting him," Sue insisted. "It's immoral."

"I think he is the luckiest chipmunk in the woods."

"Luckier than your mice that you murder with those traps of yours, I suppose," Sue continued. "I don't know how you can be so kind to one rodent and murder the other ones just because one has a cuter tail. They are all God's creatures, you know."

"Well, some of God's little mother fuckers

moved into the shed, got in the storage bins and peed all over my extra camping gear. The whole shed reeks of pee. I swear one little mouse couple can produce more pee than a dozen of the Bowery's finest winos. And Sue, need I remind you of the horrors of Mouschwitz?"

I tried a 'humane' live-capture mouse trap a couple years earlier. It worked. We caught some mice and released them in a field half way back to the City. They ran out into a field to start a new life, probably for about five minutes until a hawk saw them running around homeless in broad daylight. But it was a much better feeling than picking the dead mice out of the snap traps. But one weekend I forgot check the live-capture trap before we left. When we came back two weeks later, the little trap box was crammed full of dead and starving mice. We thereafter named it Mouschwitz and rarely speak of the horrors that occurred there.

"I don't know how you can call yourself vegan now, and treat animals like that," Sue objected.

"I'm only vegan because I'm too lazy and stupid to do math at every meal like some kind of culinary mathematical genius like my cardiologist and the Nutri-Nazi want me to be. Heck, I think food taste better the more its mother loved it. I mean, an eggplant's mother didn't love it and look what that tastes like. Veal on the other hand is more delicious than beef because by the time they are beef, their mothers aren't as enamored with them as they were when they were veal. And lamb versus mutton? No contest. I'm just a part-time vegan for health reasons, Sue – not moral reasons."

"That doesn't even count. You're vegan for all

the wrong reasons."

"What are you trying to convert me to now, Sue? Do the animals care *why* I'm vegan?" If some lion decided not to eat me, I wouldn't say: 'hey get back here, you're not eating me for all the wrong reasons.' I would quietly respect his decision."

"You know why I became vegetarian?" The Wiccan Witch of the East interjected. "I was driving home one day past the same cow pasture on Route 8 just outside of town. Every day I would see the same cow standing at the same spot by the fence. And one day, there was a gap in the fence and she was over on the other side of the road. So, I pulled over, rolled down my window and said: 'Are you supposed to be on this side of the road?' And that cow gawked at me wide-eyed in fear and ran back across the road and through the gap in the fence. It understood, on some level, exactly what I was saying. That's when it dawned on me that this is a *thinking* being I am talking to. I'm supposed to kill her for her flesh to eat?"

"That is an incredible story," I stated. "What is so incredible about that story is that you actually stopped the car and rolled down the window to ask the cow what it was doing. If it wasn't you we were talking about, I wouldn't believe it for a minute."

"There is a moral contract that we engaged in when we domesticated animals," Mook interjected philosophically. "We provided protection, safety and nourishment. The animals entered this willingly. But mistreatment of animals violates this contract, whether they can express it or not, whether they understand it or not, *we* should understand that. It has been a foundation of society. It's a foundation of religion and ethics, in India the cows are *sacred*."

"Then why do you have a bloody burger on the grill, Mook?" Sue snapped.

"American cows aren't sacred," Mook said. "Indian cows are sacred, American cows are delicious. It's just the way God made them."

**

Jim and Mook decided to fire up the sauna and the Wiccan Witch of the East decided to join them. I stood up mildly hunched over holding my chest in pain.

"Jeff, are you alright?" Nichole asked.

"Yeah, it's just the log-lifting. Methinks I overdid it a bit." I winced and stretched my arms backwards. "I think I'll go for a swim and stretch my arms and chest."

I trotted down to the dock, flipped off my sandals and jumped in the pond. I sank like a rock. I tried swimming upwards, but my strength and range of motion were shot and after an attempt and a half I wasn't quite sure which way was up. I exhaled to sink myself and kick off the mucky bottom back to the surface. I popped up, gasped a breath and tried swimming two strokes back to the dock, but I was still in an upright position, flailing, trying to swim in a standing position. I curled my body in a ball and stretched out horizontally and made the two strokes back to the dock panting and in pain. Two things were at play here: my chest muscles healing from the surgery and from an afternoon of self-imposed forced labor; and, I had lost a good forty-five pounds – forty-five pounds of highly buoyant human blubber that is – making me heavier in the water. I was accustomed to just naturally, comfortably floating around the pond like a manatee.

"Are you alright, SweetiePie?" Nichole came running to the dock. "Is it your chest?"

"Not really, I just sank like a mob boss in the East River with cement galoshes. I guess I had taken for granted that I've been wearing nature's own life-preserver and inner tube on my torso all these years. I've got to re-learn how to swim."

"Well let me get you one of the kids' pool noodles."

It felt a little undignified at first, but it beat flailing around near-drowning. With the noodle keeping me afloat, it felt great to swim at my own pace and stretch my healing chest muscles – a much more appropriate exercise for a recovering cardio-surgery patient than dragging logs up the side of a mountain like a beast of burden.

**

"CA-CAW, CA-CAW!!!" Mook shouted holding his vape pen over his head as he, Jim and the Wiccan Witch of the East emerged from the sauna wrapped in towels.

"Sure," I held my chest and leaned over the picnic table by the pond. "My chest is killing me. Besides this is supposed to be happy hour after all."

I took the vape pen and Mook trotted down to the dock and splashed into the pond. He emerged a minute later climbing the ladder onto the raft.

"He looks like he's naked," Sue observed.

"He looks like he's standing on his head, he's a got a bald head and a hairy ass," I added.

"Does that mean he's holding his beer with his foot like an orangutan?" Jim asked.

"Oh dear, where does that mean he is pouring that beer?" asked Nichole.

"What a cute little button nose he has," giggled Sue.

"Well I'm sure it's cold in there," Nichole offered in Mook's defense.

Mook stood on the edge of the raft and backward summersaulted into the air and straightened into a dive into the water.

"Was that feet first or head and hands first?" Sue pondered.

"He's going to hurt himself," The Wiccan Witch stood up to keep a watchful eye on the Mook "Jeff, what's your plan for being up here, now? With your health and all? You shouldn't come up alone. Do you want to use one of our radios in case of emergency?"

"Let's not make too big a deal of it. My cardiologist assures me I am not at risk of suddenly dropping dead. The blockages are gone. I just have to heal from the surgery and start looking out for my long-term health."

"You should keep a map and directions to the nearest emergency room in the car in case someone else has to take you there in an emergency. Remember that time you almost broke your leg on the dock."

"And I didn't need an emergency room in that case. My dad talked me out of it, remember? Besides, that wasn't even the closest I have come to needing an emergency room up here. The closest I ever came to going to an emergency room from here was when I got my penis caught in the zipper of my sleeping bag."

I had been camping out by myself on a cold November night and I woke up in the middle of the night having to pee like a racehorse. It was cold and I ran back to my sleeping bag in as mad a dash as I had run out to relieve myself. I wriggled in the bag and somehow 'it' wriggled out of my boxers as I was trying to wriggle the zipper up. The zipper came unstuck and I gave it a good arm-sweeping zzzzzzzip. YEEEEEOOOOWEEEEE!!! SHIT!!! FUCK!!! HOLY CRAPPING PISS!!! The zipper was stuck, and 'it' was stuck in it – and it wasn't budging, and neither was 'it'. And there was no way I could bring myself to just rip the zipper past the sticking point. I thought for sure I had to go to the emergency room. I started hopping to the car in my sleeping bag like I was in my own personal sack race, replete with clumsy stumbles and falls and flailing attempts to get myself back up and hopping again, screaming and cursing all the way to the car.

The mental image of myself victoriously hopping across the finish line of my own personal imaginary sack race into the emergency room did flash through my mind, and I couldn't imagine how mortifying it would have been, but I instantly dismissed the embarrassment as selfish vanity compared to the urgency of the immediate penile emergency at hand. I wriggled into the car and got the key in the ignition, but I couldn't figure out how to drive with my feet wrapped into one enormous sleeping-bag-bound foot. I couldn't even get it out of park; driving like that could not possibly have ended well. I imagined the embarrassment of the State Troopers laughing their heads off when they found my dead body behind the wheel with my mutilated pecker sticking out of my sleeping bag. And that's what stopped me long enough to come to my senses. I paused, took a breath and yanked it (the zipper, not 'it') in one sweeping motion. YEEEEEOOOOWEEEEE!!! SHIT!!! FUCK!!! HOLY CRAPPING PISS!!! AGAIN!!! And I leapt out of the sleeping bag and went running around the camp site like a chicken with his dick cut off fumbling for the first aid kit in the dark. Emergency room visit averted.

Mook retrieved his towel on the dock and much to the delight of his gaggle of onlookers, retrieved his pants from the sauna.

"A toast!" Mook proclaimed with his beer can

raised. "Long live Nicholopolis!"

"All hail Hornbullonia!" I added with a raise of the vape pen.

"And Death to Assholistan!" Nichole finished.

The sun was setting, and the coyotes began their nightly howling. Coyotes have a high-pitched yipping, yelping siren-like howl: "Yyyiiip-yeeep-weeeeop-yyyyyiiiiipeeep."

"Sounds like their rounding up the pack," Nichole said.

"Sounds like they got their dicks caught in their zippers," I replied.

"Sounds like it's time for us to head home," the Wiccan Witch gathered her clothes from the sauna, her wine and her husband and they climbed aboard the all-terrain Kawasaki Mule still in their sauna towels. The Mule puttered off around the back side of the pond and as it entered the woods the sauna towels flung up over their shoulders and onto the roll bar. And they rode off naked into the sunset, their respective wine and beer raised high over their heads: "All hail Hornbullonia! Good night!"

**

My chest was still killing me the following morning, but I abstained from any pain-relieving activities or substances since I would have to drive back home to New York City that afternoon. Mook spent the morning ensuring no pain-relieving substances or beverages were left behind or abandoned. He claimed he felt too sorry for all the little sober children in Africa and India to watch perfectly good beer and marijuana go to waste.

"Jesus, Mook. How did you go through all that? Did you wake and bake as soon as you woke up this morning?" I asked as he crawled into the back seat of the car, resuming the fetal position he arrived in.

"Yeah, I woke and boke at like 7:00am and then went right back to sleep," he grumbled. Don't judge me, I'm fine to help drive if you need me to. I've woken and boken harder than this and been fine to drive before, no problem."

"No thanks. I got it." I rolled my eyes at him in the rear-view mirror.

I thought sitting up straight in the car would help my chest, but the pain got worse and worse. Then my breathing got more and more strained. Soon, I was wheezing for air.

"Nichole, something's wrong," I sputtered. "I can't freaking breathe. I'm pulling over."

"Are you okay? Should we go to a hospital?"

"No, I think I just tore something dragging those logs yesterday." I recognized the symptoms, not the burning chest and aching arms and jaw of a heart attack but the sharp post-surgical pains that make it hard to breathe, which congests my lungs, which makes it harder to breathe et cetera and down the downward spiral we go.

"If you learned one thing isn't it to get checked out to be safe?"

"No, I also learned what a heart attack feels like and what a torn-open sternum feels like. This feels like a torn-open sternum."

And if there is one thing I was told, it was 'don't go to the emergency room, go to the cardiologist' lest I wind up admitted for a day or two to find out what we already know: I have a weakened heart and a lot of post-surgical pain. I walked around the car a couple times and gently stretched a bit and took some deep breaths. I sat back down and put a hand on my chest under my seat belt. "You're not going to believe this, but I think it's the seatbelt."

The seatbelt pressing and rubbing on my scar caused enough pain to make it uncomfortable to breathe, which made me wheezy, which exacerbated the pain, which made it harder to breathe. I drove back to the City with my seatbelt under my arm and the pain subsided. Dr. Freeman would later tell me this is common, and they actually sell felt seatbelt pads to cushion the seat belt on chest scars. I came to learn how incredibly irritating it could be – to the point of tempting me into going to the emergency room with chest pains and shortness of breath. I still don't think a felt pad would cut it, so I have been driving with the seatbelt under my arm ever since and probably always will.

Mook slept through the whole affair passed out

in the back seat and Nichole is no help at all in the driving department, she has no license. She is not a drunk, She is a New Yorker who never drove a car in her life and neither did her mother, it's just the way we are in New York.

The rest of the drive home almost drove me to the emergency room. I felt like I was dying the death of a vampire with a wooden stake through my heart. Dr. Freeman would say it was still post-surgical pain probably aggravated by tearing something from all the heavy lifting.

"Post-surgical?" I asked. "Still? What was this surgery? Did he lay me out on some newspapers and crack me open like a crab with a giant nut cracker and a great big mallet? It sure felt like it. And when is this scar going to whither away into a barely visible line as promised?"

"Honestly," Dr. Freeman answered, "maybe never. If that scar isn't subsiding by now it might never."

Spoiler alert: it never does. Some people get stuck with a bad back for life, I got stuck with a bad chest. It affects my posture, my breathing and my physical abilities. And it ruined my prospects of convalescing and medical teleworking in Hornbullonia.

# Life Goes On

## 31. Out of the Toilet

Long walks gave me a good excuse to get out of the house at least once a day, and Wally kept me company on many of them, but the rest of my time seemed to get emptier and emptier, the gaps in between minor activities were getting longer and longer and they started to stretch out in my mind further and further. Without a doctor's appointment or a walking date with Wally, and no other immediate reason to motivate myself, I was getting started later and later every day. I wasn't healed enough to spend the rest of the summer putzing on my project list in Hornbullonia like I had hoped, but I was well enough to start getting antsy and eager to get up and out and out-and-about.

Eight weeks into recovery I was able to get comfortable on the couch and I started spending hours sometimes trying to get motivated to get up and get out. Then I started having trouble finding the motivation to so much as turn on the TV or read. I have had my periodic bouts of being depressed in my life – probably more so than most people and I had long wondered if I had some related problem. Maybe my compulsion to galivant from disaster to disaster for a living is rooted in a need for challenges, or my indulgences in alcohol and dalliances in drugs rooted in a need for stimulus.

But this was different, very different. I could see it becoming a downward spiral of a problem: the more time I spent alone and inactive the more depressed I got, the more depressed I got the more time I spent on the couch. But it got to a point beyond my control. I woke up with a plan to walk to the park and it took until 4pm to get out of the house. I just could NOT physically get off the couch. It was a physical sensation of inertia akin to an all-over pain. It wasn't pain, more like an all-over inflammation or tingling, but I could easily see how it could be pain for someone with a more severe condition. I just sat there, my mind ruminating on my entire life as a history of one awkward embarrassment after another, consumed by a feeling of not just being useless but a heavy weight of detriment on everything and everyone in my life.

I had never heard of the link between bypass surgery and depression, but I had wondered why Dr. Freeman had so regularly, so pointedly asked me about my mood and energy and I suspected there might be cause to take note of such problems. It was hard to mention it even to him, those feelings of being a detriment on people around me could legitimately be compounded if I thought they all thought I was crazy.

The link between bypass surgery and depression is not understood but the incidence is much higher than following other surgeries. There is a wide range of theories as to why: Atherosclerotic plaques in the aorta breaking loose and getting stuck throughout the brain, the long duration under anesthesia or hypothermia during the lengthy surgery or simply the shock of confronting your own mortality.

Dr. Freeman settled on it being the beta blocker I was on and reduced my daily dose from 50 milligrams twice a day to 25 milligrams twice a day. It seemed to help, a lot. I still didn't have the energy I had been looking forward to after not having had any alcohol for two months at this point, and I complained about my energy level to Dr. Freeman for months to come. He reduced the dosage again and again to 12.5 milligrams twice a day and then to 12.5 once a day. My energy seemed to rebound in proportion every time. But was it the meds? The cycle of too much time isolated at home? The mysterious link between bypass surgery and depression correcting itself over time? We'll never know. But I saw my window in the first rebound and decided to pounce on the opportunity to get back to work while I could.

I needed to be around people. And my feelings of worthlessness were compounded by the reality that my career as I knew it might be over if I was unable to deploy to disaster areas. I feared that if I was even perceived as unable to deploy or otherwise do my job I would get relegated to irrelevance and sink into more depression. I needed to start getting back in the saddle, if only slowly.

**

I had become fully ensconced in the post-surgical pity-party period and developed a persona character I dubbed the bigga-da-fatta-dabumma who spoke in an Italian accent and excused himself from any possible reason to get off the couch.

"I am da-bigga-da-fatta-da-bumma, SweetiePie. Da-bigga-da-fatta-da-bumma no take out il garbaggio, da-bigga-da-fatta-da-bumma sit on il sofa and watcha-da-TV."

It was cute enough to extend the pity-party for a

while but being sedentary was getting to be unhealthy. I realized I had become too sedentary for too long when I finally got around to fixing the trickling toilet. Nichole has been asking me to call the building superintendent for weeks, and I kept promising day after day to fix it myself. Calling a super for such a simple fix was an affront to my masculinity and I insisted on doing it on my own. But, despite all the time I seemed to have to sit on my ass staring at the TV or the wall, I hadn't found the time or motivation to get to the tool box in the closet, take the lid off the tank and fix the damn thing.

After two weeks of this, Nichole came home from work one evening in a rush to get to the bathroom. She came back out and spun back around in surprise, returned to the toilet and jiggled the handle.

"Hmm," She pondered. "The toilet seems to have finally fixed itself."

Given three logical possibilities here:

1)    The husband called the super like she asked;
2)    The husband fixed the toilet like he said, or;
3)    The toilet fixed itself;

Option three: The toilet fixed itself was clearly the only reasonable explanation Nichole found plausible considering the on-going decline of my spirits and motivation and the rise of the frequency of bigga-da-fatta-da-bumma appearances. Granted, only my wife can truly appreciate the depths of my eternal husbandly bumdom. But, really?

"The toilet fixed itself?" I balked. "You find it

*that* hard to believe that your husband may have called the super like you said or fixed it myself like I said? You just *presume* the toilet fixed itself?"

"You don't have to get upset, I just thought…"

"Let me ask you," I interrupted. "Did you leave the wrench and screw driver where the toilet could reach it? Or did you also *presume* the toilet hopped down the hall to the closet and fetched the tools out of the toolbox by itself too?"

"Alright, I'm sorry," she raised her hands in surrender. "So, what was wrong? How did you fix it?"

"I dunno. I jiggled the handle when I flushed, and I guess the flap thing maybe just sort of fell back into place. Alright, fine, I guess the damn thing just fixed itself. But it is the *presumption* that I object to."

Nichole grabbed her hair, clenched her teeth and shot me that wifely glare that tells a husband when it is time to just shut up and that time was five minutes ago. The pity party was over.

The reasons why any wife would find 'the toilet fixed itself' more plausible than the husband actually did anything she asked or did what he said he would do may be a telling statement on the institution of marriage or gender relations in general, but I shan't digress into that topic here. I just took it as a sign I had been too sedentary for too long and needed to get back to work. I didn't know if getting back to work would be conducive to my health and recovery, but it would certainly be conducive to preserving my state of mind and getting on with my life.

**

It had been eight weeks since I had headed out
to work in the morning and I was out of practice and
even more disheveled than I normally was in the
morning. Fortunately, I still had my morning checklist
taped to the back of the front door to ensure I didn't
forget anything: Keys, Phone, Wallet, Money, Badge,
Bag, Glasses, Watch, FitBit, Kiss the wife.

I had gone through a long spell of being
completely unable to leave the house without running
back up the stairs once, twice or five times. I had begun
training the doorman to ask me if I had each item before
he let me out of the building, but it turns out it was not
in his job description and I had no business holding him
accountable for my groggy morning brain and generally
spacey nature. So, in a flash of inspiration I came up
with the back-of-the-door list. To verify beyond all
shadow of doubt that I had all the requisite
accoutrement to leave the house, I had a song and dance
routine to the tune of the Macarena in which with each
item I would tap each pocket, front, back pants and
shirt, wrist and shoulders as I swiveled my hips and
sang:

- Got my keys, got my phone, got my wallet,
  Macarena
- Got my money, got my badge, got my bag,
  Macarena
- Got my glasses, got my watch, got my FitBit,
  Macarena
- KISS THE WIIIIIFE, Macarena!!! KISS THE

WIIIIIIFE, Macarena!!!

This last item was important, not just because Nichole would get hyper-pissy with me if I rushed out the door without a kiss, but she had her checklist to go through as well:

- My shirt tucked in
- My hair brushed
- Matching shoes; and, most importantly:
- No socks or underwear dangling out of the bottom of my pants legs.

God forbid her husband leave the house and be seen in public without having been carefully inspected for all of the above.

I set out to return to work in a spectacular display of newfound physical fitness – on a Citi Bike. I had eagerly signed up for the Citi Bike bike-sharing when it started three years earlier in the summer of 2013. I could bike to work downtown at least as fast as taking the subway, leaving little room for excuses not to get in some exercise a few times a week. Once I started taking routes in the separated bike paths along the rivers, far more serene than the life-and-death struggle of biking through Manhattan streets, I enjoyed it far more than cramming myself into the Lexington Avenue Subway and did it as often as possible. But what was possible slowly became a more and more limited. I had gotten slower and slower despite working harder and harder. All the other bikers would sail effortlessly past me while I huffed and puffed and struggled. But now that I was recovering, shedding weight and getting fit again, I thought maybe I was up for triumphantly biking to my first day of work.

I walked to the corner Citi Bike station, mounted my trusty Citi Bike steed and set out to test my stamina. But it turned out, physical stamina was the least of my worries. Citi Bikes are a little awkward and clunky in the best of circumstances, being scientifically designed and engineered to ensure that nobody would ever possibly want to steal one. The big problem with riding a clunky bicycle with a recently bifurcated sternum is that every bump, every pothole or God forbid going over a curb poses the dilemma of bracing my arms on the handle bars and absorbing the impact with my severed breast plate or leaning back on the seat and taking it like a man. The only imaginably worse way to commute to work than this would be my fat ass hopping all the way downtown on a pogo stick straddling my crotch on a granite, nut-cracker of a bike seat.

Like all the other sources of post-surgical chest pain, it began to restrict my breathing and gave me the all-too-familiar and disconcerting sensation of chest pain and shortness of breath. Over time and through a lot of negative reinforcement, I learned to readjust my posture on the bike. I had learned some bad habits riding a ten-speed as an adolescent and was leaning far too heavily on the handlebars and using my upper body as a shock absorber. By the time I got across town to the Hudson River Greenway bike path I had balanced myself more comfortably on the bike and learned to avoid the avoidable bumps. And through some heavily negative reinforcement, I learned to keep weight on the pedals.

I fell into a rhythm and set a pace along with the other bicyclists. Soon I was going faster than some of the others and I became strangely aware of my surroundings. I was looking up, I wasn't struggling, I wasn't panting, and I wasn't the slowest guy blocking the path for everyone else. It was like one of those dreams where running becomes so effortless you begin to fly. I wasn't being passed by everyone. I used to get annoyed at the really fit people zipping passed me impatiently huffing and sneering at the fat guy holding up traffic – condescending bastards. I would have liked to kick their asses if I could have caught up to them. The only one I couldn't keep up with was a healthily curvaceous young woman who fit very nicely into her skimpy bike shorts. Believe me I tried to keep up, but she was fast. I guess you have to be fast if you are a healthily curvaceous young woman who fits nicely into her skimpy bike shorts or you'll wind up with a couple dozen guys trailing behind you like you're Lance Armstrong leading the pack in the Tour de France.

Biking was not like this before. Before it used to be like being a circus elephant on a toy bike heading uphill while the Tour de France went whizzing by me on all sides. At the time I did not quite understand that it was not normal. Had I known my new normal was normal, I would have known something was very wrong a long time ago.

## 32. And into the FEMA Frying Pan

I hated our regional FEMA office being in One World Trade Center, the so-called Freedom Tower, not because it might be a target or for the bad memories of that day. Those things bothered a lot of my colleagues, many of whom were responders at the time of the 9-11 attacks. But for me, it was just embarrassment at the stupidity of putting a response agency: in a building that's a target, in a flood plain, in a congested downtown area, on a high floor with no back-up power. Any time I told anyone, any stranger, any drunken idiot on a barstool next to me, that I worked for FEMA in New York City, they would invariably ask: "Oh? Where is the FEMA office in New York City?"

"One World Trade Center"

"Really? Is that a smart idea?" they ask.

"No, it is not." I respond, "It is an incredibly stupid place for a FEMA office." I then proceed to list all the above-mentioned reasons, mortified that every schmoe on a barstool next to me exhibits more common sense than my own agency. I had had this conversation ad nauseam, in the two years since we moved in.

It was a purely political move. The building owners and lessors were having difficulty filling the building and it would have been a political disgrace to let it sit even half empty after all the years of delay and infighting. The federal government stepped up and honored a General Services Administration (GSA) lease on the original towers, but had trouble coercing other federal agencies into the building. This surprises people but government agencies do not have to lease their office space from the government. The GSA is 'the landlord of the federal government and owns all the civilian government real estate. They also own all federal fleet vehicles with the US Government license plates and provide all manner of bulk purchases and contracts. But other government agencies are under no obligation to use their services.

In fact, GSA gets no appropriation from the Congress, they have to fund themselves with the revenue of their services. And with the pure power of bulk on their side, they do quite well for themselves – too well for the liking of some of their employees. When the Congress fails to fund the government and there is a lapse-of-appropriation shut-down, the rest of us go on taxpayer-funded furlough vacation while GSA has to go to work. Their funding doesn't lapse because they get no congressional appropriation – suckers!

Most angry taxpayers that demand "government should have to run like a business" would be surprised how much of it is. The same is true for Army Corps of Engineers. They have to sell their services and their post-Katrina reputation for levy building to countless flood-prone jurisdictions. FEMA's flood insurance and radiological emergency program staff are funded by utility licensing fees and are in the same boat.

Other agencies successfully resisted the political pressure to relocate into the tower, but the Department of Homeland Security found the symbolism irresistible and ordered FEMA into the building against the vocal protests of the then-administrator of the agency. "Over my dead body!" Administrator Craig Fugate had assured us (and we might still hunt him down and make good on that promise) but in we went.

But the thing I hate most about working in that building is the security. In a federal facility, such as the Jacob Javits Federal Building we were in before, security is provided by the Federal Protective Service and caters to our needs. At One World Trade Center, they cater to the needs of Conde Nast and their fashion publishers and we take a back seat.

FEMA is a coordinating entity, it coordinates all the federal agencies involved in a disaster response. Other federal agencies cannot enter our facility without building ID and there is little point in getting them building ID because if they let it expire by not using it for four weeks, the ID badge expires. And this is how I wound up locked out of the building upon my triumphant return.

I stood off to the side of the turnstiles as directed by the security guards after my badge failed to swing the gates to the elevator banks open.

"You have someone coming down to sign you in?" asked a security guard himself between me and the entrance.

"He's coming now," I gestured toward Nathan coming out of the elevator.

"Dude, look how thin you are! How do you feel?" Nathan bellowed across the lobby. The security guards in the lobby sneered in seeming disappointment they didn't get to throw me out of the building all together.

"Feeling sexy, Nathan. Check it out, I can see my penis again!" I shouted back as I placed my hands on my hips and made a quick downward-glancing package check on myself, past where my protruding belly had once obstructed the view.

"Hello down there little fellow." I wriggled my fingers downwards. "Long time no see." Nathan laughed and patted my shoulder in welcome. The security guards drifted away in disavowal that we might be lawful tenants of the building.

**

Nathan took me up to the 52nd floor. We stepped out of the elevator and I looked through the double glass doors and through windows at the expansive view of New York Harbor. It was so familiar but seemed like a lifetime since I had been there. I paused to ask myself if it was a good idea to be back in this environment that has been the cause of so much stress. I reminded myself what it was like at home in the frying pan and stepped straight into the fire and straight to the conference room where we were greeted by Bernard, our regional administrator and Jay his chief of staff. I set my bike helmet on the conference table and we shook hands.

"Welcome back, Jeffrey. You look great," said Jay eying me up and down. "You've lost a lot of weight."

"Best shape of my life, Jay," I replied. I placed

my hands on my hips and looked down. "I can see my toes again. Hello down there little fellows!" Nathan glared at me for making his heart skip a beat.

"Are you ready to come back, Jeffrey?" asked Jay. "We can work with you for whatever arrangement you need – medical telework, part-time, tell us what you need. We are here to support you."

"I'm good to come back but, yes, something like telework part-time would be appreciated, maybe three days in the office and two days at home. I still have weekly cardiologist appointments and other medical appointments and exercise and physical therapy routines to stick to."

"What about the team?" asked Bernard. "Are you going to be able to deploy if needed?"

"I look forward to being able to deploy with the team again," I replied. "But I have regular medical appointments to keep for a while yet."

"We totally understand that," Bernard and Jay nodded at each other.

"I've got to keep those appointments, because any appointment now the cardiologist is going to tell me I can drink again, and I am *NOT* missing that appointment." I declared with a pointed tap of my index finger on the table for each syllable.

They both smiled. "We wouldn't ask you to miss that, Jeffrey," Jay chuckled.

"But you know we are monitoring a storm right

now, right?" asked Bernard. "Hurricane Matthew is heading up the coast and the possibility of a strike in the northeast is not out of the question."

My jaw sagged as I let out a gentle exhale, resentful that they would suggest I deploy into potential highly stressful circumstances in the same breath as welcoming me back and offering to let me ease back in. I restrained myself from rolling my eyes and dropping my jaw.

"It's not likely to hit up here, Jeffrey," Jay held up his finger tips and nodded in recognition of my apprehension. "We just need someone to sit with the State emergency management at the operations center in New Jersey while they monitor – just going through the motions."

Bernard caught my eye and nodded in agreement. Bernard was the head of New Jersey State Emergency Management at the time of Superstorm Sandy when I was the FEMA liaison to the emergency operations center. Emergency management in New Jersey is run by the State Police and Bernard was the colonel in charge, reporting to the attorney general who reports to the governor – Chris Christie at the time. Bernard knew my history with the New Jersey State Police emergency operations center and understood the implications for serious and undue job stress considering my health.

Four days before landfall, I had been told to report to a national team from FEMA HQ, but they were redirected. I was told an out of region team would come but they were delayed. So, we wound up with a team with New York State, a team with New York City, a team at our own operations center and me, and me alone, in New Jersey perpetually telling them the cavalry was about to arrive for four days leading up to landfall.

Two days before landfall I received a frantic phone call from our hapless response division director, Rick. "Get New Jersey on a conference call, right now, in like two minutes! New Jersey leadership, highest ranks, right now!"

Rick had always been in over his head as division director and seemed to lose interest in trying to catch up. He was in cruise control toward retirement and had talked about little else for the last few years. He thought he would skate past the finish line, until Sandy reared its ugly head and suddenly threatened to expose his negligence and end his FEMA career. He was in a panic.

I was the only civilian not in a State trooper dress uniform in the conference room, sitting at one end of a long conference table, the colonel at the other and about twenty of the top brass of New Jersey State Police between us. Rick stammered his way through facilitating the conference call, talking to New York State, New York City and our teams in their emergency operations centers for about forty minutes before he started wrapping up: "Alright, good call. I think it was productive, informative, let's continue these calls same time every day. Talk to all again tomorrow."

The beeps from the callers hanging up from the call rang out on the speaker phone on the conference table: bee-boop, bee-boop, bee-boop. And all the top brass of New Jersey State Police stared down the length of the table at me.

"Were they aware the State of New Jersey was on that call?" asked the Colonel, sternly. "Are they not interested in our status? Our needs?"

"Of course we are Colonel, I'll relay any concerns you may have…" I spoke slowly, trying not to stammer.

"Concern number one: what resources does FEMA have on hand to support New Jersey?"

"We have established a staging area at Fort Dix, Colonel. I have an inventory of the all the food, water, equipment and teams staged there. It's ample, but we need to start quantifying your anticipated needs and directing resource to where they will be needed."

"How the hell can I quantify my needs before the storm even makes landfall? Fort Dix is as good a place as any until landfall. Who was that ass-clown trying to facilitate that call anyway?"

"That was my response division director, Rick," I replied. "I'll give him a call right now and find out the estimated arrival time of the incident management team, if you will all excuse me." And I slinked out of the room.

I stepped out to the steps leading up to the building where the cell reception was better and I had some privacy and call the FEMA regional operation center. Nathan answered.

"Are you guys fucking crazy!?" I shouted. "Rick called me in a panic having forgotten to invite New Jersey and promptly forgot they were on the call!"

"What? They were on the call?" Nathan asked, perplexed.

"Yes, they were on the fucking call," I snapped back. Nathan started laughing.

"It's not funny. Do NOT let Rick do that again!" and I hung up.

The next day, Rick held the same call. I sat in the same room. And after forty minutes of talking to New York, Rick began wrapping up the call: "Another good call, we have resources heading to New York from our staging area at Fort Dix. We'll adjust as we go along. Let's do this call again tomorrow..."

"New Jersey!" I blurted as I leaned half-splayed across the conference table flailing to press the unmute button on the speaker phone.

"New Jersey, Rick!" we could hear Nathan interrupt on the other end of the call. "What about New Jersey?"

"Oh yeah, New Jersey," Rick said. "We have a liaison at the State Police emergency operations center, FEMA HQ is staging resources at Fort Dix and we are at our alternate operations center at Naval Weapons Station Earle in New Jersey. Thanks Nathan. We'll do the same call tomorrow."

Bee-boop, bee-boop, bee-boop... bee-boop. All the brass turned their faces toward my end of the table.

"Who was that ass-clown reporting out as if he were the State of New Jersey?" asked the Colonel. The rest of the top brass stared down the length of the conference table at me.

"That was Rick again..." I mumbled, looking downward to avoid any eye contact in desperate hope that attention would turn to anyone else.

"What did they mean they are taking resources from the staging area at Fort Dix to send to New York?" one of the majors was turning red in the face. "You said we had ample commodities, supplies, teams and equipment staged there. You gave me an inventory."

"Yes, that is what we have staged but it is a FEMA HQ staging area, I never meant it was all solely dedicated to New Jersey. That's why we need to cue requests..."

One of the officers stepped forward into my personal space and spittled in my face as he yelled: "Well, Fort Dix may be a federal facility, but the God-damn New Jersey Turnpike sure as hell isn't. We'll stop that shit on the road and redirect it wherever the hell we need it if we have to. Don't think for a second we won't, we did it in Hurricane Floyd, we'll do it again..."

"Are they making a conscious effort to ignore the State of New Jersey?" the Colonel interrupted. "I want to see all correspondence you have had with this

Rick."

"I want your note pad as evidence!" barked one of the lieutenants.

"No, there is no intention of ignoring New Jersey," I tried to soften the tone. "And this is not the time for some kind of half-assed after-action review or investigation. Traditionally, our procedures are to screw things up first and blame each other afterwards. Let's not put the cart before the horse, gentlemen. We haven't screwed it up yet. We still have time to get this right. And the incident management team will be here tonight. It'll be alright."

My wit drew a few smiles and the situation was defused enough to get them focused on projecting shortfalls, submitting resource requests and we got back on track. I went back to my seat on the main floor of the operations center and a trooper was standing at attention behind my seat. He made me nervous, so I stepped out to scream at Nathan and Rick again.

"This is quickly becoming a cluster you-know-what, Rick. And if you don't know what, I mean FUCK!" I shouted into the phone. "And when the hell is that team getting here?"

"Not until tomorrow," Rick replied. I hung up.

When I returned to my work station, the trooper was gone, and so was my notepad. It would be the first of many notepads that disappeared over the next few days.

The morning of landfall I arrived at the operations center having driven from my hotel through the driving rain around fallen trees and over downed power lines. I was kicking myself for not sleeping in the operations center – what if I couldn't make it in? There was a New Jersey State trooper standing in the parking lot. "Mr. Hornbull has arrived!" he shouted to a trooper at the top of the stairs.

"Mr. Hornbull has arrived!" the trooper at the top of the stairs shouted into the door of the emergency operations center.

I climbed up the stairs and the trooper held the door for me and shouted: "Mr. Hornbull is entering the building!"

"Mr. Hornbull is entering the building!" a voice repeated from inside.

"Mr. Hornbull is coming down the hallway!"

"Alright, I think the whole building is painfully aware of where Mr. Hornbull is," I suggested to the young trooper. "Is there somewhere in particular I need to be?"

"The Colonel would like to see you in the command room as soon as possible at your earliest convenience, sir," he barked.

"Right now is convenient for me, if it is convenient for the Colonel."

"Mr. Hornbull is entering the command room!" he shouted as he held the door for me.

I stepped past him into the command room surrounded by all the top brass of New Jersey State Police standing in a U-shaped formation with the colonel standing at the head of the U and Governor Chris Christie sitting behind him.

"I need you to convey a message to your leadership," barked the colonel pointing his finger at my chest. "The amateur hour is over! We need answers! How long have you been aware of the pre-landfall disaster declaration and what good does it do us to receive this at landfall? What pre-landfall actions are we supposed to take an hour after landfall based on this?"

"I was not aware until you just said so, Colonel," I responded in a calm tone.

"Well the clown show has got to end. You tell your leadership if they want to take this political we have a very large, very loud governor right here," as he gestured toward Governor Christie sitting behind him. "And he will take it to the airwaves as soon as it behooves us to do so."

"I'd be happy to relay your message Colonel," I replied. "Honestly I think it is about time you are speaking up."

"On second thought," interrupted the Colonel, "I don't want you to 'relay my message.' I want you to use every goddamn word, and I think you know exactly who to use it to!"

The Colonel's voice faded as my mind drifted out of the moment. It occurred to me that this was sure to be a seminal moment in an historic response operation that I was bound to relive in my mind for the rest of my life. Surely it would be laughed about, mostly behind my back and at my expense, but I knew eventually I would laugh too and the humor of the situation was tempting me toward a nervous snicker.

I excused myself and stepped out onto the steps in the front of the building.

"Hey Jeff, let me put you on speaker, I've got the deputy regional administrator and Nathan and Mike here," said Rick.

"Good, put me on speaker," I replied. "I've got a message the Colonel wanted me convey to leadership." "Good go ahead, we're listening," injected the deputy regional administrator. "What does New Jersey have to say?"

"Ok, the Colonel said: 'the amateur hour is over; the FUCKING clown show has got to end…'"

"Whoa, whoa, whoa," Rick interrupted. "Did he really drop the F-bomb?"

"No, Rick, I threw that in myself, you fucking ass clown," I retorted. "He also said that…"

"Uh wait a minute Jeff, uh," Rick stammered. "Maybe we should take this off line."

"No, the Colonel specifically said to use every goddamn word," I continued. "If you assholes want to make this political, he has a very large, very loud governor who can…"

"Wait, wait a minute. I need to explain to you," Rick interrupted.

"Oh, I'm sorry Rick. Is it your turn to talk?" I replied. "Go right ahead."

Bee-boop. And I hung up.

The day after landfall we had a video teleconference with FEMA Headquarters, New York and New Jersey. Unbeknownst to any of us beforehand, President Obama would be sitting next to FEMA Administrator Fugate.

At this time, New York City's subway system was flooded, its major hospitals half underwater; the New Jersey Shore was decimated and images of the destroyed beach communities and amusement park rides sticking out of the ocean were all over the national news. Rick stammered his way through every government-speak phrase of saying 'I have nothing to say for myself': "No limiting factors or unmet needs, nothing significant to report, no outstanding requests for assistance or shortfalls."

"Why the hell didn't you tell us the President was going to be on this conference?" The Colonel barked. "Don't you think our governor might have wanted to know that? I see New York's Governor was on the conference."

"I wasn't aware, Colonel or surely I would have…"

"Is that the ass-clown you've been dealing with

up there stammering like a fool?" the Colonel asked. We smiled.

This little conference call performance would be Rick's last as it was the cause of the premature end to his FEMA career. He escaped to a different job with another federal agency before the bureaucracy could catch up to him and fire him. He made it to retirement from the Department of Commerce three years later.

Sandy was a devastating and tragic incident – nothing could make up for that. The response went well all things considered. The New Jersey State troopers never did have to go all Mad Max on the Jersey Turnpike to get their response resources. The national and state responses simply steam-rolled right over the local FEMA regional office dysfunction. It was just FEMA's local regional office that took the black eye. And my blood pressure surely took several spikes into metric blood-pressure peso territory.

Bernard and Jay's predecessors, the regional administrator and deputy also resigned shortly after – opening the way for the Colonel to retire from New Jersey State Police and become Bernard, our new regional administrator. He was impressed in the end how I handled the difficult position Rick and the regional office had put me in and never held it against me that I was the face of FEMA dysfunction for those few contentious days and I in return respected him for his gracious understanding. But the rest of the higher-ups in the New Jersey State Police were not as understanding and my blood pressure was palpable every time I had occasion to return there.

Bernard stood up from the conference table and turned briefly toward the view of New York Harbor. He understood all too well the weight of the job stress of sending me to the New Jersey State Police emergency operations center in advance of a potentially serious storm.

"We're glad you're back, Jeffrey. We'll support you in whatever you feel comfortable doing. Take it at your own pace." Bernard and Jay gave warm smiles and left the room. I was shocked that they would ask this of me in the same breath as 'welcome back, we are here to support you.'

Nathan and I walked down the hall after the meeting. "I can't believe they would ask me to do that, the day I get back." I grumbled. "Bernard knows what I went through in Jersey.

"I just dropped dead of a heart attack a few weeks ago. Well okay, I didn't *actually* drop dead. And technically I didn't have a heart attack either, but close enough."

"Yeah, and he made you team lead for the great job you did."

"I did *not* do a great job. I only arguably did a good job *considering* the depth of the bullshit I was thrown into by Rick. I respect Bernard for recognizing that, but most of those jar-headed troopers don't."

"Rob Short is the Colonel of Jersey OEM now, he's alright," Nathan offered.

"Yeah, I worked with him in Joaquin last year. He's a good guy. He's not one of the screaming spittlers, anyway." I admitted.

"So, what's the big deal?" Nathan continued. "It's not even going to hit up here."

"That's what Rick said about Sandy." I said. "I'm just a little nervous about living on high-stress, no sleep and the deployment drive-thru-diet plan the week I come back from heart surgery. Besides, where the hell is Ashley?"

"She deployed to Florida," Nathan replied with a roll of his eyes.

"What the hell? She's supposed to be covering my team lead spot, isn't she?"

"Yeah, everybody's kind of ticked off and everybody knows it's a lot to ask of you," Nathan explained apologetically. "She didn't even tell us, she just arranged it with Region Four and made no arrangements to cover the team up here. A few days ago, we weren't even in the cone of uncertainty in the forecast."

"Well, now that it is missing Florida, is she coming back?"

"No, she redeployed to South Carolina," Nathan rolled his eyes again. "But it looks like that's where it will hit, now. New Jersey will just be hand holding for the State. Can you do it?"

"Yeah, alright." I grudgingly conceded.

The following day, Matthew had changed track again – the new forecast track headed up the East Coast and making a left hook smack at the center of New Jersey just as Sandy had done five years earlier.

"Dude, you got to get a team together," Nathan cried out as he swept toward my desk.

"Get a team together? My team is ready," visibly displaying my dismay and anxiety.

"No, we already deployed the A team to Florida and South Carolina so we had to pull most of your team to work New York and New York City."

"Bullshit! Get a team for New York and leave mine alone."

"Dude, Matthew is setting up like Sandy. We might get fucked."

"And you thought it would be a good idea for us to set up like we did in Sandy? Are you fucking kidding me? New York State gets a team, New York City gets a team, NJ gets me again and I get the metric Mexican peso blood pressure again, on my first week back from heart surgery. Are you *fucking* kidding me? Are you booking for the Department of Commerce early retirement plan with Rick?"

We spent the rest of the day and into the evening franticly engaging in the human flesh trade, trading team members like they were baseball cards: "I'll trade you my planning section chief for two logistics specialists."

The following day it was all moot, null and void, the forecast track took a quicker left hook than scheduled at South Carolina and the northeast only got the rainy remnants. The national response redirected, no convoys were headed toward us. A few people rushed out to deploy down south and things quickly died back down to something more closely resembling a run-of-the-mill, hum-drum government office. I found a quiet moment to plead with Nathan: "You have got to sort out the activation and deployment rosters without relying on me. I'll always help out in a pinch, and I didn't want to bring up my chest pains because the moment I have to be accommodated, I will be benched permanently. I don't want that by any means, I'm just not ready to get back into that crazy game just yet."

Nathan paused to gather his thoughts for a moment. "How about working on some bullshit project like the Green Initiative? You just have to document measures the regional office is taking to lessen our environmental impact, like weighing the recycle bins and shit. Bernard wants us to take first prize in the agency, it's his new thing."

"Well, I have perfected the art of composting my own bodily waste in Hornbullonia. I could give people lessons on how to do that in waste paper baskets under their desks. That ought to secure our Green Initiative victory."

"Sounds more like the brown initiative," Nathan cracked himself up.

"I just need to find a way to take it easy for a while."

## 33. Bills, Bills, Bills!!!

To the casual outside observer, my job would seem to be trying to kill me. But I may never be able to change jobs again. I will forever be beholden to my job for its quite-potentially life-saving federal-employee insurance. A long-lost college friend of mine, Mark, contacted me while I was recovering from surgery, he had just gone through a very similar ordeal and understandably had a lot of questions. But none of them were about health care, they were entirely about insurance, consumer protections and employee rights. Mark had the misfortune of starting a new job with a small company the same week he turned up in the emergency room. Can his employer drop his insurance? Can his insurance drop his coverage? Can he sue? Can the hospital refuse treatment? The short answer to all of the above is, of course, yes. But fortunately for me, I had no experience in any of that. I can't imagine being in the position I was in and also having to worry about all that. Mark didn't even have time to worry about his health, he was worried about bankrupting his family and losing his health care along with his employer-based health insurance.

With the exception of your congressional representative, I have the best health insurance in the country, and yet I get headaches and heart ache (literally) over medical bills. My medical bills had been piling up for months and I kept stuffing them in an accordion file to be dealt with later. I had learned over the years that although I should not have any co-pays or deductibles as long as I stay 'in-system,' but doctors, clinics and labs just send bills anyway and see who pays. I suppose it is simply easier to send me a bill than to argue with an insurance company. At first, I used to call and argue with them and they would send me a bill for half the amount, argue some more and get a bill for a quarter the amount. Sometimes this game would result in a bill for twenty-six dollars out of an original four-hundred. Sometimes I would pay it to make it go away, eventually I learned to ignore them, and they would figure it out with my insurance company and it would go away anyway. The process is a bureaucratic version of haggling at an Arab Bazar: "Please come in, sit on the carpet and have some apple chai, we will discuss the price of your surgery."

I decided to spare myself the anxiety of confronting the bills and just let them all argue with the insurance company for a few months and then see where I stood. I gave it about four months before I sat down and opened all the envelopes and began sorting them by biller. They all followed the same predicted pattern. A series of bills over time from each biller in decreasing amounts. Were they winning concessions from the insurance company over time? Or just settling for less? Seeing what they can get out of me? Throwing shit at the wall and seeing what sticks? A veritable phishing scam? Probably all of the above. If I set up an office and started sending out bills just to see how many people paid I would do some serious prison time for fraud. Why we tolerate this nonsense from our medical community is beyond me.

In easily over half the cases, I had no way of knowing at the time who was billing how much for what. Simply by going to the hospital I went to, I was in-system and should not have had to pay anything. But each individual doctor and individual laboratory has their own rules and agreements with insurance companies. I never at any point had any way of knowing which doctors would end up billing who for what or for how much, much less any way of knowing what lab my bodily fluid samples were being sent to and how much they charge who for what.

The underlying fallacy of our for-profit medical insurance and fee-for-services health-care system, the patient as discerning consumer, is a dangerous supposition. Without the discerning consumer, market forces do not work. They do not drive down prices if no one knows what anything costs or more especially if they don't care because their health or even their life is on the line. But more dangerously is that there is no accountability to the patient. In who's interest is it that you recover? There is no disincentive for bad outcomes.

Who is incentivized to simply cure the patient? The insurance company that has to shell out money to keep you alive? The doctor who gets paid more and more, the longer you need treatment? I am not suggesting that the people involved are amoral, I am merely suggesting that the problem with incentives is that they work.

If your health insurance doesn't cover preventative care it is because the bean-counters have calculated that they will save money if you simply, dutifully fuck off and die, therefore that is the preferred course of action. Such is how we live and die under a system (or lack thereof) of private, for-profit health insurance providers.

The fee-for-services health-care providers have the opposite problem: they simply don't know when to quit. They have no monetary incentive to slow the pace of tests, procedures and drugs and nobody is monitoring the long-term effect on the health of the patient. Will Dr. Surya ever have any idea about my long-term problems? He didn't even know about my post-surgical trauma beyond me coming back to him that one day. I suspect he saw I was still walking, declared the surgery a victory and went on to the next one. I asked Dr. Freeman if he ever called him to discuss my case. "How long do you think that conversation would have lasted?" he answered. "Hi, I've got your fucked-up patient and I was wondering… click."

My medical school professor father once described his end-of-life wishes as follows: "I'm going to disappear to a Caribbean island one day. Don't hunt me down and try to drag me back, I don't want to spend my final days being pointlessly tortured to death in a hospital."

I wasn't raised with a whole-lot of faith in the medical-industrial complex.

**

As a federal employee I have a lot to be thankful for: job security, comprehensive insurance, flexible work schedule and, most importantly, a culture of trying to do everything we can to make the system work for a sick employee. But in the American system (or lack thereof), even with all the advantages I have, I fall

victim to the same underlying inefficiencies and
amoralities.

I can lose my job for being out sick for too long
and my medical insurance would disappear with it. A
for-profit health insurance industry has no incentive to
insure the ill, or to continue to provide coverage to
anyone once they fall ill. As I learned watching over my
dying friend Shakey, we can keep anyone who is not in
too many pieces 'alive' indefinitely. All our lives will
end with a discussion of whether insurance will pay for
continued care as our loved ones and doctors debate
whether to pull the plug.

America fears single-payer insurance and
socialized medical care because they, very rightfully,
fear the financial bean counters taking over the medical
decision-making process. What we fail to realize is that
that is exactly what our for-profit insurance and fee-for-
service medical care systems is: the sly fox bean-
counters ruling the roost in the medical hen house.

I am not an ideologue. I couldn't care less about
a single-payer system, socialized medical care, free
markets or private insurance. I care that sick people can
get to the doctor. It is a moral question. We should be
arguing over how to best provide health care, not
whether to provide health care. And we certainly should
not allow public or private insurance provider bean-
counters to dictate public health-care policy or
individual medical treatments – or cessation thereof.
Our national discourse on health care has been
dominated by a discourse on insurance policy bean-
counting. Just count the beans and butt out.

Our angry and ideologically-loaded national discourse prevents us from discussing the straight-forward pragmatic questions of how to get care to the sick, how to keep it affordable, how to keep medical decisions confined to medical professionals and their patients and loved ones. Our national discussion of healthcare (and anything else) is ideologically-loaded, angry and dominated by gas-lighting trolls (both witting and unwitting) for a reason: the conversation is defined by those who benefit from the status quo. Those who benefit from the status quo benefit from stifling change and change is stifled by stifling any meaningful, thoughtful or even rational discussion – enter the gas-lighting angry trolls pulling the hood over the eyes, ears and mouth of our national discourse.

I found a letter in among my heaps of bills with a header: 'Urgent: action required to ensure continuation of your care.' It referenced procedures I had undergone at a clinic I had visited. The letter was from a lobbying group representing the insurance industry urging me to call the clinic and its affiliated hospital and urge them to meet a particular group of insurers' demands on a new contract. Really? What am I a volunteer lobbyist for the insurance industry? My civic duty for today is going to be calling my healthcare provider and shaming them for their cruel unfairness in not giving Kaiser Permanente a bigger slice of the ever-mushrooming health care-industry pie? Is my insurance company trolling me?

The trolls have actually given us one answer to the biggest question facing health-care reform today: how to pay for it. The answer is now obvious: Donald Trump will talk Mexico into paying for it. If he can talk them into paying to barricade themselves inside their own 'shithole' country, surely he can talk them into paying to make the grass a little greener on the other side of the wall.

I am not attached to any one solution to our health care crisis. But I do know that in order to find the one that works for America we need to think collectively rather than individualistically. It won't be solved for any of us if we are each looking out for number one. The only ones who benefit from that are those who benefit from the status quo – and that ain't me or you.

There used to be an expression: "Hey, I'm not just doing this for my health, you know." It meant a task was not fickle and self-absorbed or useless folly, it has some purpose. Doing something for one's health has taken on a greater importance nowadays, a sense of self-importance expressed with a certain indignation of self-absorption. The reason that expression no longer makes sense in the modern world is that doing something for one's own benefit is paramount to doing something for some greater purpose.

The greater purpose of our times is this: to enter into the national discourse and into each political discussion with a determination to *not* try to win an argument. In so trying, you are taking the trolling bait, sinking to their level and generally making an ass of yourself. Thwart confrontation by showing understanding of others' points of view and never mind the damn trolls, just make sure you don't become one yourself.

## 34. Election Night

Nichole hurried me in a flustered panic to make it on time to meet my parents for my birthday dinner. She rushed me out of the house, down Second Avenue to the Writing Room, a casually swanky East Side restaurant that replaced Elaine's when it closed.

"Why don't we get a drink at the bar," I suggested as I took a breath. "They're probably waiting in there for us before they sit anyway."

"No, they said they booked a table in the back room. It's five minutes to six already. Let's go find them." Nichole hurried me through the tables, sloluming through the diners into the back room. "Let's not keep them waiting, we're almost late."

"Alright already, Rainman! What's the hurry? What is it five minutes to Judge Wapner?"

"*SURPRISE!!!*" shouted about fifty of our family and closest friends as we entered the room.

I took a step back and my jaw dropped. "Alright, you got me," I conceded, chuckling and embarrassed. "But didn't anyone warn you about throwing a surprise party for a guy with a cardiac condition? What are you trying to give me another heart attack?"

"*SPEECH!!!*" The room delighted in the success of their clandestine surprise party operation. I raised my hands in surrender until the room fell quiet. I paused to gather some thoughts.

"Most people fear and dread turning fifty. I had the misfortune of nearly not turning fifty this year and the good fortune to be eternally grateful for the good fortune to turn fifty. I hope Nichole and I will turn sixty and seventy and ninety, a hundred and more together. I think that sounds great, and I hope you do too. I nearly got choked up and didn't want to ruin the moment, so I pivoted to some humor. "Somebody else was happy to learn I am turning fifty," I held up the AARP card that came in the mail earlier the same week.

"I don't know how the AARP found me, but I think I figured out how the CIA found Osama bin Laden: they told the AARP he was turning fifty next week – they found his ass, and his address." The humor pivot worked. The crowd laughed and the mood turned back to cheerful. "And I would like to take this opportunity to announce another victory over tyranny and evil. As all of you here are aware, the fair people of Hornbullonia and Nicholopolis have lived in fear and loathing of the dreaded Shah of Assholistan for the last several years. He has threatened and bullied us, trying to extort unreasonably inflated sums to buy him out. I am honored to announce that, unbeknownst to him and unbeknownst to the Grand Duchess of Nicholopolis, I entered into secret negotiations, with a lawyer anonymously representing us, to buy Assholistan at a fair market price right out from under his wrinkly old ass. So on my birthday, I have a gift for you Grand Duchess: the proverbial head of the Shah of Assholistan on a proverbial platter." I bent on one knee, head tucked down in reverence and one arm extended upward holding the imagined silver platter. The crowd went wild. The staff looked really, really confused.

"*DEATH TO ASSHOLISTAN!!!*" the crowd roared. "*LONG LIVE THE GRAND DUCHESS!!! ALL HAIL THE EMPEROR!!!*" the crowd roared again, Mook jumped in the air pumping both fists over his head, Nichole laughed with tears of joy and hugged me tightly.

"Would anyone care to guess what all this dieting and sobriety can go do with itself tonight?" I continued. "Forgive me bartender for I have sinned. It has been four months since my last libation. For my penance I shall have two Bloody Mary's and four our-vodkas and all will be forgiven."

I was beginning to see my mid-life crisis not be a crisis at all but a celebration. A celebration of putting behind me the fear of the future I had in my youth – the fear that I will never fulfill my arrogant lofty ambitions. Put behind me the anxiety of having no money or power over my life or to control my destiny.

In my mid-life I took responsibility, a lot of responsibilities. I could easily have become overwhelmed with all the responsibilities of work, family, parents, health and bills and a suddenly tangible amount of time left in my life. Mid-life has money and no time – it lies between the arrogant ambition of my carefree youth and cruise control toward retirement.

Mid-life is when I learned to come to terms with the reality of my situation and assume most of the responsibility of my life. For most people, it is a convergence of growing children, aging parents and the acme of careers. I learned I need to be cognizant of this, understanding of my family and friends in similar positions and careful not to let personal relationships fall by the wayside and make sure I find time for them. Mid-life is a time to find a path to living a full life. And in light of all I had been through, I wanted to do get on with life and do some living – some living off the wagon, that is. I gave myself a one-night reprieve for my birthday with the promise of some occasional moderate indulgences to come.

My alcohol tolerance had dropped to the point that having a few beers actually meant only having a few beers – four if I remember correctly – but there will never be anything like that first beer in four months. Aaaaaah.

**

A couple weeks later, I decided to give myself another experimental one-night reprieve from the wagon and agreed to meet Wally and the Beave to watch the presidential election results come in down at Reif's. Wally and the Beave wanted to try the Three Little Piggies Barbeque that opened around the corner that everyone was talking about. But I was on the heart-healthy dieting straight and narrow, so I had a healthy dinner at home with Nichole and met up with them later.

Big Hans, Snake and a couple of the iron-worker union guys were finishing up a card game at one corner of the bar. A petite man we all called Tiny Timmy sipped a cocktail next to them. Wally and the Beave had spread their jackets and purses across a few stools to stake a claim to some bar-front real estate in the opposite corner.

"Ladies," I greeted them as I came in to the bar. "How was the Three Little Piggies? As good as they say?"

"Pretty good, and it definitely makes for a good tummy-lining drinking base," replied Wally. "And I am in the mood to celebrate."

Wally wasn't normally that vocally political, but she does have a feminist streak in her in a girl-power kind of way and she was in the mood to celebrate the election of the first woman president of the United States.

"This is going to be an historic night," she declared with a raised fist of feminist power. "I can't believe we are going to witness the first woman elected president of the United States. I was really beginning to think I would never live to see it. This calls for a shot."

I grimaced "Alright, but take it easy on me Wally, I'm really out of practice. Between my reduced presence in the bar and my improved posture, my elbow callouses have faded away, and my alcohol tolerance ain't what it used to be. Nichole made me promise I wouldn't drink as much as you."

"Fair enough," she declared raising her shot glass of Jameson over her head. "To history!"

"To *her*story!" countered the Beave and gave us each one of her signature dainty high fives. They threw their Jameson down their throats and slammed their shot glasses on the bar. I took a small sip and gently slid mine behind my beer for safe keeping for the next round.

"Oh my God, is this really going to happen?" asked Wally leaning on the edge of her barstool staring up at the television.

"Yeah, unless Trump wins every swing state plus one non-swing state," I replied confidently. "He can't win North Carolina, much less Pennsylvania."

"Is Trump really ahead in Wisconsin?" asked the Beave.

"That doesn't mean anything," I said. "There's still hardly any precincts reporting. It doesn't mean anything yet."

"And look, Hillary won New Hampshire," the Beave said, giving another round of group dainty high fives.

Snake swaggered out of the women's room and paused behind Wally and the Beave to glance up at the election coverage.

"Fuckin' crooked Hillary," slurred Snake. "This country's going to hell in a hand basket." The iron-worker crew nodded and scowled.

"You can't handle a woman in the White House Snake?" Wally said, scowling back at Snake.

"It ain't me. This country's fighting back. They don't like the way we're going."

"Don't like what? A woman in a position of

power?" Wally swiveled her bar stool to face Snake.

"You see the bathrooms?" asked Snake. "There's man-woman signs on both of them, now. For what? So, some tranny can piss anywhere he wants?"

"Yeah, did you see the new signs?" I asked Wally. "The new city law, no gender designation on single-occupancy bathrooms."

"Well what are you worried about Snake?" asked Wally. "Now you can beat the shit out of yourself in any bathroom you want."

"I guess now I'm allowed to shit in the women's room," Snake smirked and folded his arms.

"No," snapped Wally, "it does not mean that."

"Hey, my body, my choice," Snake retorted. "I'm just sayin' the country's not ready for this. I know she ain't gonna lose, but I didn't vote for her."

"What? You voted for that misogynistic con artist?" Wally stood up with her hands on her hips, her jaw agape.

"Let him be, Wally," I interjected. "He's wasted, angry and Kumbaya is not in his repertoire."

"BARACK OBAMA!!!" Big Hans let out in a loud burp.

"Are you rooting for him, Hans?" asked the Beave laughing. "You know he's not running tonight, right?"

"Can't we all agree on one thing in these divisive times?" Big Hans walked towards Wally and Snake with his arms raised in peace, "that Barack Obama has the most burpable name in history – or at least the most burpable name since Ali Baba."

"You seem to have a fair bipartisan point there Hans," said Wally with a raised glass.

"BARACK OBAMA!!!" Hans belched and raised his glass back at her.

"I'll buy a round of drinks if anyone can burp 'Barack Obama's Pajama's'" Hans waived one finger in the air.

"Bara…" attempted the Beave with a titter.

"BARACK OBAMA'S PAJAMAS!!!" Snake belched out.

"Another round of shots!" Big Hans proclaimed. "You too Jeff. Finish that up you got another one coming."

"Alright, but a second one for Wally on me, please. Nichole made me promise not to drink as much as her."

"Hell, if it makes you feel better and you're buyin'," laughed Wally as she knocked back her shots back to back.

"They're saying Trump won Ohio," the Beave said with concern.

"Yeah but Hillary's got Virginia," I retorted. "So, he didn't get all the swing states, he's fucked."

"Oh my God, they're calling Wisconsin and Michigan for Trump," observed Wally her voice cracking.

"It's ok, Hillary got Illinois," The Beave tried to reassure her with one of her little tiny high fives.

Wally obliged her with a token high five and turned to me teary-eyed. "Oh my God, if she gives me one more high-five, I'm going to plant one right on her forehead."

A pit of nausea began to grow in my stomach as the realization sank in. Soon that pit spread across the bar, onto the TV screen and across the nation. But for me it was different. As much as I disliked and disagreed with Trump's politics, there was a big difference for me between what I didn't like and what scared me. The possibility of a Trump victory entered a whole new realm for me. I had a front row seat to the resurgence of despotism that grew out of the ashes of hope in eastern Europe following the collapse of Communism. I had seen the playbook before: denigrating the media to justify false narratives, delegitimizing and even criminalizing his political opposition, disregard for the rule of law, confusing the difference between the nations interests and his own. Trump had shown all these signs in the 2016 campaign with his cries of 'fake news' and 'lock her up,' his call for foreign election interference and his continual profiteering. But I had never really considered that he might actually win, that it actually could happen here. For all our peace and prosperity, Americans had become quaintly naive to the hazards such demagoguery could pose to a nation. Political issues as Americans knew them paled in comparison to the threats this kind of behavior posed to democracy. For every institution he denigrated, every norm he shattered would put American democracy another step down a path toward demagoguery. Our national political discourse and so-called culture wars suddenly seemed so trite. And the events of the night became frighteningly sobering.

"Can I get a shot for me and two for Wally?" I asked. "It's going to be a rough night, Wally. I'm going to need to get you really shit-faced."

"You got it," she replied pushing her empty shot glass toward the bartender, her head hanging low. "Happy to oblige."

"Sorry Wally, I didn't want the dumb fuck to win, I just wanted that bitch to lose." Snake tried to console.

"That's it, isn't it?" said Wally. "This country just can't handle a powerful, successful woman. A strong woman is a bitch. They think she's a bitch? Imagine if she acted like him. This country just regressed 50 years backwards in the progress we have made."

"Imagine how fast our rights are going to backslide in the LGBT community," lamented Tiny Timmy, a petite man with the wind taken out of his normally peppy sails.

"Sorry for your loss," Snake offered. "Let me buy you a consolation drink."

"No thank you," Tiny Timmy snapped. "I'm going home. I don't exactly feel like celebrating right now."

"C'mon, don't be such a homo," Snake said.

"*What* did you just call me?!" Timmy barked.

"What? I didn't mean nothing, I'm just trying to buy you a drink," Snake stepped back, the iron-worker crew raised their hands as if to surrender.

"Yeah, he's just trying to buy you a drink because you're our friend," One of the iron workers said apologetically.

"I'm your *homo* friend? No thanks, I'm outta here." Timmy gather his money of the bar and his jacket off of the back of his barstool.

"What? I didn't say there was anything wrong with being homo," Snake backpedaled faster. "I even always said I wouldn't kick Mick Jagger out of my bed for eating crackers."

"Mick Jagger? Gross!" Timmy snapped. "The man's mouth looks like a screaming vagina. Ew! You're a homophobic bigot and you have no taste in men," Timmy scampered out hurriedly threading his arms through his coat sleeves, his nose in the air in contempt.

"And I'll buy my own drinks, thanks," Wally

slurred in defiance.

"I don't think more alcohol is the answer," the Beave diplomatically suggested.

"More alcohol is never the answer," Wally replied. "More alcohol is the question. 'Yes' is the answer."

Wally continued to make good on my promise not to get as drunk as her for the next hour or so until that wave of nausea sweeping across the nation hit the west coast, sloshed back across the continent and the broke right on top of her head. She slid off her barstool and knocked it over backwards and plopped onto the floor in an upright sitting position.

"I think…" she paused to hiccup, "I'm going to throw up,".

"Oh, I've got a scrunchy for your hair," Said the Beave, rifling through her purse.

I held Wally by the arm and led her towards the bathrooms as the Beave trailed behind holding out her scrunchy.

"Look on the bright side, Wally," Snake shouted after us. "You can puke in whichever toilet you want now. That's progress."

I stood behind Wally as she knelt over the toilet and the Beave stood in the doorway holding her pony tail up in the air as Wally retched up her dinner into the toilet.

"So, I see you had the bar-b-que beans at Three Little Piggies tonight, huh Wally?" I observed. "How was that?"

"Better going down, I hope," the Beave chuckled.

"Is that pulled pork I see?" I continued, giving the Beave a wry smile.

"Fuck you both" Wally sputtered raspily as she coughed and gagged.

"Hey what's going on in here, I got to use the bathroom" Snake interrupted loudly. "What the hell are you doing? Performing an exorcism on Wally?"

Snake shook his beer bottle at us spreading a few dashes of beer: "The power of Christ compels you! The power of Christ compels you!"

"Your mother sucks cocks in hell, Snake!" Blurted Wally in a gravelly, barf-throated voice, before she retched one final time.

The Beave and I each held an elbow as we slowly walked a weaving Wally out of the bar. Snake, Hans and two other construction workers were laughing and chanting at the bartender: "Four more beers! Four more beers!"

"Is Dan home?" asked the Beave gently as we walked Wally home around the corner.

"He went to watch the election at Johnny's," she replied tearily.

But Dan had left Johnny's some time before to wander the streets stoned, drunk and despondent screaming "FUCK TRUMP!" at the top of his lungs. He was at the apartment building entrance, red-eyed and haggard, with his keys drooping out of his hand as we came around the corner. Wally broke loose and ran to Dan for a hug. Dan-Dan cried in each other's arms.

Dan-Dan held each other as they walked abreast through the door. Wally sighed: "Just wake me up when America is great again."

I walked back around the corner with the Beave.

"Well, you managed to not drink more than Wally," said the Beave, thankful that she didn't have the two of us to contend with in that state.

"Nichole will be so proud," I replied

"So, are you going back on the wagon again after this?" she asked.

"Oh, I think maybe tonight's events call for extending my little one-night hiatus from my hiatus for, I dunno, another four years or so." For better or for worse, getting on with life was going to mean getting back to drinking. Kept in any semblance of control and moderation, it would be for the better for enjoying life, and for the worse for a coping mechanism with potential to spiral out of control. But such is life.

## 35. Third-World Subsistence Farmer

Dr. Freeman greeted me with an enthusiastic rave review from the lab: "I got your blood work back– fantastic. You've got the cholesterol level of a third world subsistence farmer." He said smiling, his eyes open wide and his eyebrows raised.

"Great," I replied, "What's the life expectancy of a third world subsistence farmer?"

"Well, they have a different mortality structure influenced by infectious diseases. That's not the right comparison," he said. "I just mean to say you are burning off fat and cholesterol as fast as you consume it before it can build up in your blood stream."

"I know, I get it. I was just joking. I understand demographic mortality structures. That was my graduate dissertation."

"Really? What was it about?"

"Declining life expectancy in Hungary," I answered

Hungary was the only country in the world at that time without a war or famine that had a declining life expectancy. Not true anymore, now they have been joined by everyone else in Eastern Europe. The causes of death were all life-style related: Lung cancer, liver cirrhosis, heart disease. And they were related to other statistics oddly unique for such a small country. At one point or another in my 30-year study period from the sixties to the nineties Hungary had the highest per capita consumption of tobacco, alcohol and fat. They had the highest divorce rate, the highest accidental death rate, highest suicide rate. In short, unhealthy lifestyles and indicators of stress.

And they weren't just any indicators of any old unhealthy lifestyle, they were indicators of my unhealthy lifestyle. It was palpable to any Western foreigner who set foot in Hungary in that time. Long before I knew the statistics, the prolific cloud of cigarette smoke, the ubiquitous drinking and the diet of pig fat were shocking. They eat little cubes of raw pig fat for breakfast over there – they call it *szalonna*. It sounds so classy, like a finger food in a pig fat salon.

I ate it all the time. I considered it a symbol of my cultural immersion. And when I was in graduate school in England, I worked on a World Health Organization project pairing English health authorities with Hungarian ones to advise on public health strategies. When I brought a group of NHS health officials on a tour of Hungary, every single public health authority office, every single hospital, greeted them with a silver platter of god-awful Hungarian cigarettes and shots of home-made weapons-grade moonshine and fed them pig fat, salted, dried, pickled or just straight-up raw, weapons-grade pig fat. The English doctors couldn't believe it. They didn't want to be rude, so they got shit-faced and ate pig fat at every meeting. One of them started smoking again for the first time in ten years. I was worried I wouldn't return them all to England alive.

It was a topical issue in the news at the time when I lived in Hungary. And it dawned on me that I was a walking, living laboratory conducting a long-term multi-decadal study of whether a foreigner living a Hungarian lifestyle would fall victim to the same risk factors.

At the time, I firmly believed nothing I did in my twenties would kill me in my fifties. I mean, as frightening as the statistics were, the deaths increased beginning age 40 and not really taking off until after 50. That's why I quit smoking at age 39 after 19 pack years: I thought I was in the clear. I still don't know if those years had an effect on my fate or not. I mean, if it was the lifestyle factors that led to my near-demise, of the thirty years between the ages of twenty and fifty, was it the fifteen years in which I smoked, ate like a Hungarian, drank like a Hungarian, occasionally delved into cocaine and grew terribly out of shape? Or was it the fifteen years immediately preceding my near-demise in which I quit smoking, started exercising, drank less and ate healthier? It's starting to look like it was the first fifteen years came back to haunt me.

And now that I look back at it, I was showing some subtle early symptoms back then, twenty years before they all came crashing down around me. My psychiatrist friend, Agi, took me to a cardiologist. I after I had complained to her about trouble sleeping because of breathing problems and some irregular heartbeats, like my heart was skipping and starting again with a chest-thumping ker-thump.

In fine Hungarian fashion, the Hungarian

cardiologist had a cigarette dangling out of his mouth while he read the EKG and said: "I think I see of what you are complaining of, but I think it is just from smoking."

"Just from smoking?" I balked. "Smoking just kills half a million people a year in my country, what the hell does it do in yours?"

"I think it is nothing," he answered dismissively. "But if it worries you, quit smoking and quit caffeine and I think it will to go away."

I quit caffeine and in fact it did mostly go away, so I figured he was right that it was nothing and procrastinated quitting smoking for another ten years. The ungodly amounts of caffeine I was consuming was having a bigger effect on me than I had realized. I had been drinking a dozen double Hungarian weapons-grade espressos a day. At first, I only wanted to cut down but the more I cut down, and the more my caffeine tolerance dropped, the worse the hype-ups and crash-downs got. I realized I was drinking so much because I was susceptible to crashing after the buzz wore off and I'd want another and crash harder and want two more and so on. The reverse happened when I started cutting down, I could handle less and less until I quit altogether. I just couldn't handle it anymore. Now the only caffeine I ever consume is a sip of my wife's diet Pepsi when I'm driving tired and that's enough to get me wired. Once I quit caffeine altogether most of the symptoms went away, but some residual ones stayed and only disappeared after the surgery.

Doctor Freeman listened to all this intently

leaning forward across his desk, never losing his penetrating eye contact. I had mentioned my youthful lifestyle indiscretions before, but I have a tendency for understatements, and he was only now realizing he had underestimated what I meant by 'I drink but not like I used to.' And even though I had quit smoking ten years earlier and caffeine twenty years earlier, these still could be contributing factors.

"Could I have been picking up on early warning signs twenty years before it came to a head?" I asked him.

"I suppose it could. What was the conclusion of your dissertation?" Doctor Freeman asked.

"Fat, drunk and Hungarian is no way to go through life." I answered.

## 36. Winter Solstice

The ever-darkening days of late Autumn had a terrible effect on my mood and state of mind. I took advantage of a telework day on a sunny day to take a walk in the park and keep my FitBit happy, followed by a lunch date with the ladies who lunch. We met at the Hummus House, an Israeli Mediterranean restaurant full of delicious and nutritious vegan options for my heart-healthy diet.

"Do we have to eat here?" the Beave whined. "Why can't we go to Three Little Piggies?"

"My cardiologist would have a heart attack if I ate at Three Little Piggies. I mean, I'm not a picky eater, by any stretch, sometimes I salivate over the thought of bacon grease coursing through my veins, but my cardiologist is the pickiest mother fucker you ever want to meet."

"Your cardiologist will never know, it'll be our little secret," the Beave briefly clutched my fingers and promised.

"He'll know. He makes me wear this ankle bracelet that alerts the authorities any time I enter a bar-b-que joint and it delivers a sharp electric shock if I go through a drive-thru or come within fifty yards of a Waffle House. Besides, one mis-step and my weight loss could do an about face and start heading upwards again, one pork rib and I could go back to hyper-inflationary cholesterol, one beer too many and my beer belly could re-inflate like an air bag: POOF!" I puffed my cheeks and held my hands out in front of my belly

"Can I take your order?" the waitress interrupted.

"What can I eat here?" the Beave complained.

"How about the eggplant stuffed with quinoa," Wally suggested.

"Fine," the Beave said.

"I'll have the babaganoush and the roasted cauliflower," Wally requested.

"Mushroom hummus and a whole-wheat pita for me, please."

"But you know you would rather have some bar-b-que," the Beave huffed.

I guiltily looked down and sighed shamefully admitting she was right. "Bar-b-que was an important part of my life before my cardiologist was an important part of my life, but I can't eat it. I could order some just to throw it on the floor and roll around in it like a pig, but I can't eat it."

"Good for you, Jeff," Wally shot a glare at the Beave in my defense. "Your efforts show, you've lost so much weight, I didn't recognize you when you came in. I've lost weight too, if you haven't noticed." Wally did a half turn in her seat with her arms raised.

"Are you keeping up with your FitBit's daily needs?" I asked.

"That, and I found the silver lining to Donald

Trump being elected. I was so sick with stress for weeks afterward, I couldn't eat. I was so upset, I couldn't drink alcohol. I think Trump being elected lost me ten pounds."

"Great," said the Beave rolling her eyes. "Run to the scales and rejoice, America! Can we elect Trump again after the holidays? I could lose another ten myself."

"It takes more than that if you want to get *this* sexy," I sat up straight gesturing at my flat belly with both hands. "You have to treat your body like a temple."

"I treat my body like a temple," the Beave ran her hands down her sides. "A Satanic temple of debaucherous indulgences, perhaps, but a sort of temple."

"How about getting a FitBit," I held up my arm and pulled my sleeve back. "I got my 10,000 steps in walking around the park before lunch today."

"So, this is a telework day?" asked Wally skeptically. "A walk in the park and being a lady who lunches? Where does the 'work' part fit into this 'telework' of yours, anyway?"

"Sounds like a 'tell-em-you're-working' day, to me," the Beave laughed.

"Well, I'm so sorry you are so dissatisfied with my job performance, ladies. But I did get my shit done today, some at home this morning, some on my e-mail and phone while walking around the park, but the shit is done all the same and I don't think the rest of it is of any concern of yours, my boss or the American taxpayer for that matter. Besides, this is *medical* telework and it is important for my state of health and mind to get out and about during these limited daylight hours."

"The winter solstice is coming up, you know," said Wally with a wry smile. "You're going to have to have that surgery again so we don't all get plunged into eternal darkness,"

"I think I did my part," I retorted. "Somebody else's turn to step up this solstice."

"Maybe we can fuck a virgin and throw her into a volcano instead," the Beave whispered, glancing over her shoulder to make sure nobody was eavesdropping.

"Yeah, you," Wally laughed. "When was the last time you granted the penile member admittance into that exclusive club of yours, anyway?"

"Not so long that my virginity grew back, thanks," the Beave scowled at Wally.

"Well you did say your body is a Satanic temple," I added. "Princess of Darkness? I think you might be just what the volcano ordered."

We all fell silent and innocently looked down at our food as the waitress approached. "How was everything?" she asked cheerily.

"Just wonderful," I answered enthusiastically as

Wally nodded and the Beave grimaced.

"Yeah, he loved his hummus so much, we think he might be a hummus-sexual," the Beave quipped.

"Not that there's anything wrong with being sexually attracted to one's hummus," I said. "I don't ask what you do with your filthy piggy parts, don't pass judgement on me and my hummus."

"Don't ask, don't tell. Please," the waitress said as she slapped the desert menu on the table. I picked it up and gave it a guilty glance.

"Jeffrey, don't tell me you're going to set back your progress by looking at the dessert menu?" Wally scolded.

"Certainly not, there are no calories in just looking. Hell, I can have one of everything if I'm just looking. Besides, I can imagine any dessert being so much better than it could actually be, so I just meditate on each one for a moment and move on. It's my zero-calorie Zen dessert diet."

"Having anything for dessert?" the waitress interjected.

"I've got to try the vegan pudding," I said, slapping the menu on the table like I was folding a poker hand. "I simply can't imagine how good that must be. It's dairy free, right? Is it almond milk based?"

"I'm not sure, are you vegan? Do you have any allergies?" the waitress asked.

"I just have an allergy to math. Just bring the pudding and let me meditate to my Zen pudding fantasy."

"Do you need to be alone with your pudding?" the Beave asked. "I'm totally telling on you to Nichole."

"Nichole knows all about me and my vegan pudding affair. Besides, I watch out for my heart health and the pounds will follow. There is nothing heart-unhealthy about my vegan pudding, and I can indulge in a bit of sugar now and then if I want to."

"How much weight have you lost anyway?" Wally's enquiring mind wanted to know.

"Over sixty pounds," I replied. "Maybe over seventy by now, it's a little hard to tell by the bathroom scale. It's prone to telling me sweet little lies. I thought I had hit the seventy-five-pound mark until the cardiologist burst my bubble last month with his calibrated medical scale. I have come to discover that I can get my weight to vary by up to twenty-five pounds by moving it around on the bathroom floor and leaning my weight backwards or forwards on the scale."

"Wow, where can I get a scale like that?" the Beave asked. "My scale doesn't tell me sweet little lies, it hurls vitriolic insults at me. Last week it made me cry." She pouted her lips.

"I need a scale like that," said Wally. "Attacking my self-esteem is the only way to motivate me. It doesn't even have to give me a number of pounds, it could just make farm animal noises like a Fisher-Price toy: 'You are a fat cow. You say, MOOOooooo.' 'You look like a pig. You say, WEEEeeee, weeee, weeee.'"

"And you lost all this weight by eating a vegan-pudding-inclusive diet?" asked Wally skeptically.

"No, I can get away with dietary murder with the amount of exercise I'm getting lately. Ten thousand steps most days and I'm Citi-biking to work almost every day. Now that I'm not squeezing my circulatory system through the width of a human hair, I can just shovel the fat into my metabolic furnace like coal into a steam engine. My only limiting factor is my baboon-injured knee." I glared at Wally.

"Don't try to pin that baboon injury on me," sniped Wally. "You're going to get a worse injury than that riding a Citi Bike in the dark at rush hour now that the days are so short."

"I can't be missed in my Citi Bike get-up," I replied" My helmet has so many reflectors it looks like I have a disco ball on my head, and I've got all these little clip-on flashing LED lights. I look like the Electric Horseman."

"Well, I hope you're careful, not like one of those crazy cyclists you see weaving through traffic and blowing through red lights," Wally scolded.

"Sometimes skipping red lights is safer than vying with the turning cars. And sometimes you simply have to take a leap of balls with the traffic," I explained.

"A leap of balls?" the Wally asked her head quivering and the Beave looking up from behind her coffee cup.

"It's a phrase I added to the English lexicon when I consented to my surgery. It's like a leap of faith but without the confidence it will all come out alright. Nobody gets out of your way because you look like you have faith that everything will be fine. People get out of your way when they see you have the balls to cut them off even if it kills you. 'Whoa, look out for that guy, he's taking a real leap of balls!'"

"Of course, sometimes your balls leap out in front of a Mack truck," Wally retorted.

"I'm not as worried about the physical danger as much as I am that the stress is negating any health benefits of the exercise," I replied. "I can't believe the controversy and animosity in this city over people riding bicycles. It's all you anti bike-ites walking out in front of me staring at their phone with ear buds in and then yelling at me that get me all riled up. I ring my dingy bell at those mother fuckers."

"Your dingy bell?" the Beave giggled.

"Some people take serious offence to the dingy bell, I don't know what they think it means, to me it means: 'ahem' or 'please be careful. But some people are like: 'what's your fucking problem?' I tell people sometimes: 'That was just a warning shot. This bike comes equipped with a dingy bell for a reason and I'm not afraid to use it. I'll riddle your ear drums with a salvo of ringy-dingy-pingies you won't fucking believe, man.'

"You really think people are that afraid of your dingy bell?" Wally asked.

"Some jerks get downright confrontational about a simple dingy bell ping: 'Who the fuck you dinging at?' And I say:

'Do not ask for whom the dingy bell pings;

It pings for those we cannot see;

Not like a ghost or spirit, you see;

more like a guy behind a lamppost or a tree.'

"That always makes a quick ending to any dingy bell confrontation. It gets the toughest New York City goombah sidling away from me really quick."

"You can't control your environment on busy New York streets with a dingy bell."

"I'm telling you, the dingy bell commands attention," I insisted. "I was thinking of bringing it to work and dinging it in meetings when I want to get everyone's attention, like a paralyzed stroke victim communicating all his thoughts and needs with a dingy bicycle bell on his wheel chair.

"I'm sure you are not one of those crazy reckless bicyclists," Wally said. "And I am not one of your confrontational clueless pedestrians. I look where I am going and cross carefully and some of those bikers…"

"Oh, you people are even worse," I cut Wally off. "The last thing I need is some fine, upstanding, law-abiding asshole getting in my way when I'm taking a serious leap of balls to evade some Kamikaze cab driver."

"You know who's the worst?" I asked. "The little old poodle-walking ladies in Central Park off Fifth Avenue. They're all millionaires who donate to the Central Park Conservancy and think they own the park. I cut through one little corner of path to get to the Park Drive and they yell at me every morning: 'You have to walk your bike on the path! Can't you read the sign?'

"Yeah, I read the sign. I read the fine print on the bottom that says Central Park Conservancy. They don't make laws, they make suggestions. The ones that say New York City on them say: 'Cyclists must yield to pedestrians.' Thanks for the suggestion, but I got to get to work. One of them said: 'Maybe you're too young to remember Central Park before the Conservancy took over operation, but you have a lot to thank the Conservancy for.' But yeah, I do. I remember when we could do all kinds of things in the park other than walk a poodle, like playing football when I was a kid, I remember when families in Harlem would have large family picnics and cook-outs, the Latin Americans and Europeans would play soccer, I remember as a teenager I could drink beer and smoke pot in the park, and I remember in college I sold beer in the park and now I can't do any of those things and now you're telling me I can't even ride a bike to work through the park? The Conservancy has really made the park into a great place to walk a poodle and everyone else can get the hell out.

Thanks for nothing."

"You don't really yell at the little old ladies?" Wally balked like she was going to put me over her knee and give me a good spanking.

"No, my mother raised far too polite a young man to yell at little old ladies in the park, Wally," I assured her. "When one of the poodle walkers says: 'You have to walk your bike,' I just politely say: 'at least I don't have to pick up its poop,' and keep riding."

The stress of being yelled at by confrontational sanctimonious little-old-lady poodle-walkers in the park and anti-bikite goombahs on street corners was really sucking the joy and possibly the cardio health benefits out of my bike riding. One day, I was cutting a corner through Central Park heading south toward the midtown skyline against the flow of the jogger and bicycle traffic. A group of Japanese joggers was running north and yelled at me: "wrong way!" I wanted to yell back: "What's wrong? Is Godzilla chasing you all out of midtown?" I thought of it with such quick comedic timing it was bound to draw uproarious laughter from Louis C.K. had he happened to be hiding in the bushes watching all this transpire. But my mother raised far too polite a young man to hurl ethnic stereotype insults at strangers in the park, so I just yelled: "Merry Christmas" and ended the encounter with them and myself smiling.

I decided this was a far lower-stress strategy to deal with anyone and everyone stressing me out on my way to work in the morning. After all, what is the point of screaming 'fuck you' back at someone who screams 'fuck you' at you first thing in the morning? It just puts a damper on the whole day. I just started shouting 'Merry Christmas' at all the anti-bikites and reckless drivers and pedestrians I nearly collided with – always drawing a smile. I became like a sort of half-assed George Bailey running home at the end of It's a Wonderful Life: "Merry Christmas, you old crack head wino!" "Merry Christmas Kamikaze cab driver! Merry Christmas!" "Merry Christmas you muscle-headed goombah! Ping-ping-ding" And I biked past Trump Tower yelling in my best Jimmy Stewart: "Merry Christmas you scurvy little orange spider! You're going to jail, isn't it great?!"

After the Christmas season had come and gone, I couldn't think of a better smile-inducing response to the steady onslaught of "watch where you're fucking going asshole" and "screw you" so I just kept answering with "Merry Christmas." The later in the year it got, the funnier it got. By July I was drawing audible laughs.

I would answer every "Fuck You" with "Merry Christmas" and a ringy-pingy of the dingy bell all year every year from then on out.

## 37. There's a Philosophy in My Pants

Having continued to lose weight for six months at this point, I treated my skinny self for yet another shopping spree for ever-skinnier, skinny pants. Nichole and I made a trip to the Great Outdoors Emporium Cooperative to get ourselves some activewear for our newly-active selves. It was sharply cold and unusually bright for the winter solstice, the darkest day of the year. We proudly walked the five miles downtown to SoHo like we were taking a victory lap around Manhattan, walking briskly to keep warm. As we closed in on our destination on Prince Street, we grew a little giddy with anticipation, walking faster as we approached.

"How much weight have you lost?" Nichole asked, eyeing my figure like she was checking out a stud in a singles bar.

"Seventy pounds," I said with a twist of my hips.

"Looking sexy, SweetiePie."

"Well my pants are falling down," I wiggled my eyebrows and hips. "But it is annoying the heck out of me that I can't find a pair of pants that fit. I just bought a whole mess of new pants, where the heck do they all go?"

"I DO NOT steal your pants," Nichole insisted.

"I never said you did. I just simply pointed out that I used to have pants that fit and now I don't, and there are only two of us living in the apartment, that's all. That you doth protest so much does not help your defense in the face of any possible tacit insinuations of wanton pants thievery."

"Maybe the world-renowned pants-thief cat burglar has been breaking into our apartment along with the blankie thief that steals the blankets off of you in your sleep."

"Perhaps, the blankie thief and the pants thief are one in the same," I raised my chin and index finger in contemplation, then pointed it at her in accusation: "and maybe the blankie thief, pants thief and my cute and precious little unassuming SweetiePie are all one in the same. Maybe that's how the blankets wound up on the floor last night."

"No, that was the hanky-panky blankie thief and we like when he comes around, don't we? Otherwise, the way the blankets wind up on the floor is when you sleep on your stomach and fart them clear off the bed."

"None of this explains why my well-fitting pants keep disappearing. *J 'accuse*!" I glared accusingly down my nose at Nichole. "And you can keep the double and triple XL's. I have no use for them."

"You should probably hang on to some just in case you regain some weight in the future."

"Nichole, if I regain enough weight to fit into those pants, I'm going to need a coffin and a hearse not a fat pair of pants."

"Well, you at least owe me a thank you for taking you out to buy yet another round of skinny pants. I am so thrilled with my twenty-five-pound loss I am going to wear my new pants like a badge of honor," she said with a half twirl. I have to get refitted for new bras too."

"Whoa, whoa, whoa, are you suggesting I am getting stripped of my status as a double-D husband?" I balked. "A wife's double-D's are a badge of honor for a husband. I demand to be consulted on a decision like that."

"When you lug these things around all day every day, you can lug them around in anything you want. I am getting some clothes that fit. And we get to wear hiking clothes again."

We entered the Great Outdoors Emporium Cooperative like prodigal fat children who had been shamefully banished from the kingdom for being too obese to fit into their active wear for the past six or seven years. During our time in exile from the land of camping clothes, we were relegated to shopping for outdoor clothing at purveyors of hunting apparel.

There is a chasm of a divide in this land of ours that separates the hikers and the hunters – a divide that runs so deep to our core values that we cannot even bear to shop for clothes in the same stores. Much of the clothes are the same brands, same materials, just different stores that sell either yoga mats or guns along with the outdoor clothing. The divide between hiker and hunter, of course, is reflective of a deeper foundational divide – body type. You can be too fat to shop in the hiking store and too skinny to shop in the hunting store. I don't know why, but apparently there are no skinny hunters and no fat yoga hikers and never the twain shall meet in the outdoor clothing store. Purveyors of active wear do not want their products to be seen on fat people, it ruins their marketing image of active outdoor recreation, so they just don't make them in plus sizes – no matter the effect this has on their market share or the self-image of overweight people. Marketers of hunting apparel don't sell to skinny people because they don't want to project an image that might imply you can't catch an animal in these pants and you will starve and wither like the skinny guy in these pants.

"What do you think of these?" Nichole held up a pair of Kuhl pants.

I reached for the tag looking for a price and found a little booklet explaining the philosophy behind the pants: "Oh my God," I gasped in disbelief. "my pants have a philosophy: 'These pants have an independent philosophy of free will and adventurous exploration,'" I read aloud.

"Free-spirited pants?" Nichole asked. "I hope they don't run off without you, chasing some hapless skirt or something."

"It's making me feel a little inadequate, my pants have a more well-thought-out philosophy on life than I do."

"I thought all men's philosophies on life were in their pants. I still don't understand how you guys walk around with those things."

"We don't SweetiePie, they walk around with us. Most men's thoughts and emotions indeed come from within our pants. – a phallusophy on life."

With all my weakened heart has been through, I can see why people long associated the heart with the essence of our being – the home of our souls. Emotions weigh heavy in the heart, you can feel that. The heart is where you feel love and fear and where stress takes its toll. Your emotions are felt in your heart even if you are cognitively aware that your thoughts reside in your brain. In modern times, our scientifically linear-thinking minds see ourselves as living in our brains, peeping out at the world from behind our eyeballs. But in viewing the world from our modern cerebral standpoint, we have lost sight of our emotions as the essence of who we are.

From an evolutionary standpoint, we evolved from our earliest animal ancestors, primordial worms that grew teeth on one end and legs underneath. The rest of our bodies and minds evolved to nurture and care for the primordial worm within. So, if you really want to get in touch with your basic essence, I guess you need to get in touch with your inner worm – or at least get your mind out of the little worm in your pants.

** 

I had come a long way in the six months since the surgery. The scars on my arm and leg where they harvested the extra veins healed, I could wear my watch again and no longer worry that people thought I tried to commit suicide when they saw the fresh angry red scar running up my wrist. My chest scar would seemingly never fade, but it kind of grew on me anyway. It was a reminder of all I had been through, and I had come through just fine, even better than I had been on many levels. With my improved diet, I no longer had chronic heart burn and didn't need to sleep with a jar of Tums at my bedside. With all the weight loss, I no longer snored, and Nichole didn't have to keep a baseball bat by her bedside. With a working biological cooling pump, I no longer profusely sweat from minor exertions. The dieting, the moderated drinking, the exercise and the quitting smoking were all finally paying off. I had escaped the vicious downward spiral at last. I may have gotten myself into that spiral as a result of my inner flaws, but in the end what kept me stuck in the downward spiral wasn't a moral failing, it was a clogged pump, faulty plumbing that had kept me down.

I have a lot to be thankful to the medical-industrial complex for. But, there is something fundamentally wrong with a fee-for-services, for-profit health care system. No one is looking at the whole, no one is accountable, and it is not a self-correcting process. I have had an ER doctor, a surgeon looking out for my coronary arteries, a cardiologist looking after my heart, an orthopedist looking at my knee and my wallet, a dietician looking after my diet, a dentist looking after my teeth and gums, a sleep clinic looking after my circadian rhythm, they each look after their part. But who is looking after Jeffrey Hornbull? My life? My happiness? My job affects my stress, my stress affects my sleep, my sleep affects my exercise, my exercise affects my weight and diet, all of which affect my happiness, my job, my stress and round-and-round we go. Dr. Will Mayo, who founded the Mayo Clinic told his apprentice sons: "Don't treat diseases, treat people."

That philosophy founded what would become
the world's most renowned health care facility but
doesn't seem to have traveled very far outside of it. You
don't have to be a phoo-phooey New Age faux
spiritualist to see that Western medicine fails at being
holistic, you just have to be run through the wringer of
the medical industrial complex, most of which is just
trying to make a buck of your particular disease and
doesn't give a damn who you are or what truly ails you.
Nor do they have any mechanism to find out what ever
happened to you after you have paid the bill.

I have been reflecting not just on my health as a
whole but my life as a whole as well. How do I want to
live my life? What am I going to do about my job, my
stress, my lifestyle? I'll mitigate risks as best I can, but
I've got to get back to living and enjoying life as well.
There is value added from occasional, moderate alcohol
intake, I get a deep satisfaction from my job even if it is
trying to kill me. I can't just spend my life making sure
I don't die, I have to get on with living.

I have chest pain all day every day, usually of
the presumably harmless but acutely painful post-
surgical type, sometimes of the more disconcerting sort
that drove me to the emergency room on the fateful day.
While I learned to pay attention without dramatizing or
panicking. A trip to the emergency room would only tell
me what I already know: I have a problem with my
heart. Could it be something acute this time? Sure. But
could they even do anything about it in the ER at that
point? If I have been addressing the long-term problems
all along, there probably isn't much the ER could do. I
don't want to spend my life in an ER waiting for that

day. I'll just take care of myself, enjoy my life and when that day comes, it comes. At this very instant, you are older and wiser than you have ever been and younger than you will ever be. Enjoy this moment, it is very special.

If your health is good for now as far as you know, that is as good as it gets. It's true for everyone on Earth, it's been true for you your whole life and it always will be – you just never knew it. Life is hard, life is painful, and life is short. Life is good. Live life to the fullest in each moment. Revel in being good for now as far as you know.

I have been looking at things differently in light of everything I have been through. I have been seeing my life as a whole – looking back and looking forward at the same time. The present is just one passing glimpse of a complete whole life. Time is just another dimension passing through our otherwise static three-dimensional existence, only we get to see it unfold one slice of present at a time.

I have been looking back trying to figure out when and why my health problems started. I've thought all the way back to eating twinkies and other trans-fat laden foods of the future as a kid in the seventies. I felt vulnerable being so scrawny as a kid I used to stuff myself full of doughnuts and ice cream to gain weight as a teenager. Did that set my metabolism on bad course? Begin to clog my arteries? I remember when my friend Russell's father ran a marathon, all the kids on the block jumped on the Jim Fixx fitness bandwagon and started running. I just never improved, never gained any stamina, which may be all the better – Jim Fixx kept running and dropped dead of a heart attack while running at the age of fifty-two. Why was I unable to gain any endurance at such a young age? Was that the twinkies taking a foothold in my arteries? A preview of a genetic disposition? When exactly did I start on that collision course with the cardiologist?

And I've been looking forward at my life at the same time. Where will these heart problems lead? Maybe nowhere, maybe I'll never hear from them again, or maybe today is the day I'll drop dead.

If I were to drop dead now, I would be grateful to the people around me sharing my last moment. If it is a miserable moment, I have no one to blame but myself for not having been living my life as I should have chosen. Get to work making a life full of moments to be grateful for. Just try to enjoy the present. The present is only one glimpse into one moment of your life as a whole. Any one moment is as good as another, even if it is your last one. Rest assured your life as a whole remains intact as one complete creation.

Nobody knows how much time they may have in life, but I have reflected on the quality of my life and those things important to me and that make me feel good: eating healthy, being fit, friends, relationships, family – it's really a blessing that I went through what I went through to end up with a new outlook on life.

\*\*

The history of the Universe is a sphere. A static shape suspended in stillness. Time is a plane passing through the Universe revealing one glimpse of one moment, one layer at a time like an MRI image. Once time passes through it still remains as intact as it was before, eternally forever after you're gone. Only you are not there to perceive it anymore. Just as you are not there to perceive any of the moments that have already passed you by. Your last moment is just a moment as good as any other in your life. I never bemoaned missing out on all the time that passed without me before I was born, why should I bemoan all the time that will pass afterwards? It will all unfold just fine without me.

Time is relative after all. As far as somewhere on the other side of the Universe is concerned, you haven't even been born yet, and deep in a black hole somewhere, you always will be. And if there is more matter in the Universe than we realize, it could collapse in on itself and time could run backwards, and everything could happen in reverse. This is why I never spit gum in the toilet. If the Universe collapses and the history of everything runs in reverse, that gum could wind up back in your mouth. And as far as I can tell, gum can neither be created nor destroyed, it even survives the digestive track, so it really would be the same gum – so don't swallow it and dispose of it somewhere sanitary, please.

Not to say there is no determination in life, there is. Time isn't everything. Our choices matter very much to our happiness and to others. We are evolving. Genes are weeded out through selection according to what works in the physical world around us. But thirty thousand genes aren't controlling trillions of neurons in the network of our brains. As our brains develop, neural nets evolve as our minds form, self-selecting for pathways that work to, experience, understand and enjoy the world around us, a sort of internal evolution. We learn, and we pass down lessons to those around us and those who come after us. Our collective consciousness is evolving as well. There is an arrow of history. We are heading in a direction of better understanding and mutual compassion. Or at least we have the ability to embark on that course, and to individually contribute to that course. That is our purpose. To improve on our consciousness and pass it down, to an eventual Utopia. We certainly have that ability. Will we choose that destiny? Will you choose that course for yourself? You can start by not dwelling on all this sappy philosophical shit I have been writing here. Just have fun. Take care of your Self. Fat, drunk and philosophical is no way to go through life.

# About the Author

The author does not actually exist. I wrote under a pen name because I am a federal official in my other life, whose name could wind up on official legal documents and communications between the federal government and governors. I am guessing that whenever a governor receives a document from the federal government with someone's name attached, someone on his staff Googles the name. I struggled a bit imagining the conversation that would ensue in the governor's mansion if this book was the top of my Google search results, but I think it would go something like this:

"Okay team, what did you find out about this Hornbull character?"

"Well, Governor, the intel we assembled shows that he went through most of his life fat, drunk and stupid, dallied in drugs, may have tried to fuck a house cat and once engaged in a battle of wits with a poo-flinging monkey – and lost."

"Great work, team, with a putz like that representing FEMA we can take him and the federal government for every dime they got. Excellent. Show him straight in."

Starting off a relationship with a state in times of disaster on this note could make for an uphill battle as a good steward of the tax-payer dollar and cost Joe Federal Tax Payer a good portion of his paycheck. I don't plan on keeping my authorship too much of a secret, just off the top of my Google search results – at least until such time as FEMA comes to their senses and fires me, I come to my senses and quit or my wife comes to her senses and makes me choose between her, FEMA or a divorce settlement I could retire on. (I'd pick her of course. (Phew, that was close.))

But let's start you from the beginning. I was born and raised in Brooklyn, New York. I grew up plagued with erratic sleeping disorders but I never at any time tried to fuck the cat. Went to college in Beloit, Wisconsin where I did not study anything related to writing, but I wrote a few well-received articles for the college paper.

I went to Hungary on an exchange program and wound up spending the better part of the next nine years there. I taught English, edited for and contributed to an English-Language Newspaper called Budapest Week. I went to graduate school in Liverpool England where wrote a dissertation on declining life expectancy in Hungary. I concurrently worked on a World Health Organization project and wrote a report for the same topic. I once wrote 20,000 words in a couple weeks and thought I could write a great novel of our times at this rate.

I lived on the island of St. Croix for a while and began writing one of the great unfinished unpublished novels of our times. I never finished it, but I did learn a lot about why great novels go unfinished and unpublished – it's because they suck, they are not actually great at all.

I really did quit smoking by paying an Alaskan

bush pilot to strand me a hundred miles from anywhere in the Wrangell Mountains of Alaska. I wrote a detailed 12,000-word essay about it that did not suck at all, but I lost it to a hard-drive crash and that sucked.

I have spent over twenty years working for FEMA writing reports from disaster areas, writing emergency plans, public speaking and as a team lead for an advance team. And of course, doing some creative writing in my hotel room at night.

And yes, I really did drop dead of a heart attack and have immediate emergency open heart surgery on June 21, 2016. And the rest is history.

Made in USA - Kendallville, IN
22220_9781658896245
12.07.2021 1403